Also by Karina Halle

The Experiment in Terror Series

Darkhouse (EIT #1)
Red Fox (EIT #2)
The Benson (EIT #2.5)
Dead Sky Morning (EIT #3)
Lying Season (EIT #4)
On Demon Wings (EIT #5)
Old Blood (EIT #5.5)
The Dex-Files (EIT #5.7)
Into the Hollow (EIT #6)
And With Madness Comes the Light (EIT #6.5)
Come Alive (EIT #7)
Ashes to Ashes (EIT #8) – Winter 2013
Dust to Dust (EIT #9) – Spring 2014

Novels by Karina Halle

The Devil's Metal (Devils #1)
The Devil's Reprise (Devils #2) – Fall 2013
Sins and Needles (The Artists Trilogy #1)
On Every Street (An Artists Trilogy Novella #0.5)
Shooting Scars (The Artists Trilogy #2)
Bold Tricks (The Artists Trilogy #3)
October 2013

Perception

*A Paperback Collection of
Experiment in Terror Novellas:*
#2.5~ The Benson
#5.5 Old Blood
#5.7 The Dex~Files

∞Karina Halle∞

\m/ Metal Blonde Books \m/

First edition published by
Metal Blonde Books September 2013

Publisher's Note: This is a work of fiction. Names, characters, places, and incidents either are the product of the author's imagination or are used fictitiously. Any resemblance to actual events, locales, or persons, living or dead, is entirely coincidental.

Copyright © 2011-2013 by Karina Halle
All rights reserved, including the right to reproduce this book or portions thereof in any form whatsoever.

Cover design by Najla Qamber

ISBN-13: 978-1492374848

Metal Blonde Books
P.O. Box 845
Point Roberts, WA
98281 USA

Manufactured in the USA

For more information about the series
and author visit: http://khalle.wordpress.com/

FOR THE HARLOTS

THE BENSON

I have never been inside The Benson hotel before. Looking back, it's kind of weird since I've lived in Portland for my whole life, but I guess there are a lot of things in your city you never see. Not the way the tourists do.

Tonight though, I decided I would be a tourist. Having a camera at my side would certainly help in that pretense. I smile up at the doorman as I make my way up the sidewalk, pausing briefly at the bronze plaque on the ground as I have many times before when walking throughout downtown, and then timidly walk up the steps inside.

"Good evening and welcome to The Benson ma'am," the doorman says to me, cheery enough in his fancy, gold-gilded uniform. Still, I feel like he's judging me and what I'm wearing; my Doc Martens still muddy from the morning's rainfall, my maroon leggings with a hole in them and a scuffed leather jacket. I'm obviously not a guest here, not at one of the most prestigious hotels in the state of Oregon.

I give him a tight smile and walk past him into the revolving doors which sweep me inside. The lobby is surprisingly busy for nine p.m. as there's a line at the vast checkout counter a few people deep, and the bar/lounge to the right of me is crammed full of swanky patrons swilling martinis. I barely have time to take in the understated grandeur and opulence of the lobby – which totally reminds me of the golden age of Hollywood – before a waving movement brings my attention to the bar again.

In the corner, swilling what can only be a Jack Daniels and Coke is Dex. Actually, he's not swilling it. Rather, downing it in fast gulps and as soon as he sees he's caught my attention, he waves the prim waitress over and orders another one.

I swallow hard, feeling all sorts of strange feelings rush up in my body. I'm nervous, I already was, but I'm excited too and though my breath catches slightly when I see him, it eventually flows out all hot, ragged and sparkling with nerves.

I haven't seen Dex since we parted ways at the airport in Albuquerque. It wasn't long ago, but it still makes me feel like I'm going on a first date all over again. Not that we ever were dating and not that (with his girlfriend Jenn) we ever would. But I can't help the way I feel. Stupid. And in love with my partner.

I smile, broad and completely natural for him, and make my way to where he is sitting, at a small, white clothed table just big enough for two. Before I reach his side, I wonder if he's going to hug me and before I can finish the thought, he stands up, stepping around the table. I am quickly enveloped into his arms. He smells like Old Spice and a bit like the hand-rolled cigarettes he picked up in New Mexico. His arms are strong and firm around my back. The hug is close, tight and genuine. I relax slightly, wishing we were somewhere else and not this busy lounge where people watch us with disinterest.

I am the first to pull apart, though I could have stayed in his arms all night. I give him the once over now that I am up close.

He looks pretty much as he did in New Mexico. The cuts on his face from the shapeshifter's attack are faded; his moustache has been trimmed, almost gone, as is the scruff beard under his chin. His eyebrow ring glints from his black brow. His cheekbones are high, perhaps higher than before. I take another step back and see that he's lost a little bit of weight. It shows in his face most of all.

"Checking me out again?" he says, his voice low, his lips snaking to the side in a smirk. There's something off about him, but I don't know what it is. Maybe it's because, despite the closeness of the hug, there's an awkward distance between us, like we aren't sure how to act around each other now that the skinwalkers and Maximus and sharing a bed for a few nights are gone. We both almost died in New Mexico – I know it had an impact on us, but it doesn't seem to have any bearing here in the swanky Benson hotel.

And then there are his eyes. Dex's eyes are his focal point, the part of him that wins people over or drives them away. Dark chocolate, enigmatic and emotive. Sometimes they are ruthless, sometimes seductive. They are a mystery as much as he is and the one thing I can't help from drowning in over and over again.

But here, tonight, they are clouded. No, that's not quite it. Not clouded but subdued. The sparkle and zest that roam in them, no matter what his mood, are gone. They are handsome, beguiling eyes but not his.

I think back to Red Fox and how he had gone so long without his anti-psychotic medication that he began to actually feel again. It was scary for him, no doubt (and for me, let's not kid ourselves) but in the end...he was free. Or so I thought. Now it seems that sparkle and life, the manic highs and lows, are gone. As destructive as they were, they are an important part of him.

"Sorry," I mutter to myself, dropping my eyes quickly to the table just as the waitress comes by and puts down his drink.

"What would you like, Perry?" he asks me. I look up at him and the waitress. Her name tag states her as Prudence. She has white hair and a friendly smile but a stance that says I better be quick with an answer.

I don't drink normally, especially not on the job – which is what I am doing here tonight with Dex – but I say, "A glass of the house red, thanks."

It's the cheapest and will relax my nerves. Prudence leaves with my order after Dex gives her a quick wink. He then turns to me as we sit down.

"So how are you, kiddo?" he asks, peering at my face, trying to read me before I say anything. "Is it nice having me in your neck of the woods again?"

"It's just nice to see you again," I say honestly. With Dex living in Seattle and me in Portland, I only ever see him when we film. And in the between time, I miss him.

A blush starts to creep up my neck. I can feel it.

He gives me a smile that reaches his eyes and shows perfect teeth that are quite white for a smoker. "Well, it's nice to see you. Too bad you're not bunking with me tonight at my motel."

I give him a sharp look, not sure if he's kidding or not.

He smiles again, almost leering. "I'll probably be shaking in my boots after tonight with only my pillow to hug."

The waitress comes back and gives me my wine. He gives her the same kind of smirk. This is how I know he's messing with me.

I roll my eyes. "So what is our plan for tonight anyway? Are we just going to sit here and drink and wait for the ghosts to show up?"

"Patience, Perry," he says and takes another gulp of his drink. He gestures to the wine and nods at it. "Have some of that and relax."

I take a sip of the acidic merlot and look around me. As gorgeous and old-fashioned as the hotel is, there are so many people about, and I can't imagine how on earth the place could be haunted. But apparently it is. In fact, Portland has a few ghost tours that come around and poke their heads in the hotel a few times a week. I doubt anybody ever sees anything, though.

"Are we the first ghost hunting show to come inside here?" I ask Dex.

He coughs on his drink and shakes his head. "Fuck no. We're a bit behind on this one. I think just about every ghost hunter has been in this hotel at some point or another."

"Do they ever find anything?"

He gives me a wry look. "What do you think? Of course not."

"What makes you think we will?"

He smiles again and reaches over with his hand to pat me softly on the head. "Because I've got you, kiddo. You're my little ghost bait."

I think back to Red Fox, to a moment when Dex said I might be offered up as bait to the skinwalkers. The idea bothered me then and it bothers me now. I take a longer sip of the wine this time.

He's watching my face closely, as usual, and he still keeps his hand there. I'm not sure if he's trying to comfort me or what. I shoot him a deadly look from the side of my eyes.

"I'm joking you know," he finally says, his voice less rough, less gravely. "I just mean, well, you know there's something about you, something that attracts these things. You're like a secret weapon."

"Some weapon," I scoff and look down into the glass, my vision becoming a blur of deep reds. "What's the point of just attracting these...things? These people? If I could use this...power...whatever it is, for good...that would be a different story."

He shrugs and takes his hand away, his attention back to his own drink. The back of my head feels vulnerable without his hand there. "You never know. There's supposed to be a shitload of ghosts in this hotel, maybe you can help one of them."

I raise my brows at him.

"A shitload?" I repeat. "Where do you get your information, Mr. Foray?"

"Wikipedia. That thing is never wrong," he says without irony. He looks around him and takes in the scene. "We're supposed to meet the night manager, Pam, in a couple of minutes. She said she'd find us. She'll give us a tour of the place; hopefully give us the real story. I want that on film."

"And what do you want me to do?" I ask. Once again, we're going into a film shoot more or less blind. And by we, I mean I. Dex always knows what's going on and I'm always in the dark. I did research The Benson before biking over here and all that, but I have no clue what to do or say. There is no storyboard, no script. We just wing it and I usually end up looking like an idiot.

"Just be yourself. Ask her questions. I'll film both of you. We'll wander around the hotel. Then we'll probably be allowed to go off on our own and do some exploring. I'll give you the infrared camera this time so we can see if we pick up any hot or cold spots."

I shiver at that thought. Using the infrared meant we'd be wandering around in the dark. Whether I'm in a lighthouse on the coast or in the New Mexican desert, the darkness still gives me the creeps. Especially now that I know there are things out there that want to hurt me. That know I'm a sort of "bait."

By the time Pam shows up, I have finished my glass of wine. It has only left me anxious, not relaxed.

Pam is on the overweight side, similar to the way I was in high school, but unlike me, she seems to bustle with confidence. Or bustle with something. Her wide, cheery face gives her the appearance of being younger than she probably is and she speaks a mile a minute.

"You must be Perry and Dex, I recognized you!" she exclaims, beaming at us and holding out her hand. We both give it a quick shake. She points to the name tag on her black suit. "As you can see, my name is Pam. Pam Gupta. I'm the night manager here at The Benson."

"Thanks for having us," Dex tells her sincerely, reaching under the table and bringing out a backpack and a camera bag.

"No, thank you," she says putting extra emphasis on the words. "As soon as you told me who you were, I looked up your ghost show and immediately fell in love with you guys."

Dex and I exchange a quick look.

"I mean," she corrects herself and lets out an awkward clip of a laugh, "I was scared witless at the Darkhouse episode and the one in Red Fox but I was so drawn in by you two. You're just so...so..."

"Handsome?" Dex asks, flashing her a smile and stroking his chin scruff.

She blushes and giggles. "Well, yeah I guess you are."

I roll my eyes. Dex doesn't need any more encouragement.

"But," she continues, "you're both just so...lucky!"

We look at each other again, even more confused.

"Lucky?" I ask.

"How about I explain as we walk? I don't have much time to show you around before I start my shift."

We get up, Dex giving the backpack of equipment to me, and we follow Pam through the lobby. For a larger woman she walks like a sprite, moving quickly between people and showering her big smile on all of them. The guests eye Dex and I curiously, intrigued by the camera he has placed up on his shoulder.

We stop before a grand staircase leading up to the second floor. I eye myself quickly in the mirror on the landing. My floral dress is sticking to my leggings in static cling, and my black hair is a mess from my motorbike helmet (and Dex's hand). I don't look camera worthy at all. I shrug helplessly at my reflection and look to Pam who is pointing up at the stairs.

"There's been many sightings of one of ghostly guests walking up and down this very staircase," she says, sounding like a chipper tour guide talking about museum pieces and not dead people.

I look at Dex beside me and see the camera is going, picking up everything Pam is saying. Sensing I'm staring at him, he reaches out and pushes me toward Pam, into the frame. I know he wants me to start acting like the host I am.

I smooth down my hair and clear my throat, stepping into the shot. "Have you seen any ghosts, Pam?"

She shakes her head quickly and looks wistful. "No, I haven't. Come on, let's go to the next floor."

Not exactly the answer I was hoping for.

She scurries up the stairs and we follow, my short legs straining to keep up with her quick busybody motion.

We walk toward the elevators and as we are waiting she says, "I think you two are lucky because I've always wanted to see a ghost. I believe in them. So badly. But I've never seen one. Weird, right, considering that I run The Benson. At night."

The elevator dings and the doors open. There's a couple inside who eye the camera with trepidation, but we step inside with them anyway. Pam makes small talk with them as she pushes the button for the 8th floor and doesn't mention ghosts again until the couple get out at the 5th floor.

She tilts her head at us. "I don't like to discuss the ghosts around the guests though. People can be pretty strange about things like that."

"I don't blame them," I find myself saying.

"I guess you'd know," Pam says as the elevator stops at the floor, and she leads us out into the hallway, past a rotary phone resting on top of an antique table.

She notices me eyeing it and gives it a quick wave with her hand. Her bracelets jingle with the motion.

"We try to keep all the original furnishings from the hotel. Adds to the class and elegance of the place, don't you think?"

I nod, not really needing to be sold on the hotel as a whole.

Pam takes us to the right, and we walk past the rooms down to the very end of the hall. Dex keeps filming, even though he takes his head away from the camera.

"So, if we show The Benson in a good way," Dex says to Pam, "any chance we can score a free hotel room for the night? I'm staying at a roach motel outside of the city, and I'm getting itchy just thinking about it."

Pam turns around briefly and smiles at him but then spins around and keeps walking without missing a beat.

"We'll see. Would you two be sharing the room?"

Dex automatically grins and looks down at me as we walk. I shake my head, not amused.

"No, Perry snores and kicks in her sleep," he says.

I smack him on the shoulder and the camera shakes.

"I do not!" I protest.

"Oh, and drools," he adds quickly.

"So you two are a couple?" Pam asks, not looking at us this time but slowing down as she nears the end of the hall.

"Only in certain situations," I mutter under my breath.

"No, we are not. Perry is far too good for me and I am forced to make do with my Wine Babe girlfriend."

Finally Pam stops walking and looks at him. "Wine Babe? You're with someone from that show?"

"You've seen it?" Dex asks, his eyes wide and hopeful.

"Yes," she says slowly, and for once her chipper look is gone. Her cheeks sag a bit. "My ex boyfriend used to drool all over that skinny, exotic one."

"Yeah, that's his girlfriend. Jennifer Rodriguez," I inform her. She eyes me and sees that I'm none too thrilled about it either. Nothing like a hot woman to make two chubby girls feel like they're having a bonding moment.

"Well, I'm just glad some women watch it," Dex says, turning his attention the camera, perhaps feeling the animosity and low self-esteem just reeking from our pores.

Pam laughs and the cheery façade returns. "Don't be silly. I don't watch that dreadful show. They pair shiraz with Kraft Dinner. Only an idiot would watch that. Like my ex-boyfriend."

Dex opens his mouth to say something, but I know he completely agrees. That's the reason he quit doing camera work on Wine Babes and started up Experiment in Terror with me instead.

"Anyway," she continues, "here we are."

I look at the door we've stopped in front of: Room 818.

"Where are we?" I ask.

"This was Parker's room," she says ominously.

"Who is Parker?" Dex asks. I'm surprised that he doesn't know something for once.

"Parker..." Pam starts and then trails off. She takes her keys out from her pocket; the noise of them rattling fills the hallway. It suddenly seems very empty and hollow and a weird, familiar feeling washes over me, causing the hairs on the back of my neck to stand up.

The lock turns, and the door slowly creaks open. Only blackness and dust come billowing out of the room.

"After you," Pam says.

Dex shrugs and then nudges me in front of the camera, indicating that I am to go first. Of course. I always have to be the first to walk into everything when I'm on camera. And sometimes when I'm not on camera. It depends on how sadistic Dex is feeling.

I take in a deep breath and push the door aside. It slowly swings open with a low groan, and I walk blindly into the swirling dark.

"Should I be putting on the night vision?" Dex asks no one in particular. I hear him fiddle with the camera settings but before anything happens, I am blind. Pam has walked in beside me and switched on the lights.

"No sense in scaring ourselves yet," she chirps, and I can barely make out her round face.

Dex comes in and Pam shuts the door behind him. Once my eyes adjust to the light, I see that we are in a hotel room that probably looks the same as any other hotel room, albeit a large and very pricey one. Aside from a heavy chill that seems to hang in the air, there's nothing too off-putting about the place. The bed is made, there seems to be a separate room with a living area, divided only by a Japanese-type paper partition, and I can just see a rather opulent looking bathroom jutting out to the right.

"As I said, this is Parker's room," she says. "Well, it was his room. I say this because some guests who stay in here say they still see him. But it happens very rarely."

"And once again," Dex repeats, sounding bored, "who is Parker?"

Pam walks over to the king-sized bed and sits down on it. It sags a little from her weight; the mattress is not as springy as it was back in the day.

"We have a lot of ghosts in this hotel. Parker isn't the most well known of them, but he is the most real. Because he was a real person and his story is terribly tragic. Tragic, but all too common."

I go over to the bed and sit down beside Pam. Suddenly, that slightly see-through partition between the bedroom and the living area is giving me the creeps, like I can sense someone standing behind it.

Dex looks like he picks up on the vibe too. Although he is standing in front of Pam and I, with the camera in our faces, his eyes keep flitting over there and his head is cocked slightly as if he is listening. I stifle the urge to shiver—I don't want to look like an amateur—and keep my attention on Pam.

"What happened?" I ask, trying to keep my voice light, trying to ignore the goosebumps I can feel rising underneath my jacket.

"Parker, Parker Hayden, was a ship owner in the '30s. Back then, Portland was a very different city. The ships were its lively hood. There was a lot of money, a lot of crime, a lot of... well, scandals, I guess. Think Vegas, but on a river. Anyway, Parker was just one of the many wealthy ship owners. He spent half his time here, half somewhere on the east coast. He rented a room, this room, spending an obscene amount of money every night. He was a ladies man too, no surprise there! He was also a bit nuts. But because he was rich, you called him eccentric. There were rumors he was having an affair with a maid or two; sometimes he'd be caught stealing tons of toiletries and hording them in his closet. In this day and age we'd call him a weirdo but back then, he was just rich and powerful and you let him do what he wanted."

"Doesn't sound too much different from nowadays," Dex says softly, keeping the camera focused on Pam. He's paying less attention now to the other room, which makes me feel a smidge better.

Pam laughs. "You're right about that. And it was the same kind of outcome. Back in 1934, Portland was hit hard—really hard—with this strike. I think it was called the West Coast Waterfront Strike? Anyway, there was the strike, his ship was basically inoperable, and he lost a lot of money. Really fast. According to the records, he was kicked out of the hotel because he couldn't pay his bills. Not for this room, not for any room here."

"And what happened?" I push.

She sighs and rubs her face quickly, looking uneasy for the first time tonight. Lines appear on her youthful face.

"He wouldn't leave. He was kicked out several times, out on the street even. Publicly humiliated. All unshaven and messy, like a vagrant. He said people were after him, wanting money and that he was afraid for his life. Then the hotel staff found him. Dead. Hanging in the maid's laundry room, from a noose made out of towels. The strike ended two days later. How is that for irony?"

She smiles at me, but it is forced and I can't be bothered to return it. The story stirs something in my gut.

I look up at Dex and see that his attention is back on the other room again.

"What is it?" I ask him. I can't help myself.

Pam's attention goes to him, and we all look over but see nothing.

"The guests who have seen him," she puts in, her voice low, her eyes on the partition, "they say they see a man pacing anxiously in the other room there, muttering to himself. Once he notices you, he tries to say something or write something down. But no words come out and as the guests get more scared and confused, the ghost gets frustrated. Sometimes he disappears, sometimes he rushes at the guests and then... poof."

"Well doesn't that make for a memorable stay," Dex comments underneath his breath.

Pam giggles nervously at his lame joke and then gets up. "I'm afraid I will have to leave you two now. Duty calls."

Dex lowers the camera and touches her arm lightly, causing her to pause mid-bustle. It's obvious she wants nothing more than to get out of the room. I have half a mind to join her.

"Where is the laundry room?" he asks.

Pam looks down at her feet quickly. "The laundry room? Why?"

"Well, we aren't ignoring the place where the man hung himself. With towels, mind you. I mean, I can make a swan out of towels, but a noose?"

"I'd show you, but I really must—"

She looks at me for support as he reaches forward and plucks the keys out of her hand.

He holds up the keys in front of her face. "Just tell us which key will get us into the laundry room and we'll have no problem finding it on our own."

"Dex," I begin, not wanting him to step out of bounds. He can be relentless sometimes.

He ignores me and flashes Pam a smile that usually makes me weak at the knees. "Come on, Pammy, you know you want our little show to succeed here. Parker would want us there. Give the man some closure."

Her mouth twitches while she thinks it over. Dex gives her a quick wink and she blushes slightly. I can't help but roll my eyes again.

"All right," Pam mumbles and takes the keys from him. She goes through them in a blur and pops one off the ring and into his outstretched hand. "It's in the basement. This will open the freight elevator at the end of the hall and take you right there. But I want this back, OK?"

"But of course." He grins and closes his hand over the key before she has a chance to change her mind.

She looks at me and I give a little shrug.

"We won't wreck anything or scare the guests," I say. I want to add, "We promise," but I know we can't promise anything. Destruction and fear seem to follow Dex and I wherever we go. That is the nature of the ghost hunting business, even one that's only on the Internet.

I can see Pam isn't comfortable with the situation, but she doesn't say anything else. She just leaves the room and shuts the door behind her. The movement causes the dust to fly off of the nearby lamps.

I slowly let out my breath and look at Dex. He's watching me carefully.

"What?" I ask.

"Do you want the lights on or off?"

He raises his camera a bit and I get it. Are we going to shoot this in the dark or in the light? I know what I'm going to say, and I know what he's going to say.

"Leave the lights on," I tell him.

"I think we should have them off."

I knew it. "Why do you even bother consulting me if you're just going to do what you want anyway?"

"I like you to feel like this a partnership," he says, and sounds strangely sincere. He tucks the key into his cargo pants and gives me a quick smile. "And you know that shooting in the dark adds to the tension."

"It also adds to my ever-building threat of dying young," I point out.

"Twenty-two ain't so young anymore, kiddo. I mean, you've almost surpassed James Dean. If you kick it now—"

I raise my hand in the air. "That's enough. Let's just get this over with."

"Perry's famous last words."

"Dex. Shut up."

It's his turn to roll his eyes. I feel a cold waft come in from the living room area, and I automatically rub my hands up and down my arms. There's definitely something going on in this place, and I am in no hurry to find out. But of course, it's my job to find out.

"What if we just leave this light on here?" I say, pointing at the lamp. The rest of hotel room, including the bathroom and the living area, are only lit by residual light. It's just dark enough to be spooky over there, but it's not so black that I'd be having a panic attack.

"If you wish," Dex says and I hate how unafraid he sounds. Then again, he always gets to view things through the lens. He never has to be the one seeing the horrors face-to-face.

It's a catch-22 with my job. On one hand, I'm often scared shitless at the slightest thing and pray that I don't bump into a ghost (or a skinwalker, now that I know those things exist). On the other hand, if I don't run into anything, it makes for a pretty bad episode. I mean, most ghost hunting shows don't have much to show for themselves, anyway, but that's also the point: We don't want to be like most of those shows. We are above and beyond that, at least that's what Dex rattles off half the time. I don't even know if he believes what he says, but the fact is that when we do capture some unexplainable stuff on film, the views go up and we look good.

It's too bad our looking good comes at the cost of me nearly peeing my pants every time.

"So…" I begin.

"So, just come here." He places his strong hands on the sides of my arms and physically moves me over so I'm right in front of him and the camera. I don't want him to let go but he does. "I'll roll it, you give a quick spiel based on whatever Pam just said and then walk into the other room. I'll be right behind you."

"Don't I get a flashlight?"

"I'll be your eyes. Ready?"

I nod, square my shoulders and take a deep breath. We usually go in just one take and I give a very quick overview of what we are doing in The Benson hotel and what we hope to find in room 818.

Then I turn around and face the darkness of the living room. I don't know how it's possible, but it seems to have grown darker in the last few minutes. Before I could make out a couch and a table, as well as the entrance to the fancy bathroom. Now, I can't see anything at all. Just the partition with its slightly transparent sheets of fabric paper and that terrible feeling that there is something, or someone, just beyond it, waiting for me to enter its clutches.

Dex clears his throat, a signal that I need to move. I feel frozen on the spot but will my legs to step forward, even though every part of me is screaming not to.

Somehow, I do it. I step into the void and feel a rush of frigid air flow around me. No, flow is too gentle of a word. It slams into me like an invisible hand.

I pause and take another step, trying to pick up where the bed should be. I still can't see anything, but Dex says in a low voice, "Move to the right a little. The bed is right in front of you."

I do as he says and stop. Dex sucks in his breath in one sharp motion.

"What is it?" I whisper uneasily. I wish I could see what he is seeing.

"Do you not see it?"

I turn around and see his silhouette against the light. "See what?" I feel the symptoms of a panic attack poking around my spine.

He doesn't say anything but keeps the camera trained on me while reaching into his backpack. He pulls out what looks like the small infrared camera.

"Here, turn the switch on, it's on the side," he says and hands it to me. I fumble for it, feeling around for the button.

It comes on and then I can see again. Well, kind of. It's aimed at the floor and I can see the shape of my feet and legs glowing a hot red against the blackness. I feel a lot like I'm in Predator.

"Now turn around and aim it straight in front of you."

I hesitate for a second, afraid of what I'm going to witness. Then I turn on the spot so I'm facing the black room and look through the infrared camera.

I nearly drop it.

Right in front of me, to the side of the bed, is a tall, long shape of pale blue light. A hazy silhouette. The outline of a man who isn't there.

"That's unbelievable," I hear Dex say from behind me. I can't form the words to agree. The fear is overpowering my fascination. There is someone standing right in front of me. Parker Hayden.

"Talk to it."

"What?" I whisper hoarsely, my eyes flitting from the screen to the blackness in front of me. If I walk forward, will my hands grab onto a desperate dead man? Or will they pass through them, like no one is there at all? Do I even want to know?

"Mr. Hayden," Dex speaks in a gentle voice, void of any self-consciousness. "Mr. Hayden, we can see you. Would you like to talk to us? Would you like to tell us something?"

The shape on the camera shakes vigorously on the spot, like the picture on a television that's being hit from the side. Then it stops and in a blink of an eye it bursts out of the screen, screaming past us in a blur of cold, miserable energy.

And just like that, all the lights in the room come on and it's just Dex and I left staring at each other, cameras in hand, feeling cold and dumbfounded at what we just encountered.

I manage to shut my mouth so I don't look like a drooling fool on camera and look back down at the infrared.

"We need to follow him."

I look up at Dex with the most incredulous stinkeye I can muster.

"We need to follow him? We don't even know what that was. Or who that was. Or where he went. Or if he wants us to follow him…"

Dex turns around and heads to the door.

"Dex!" I yell after him and grab onto his sleeve. I look up at his eyes but I can see he's already gone, thinking in the mind of a ghost, plotting where Parker would have gone next.

"Perry, we can't just leave it at that."

"I don't know, I think what we just captured is some pretty awesome stuff. Maybe that's all we'll get for tonight. Maybe it's time to go home."

The side of his mouth twitches and before I know it, he's grinning at me. "Why Perry, I thought you'd turned into quite the little fearless ghost hunter back in Red Fox. Getting cold feet, are we?"

I wish I had a snappy rebuttal for that, but I don't. The truth is, I'm scared. It doesn't matter how many times you've seen a ghost; it's still scary. And considering how often these supernatural beings have tried to kill me in the past, I think I have every right to fear each one I encounter. Every chance I get to get out of the shoot alive is a chance I want to take. I mean, deep down inside, I'm just an ordinary, 22-year-old girl who likes to listen to metal and dreams about chocolate on a nightly basis. Just because I'm ghost bait, doesn't mean I have to exploit it.

But I don't say any of this to Dex. Even though he's just my partner (and I'm usually the sane one), I can't bear the thought of losing face with him. He took a risk by creating this show and by putting me in it. I took a risk by giving up my old job to make something of my life. I want to be the person that he thinks I am, that fearless, brave girl—woman, even—who laughs in the face of danger. Something more than ordinary.

"Cold feet?" I repeat, my voice hard. "You're the one who is showing up all icy on my infrared."

He studies me for a second, sucking slowly on his full lower lip, trying to read me. I hate it when he does that. But instead of looking away as I often do, I hold his gaze, challenging him.

"OK, kiddo. Glad to see you're still up for the challenge," he finally says.

"I deal with you every weekend, don't I? Anything after that is a piece of cake."

He flashes me a quick smile and opens the door. I follow him into the hallway, take in a deep breath and try to calm my nerves, which are firing all over the place and causing me to shake internally. My bluff worked. Now all I need to do is keep up appearances.

As we walk down the hallway to the freight elevator, I already know where Dex is planning on taking us: the laundry room. I don't want to think about the horrors that might lie there, so I ask him, "You told me you saw something, before I turned on the infrared… what was it?"

We stop in front of the elevator and Dex inserts the key, giving it a turn and pressing the down button. The elevator purrs loudly, as if it hasn't been turned on in decades. I'm reminded of The Shining for a brief instance and hope a river of blood doesn't come flowing out of it.

"Just some really weird lights dancing around. You know how you can get those orbs on screen, like the ones we saw at the lighthouse? Same kind of thing but they were jumping up and down, like balls in a lotto machine or something."

The elevator button light goes off, and with a loud metallic groan, the doors slide open to expose a larger than average elevator behind them.

"Ladies first," Dex says, but I shove him forward. Not this time.

We get in and press the button for the laundry level, which is marked, thankfully. It's also below the first floor and the first two parking levels, which is a slight cause for concern. Just how far down are we going?

I give Dex a nervous smile, which he returns with a mischievous one. An agonizing minute later, we lurch to a stop on the laundry level.

The doors shudder slightly, then open as if being pried by invisible hands. In front of us lies a long hallway, poorly lit by buzzing overhead lights, casting shadows on the few doors that lie along the way. Not the most welcoming place.

Dex steps out first. He grabs my hand, his grasp on mine firm and warm, and I let myself feel the momentary wash of comfort that only he can provide for me. I let him lead me into the hallway. The elevator doors remain open and waiting for the next passenger, only on this empty, quiet floor, there is none to be found.

Dex hoists the camera onto his shoulder again and motions for me to turn on the infrared.

"Might as well start filming this now."

"Where is everyone?" I ask. "I mean, the hotel runs around the clock, doesn't it?"

"But which clock?" he answers in a statement, not a question.

I sigh and flip on the infrared again. My body glows a vibrant red but when I aim it over at Dex, he only comes up orange.

"What?" he asks as I purse my lips, thinking.

"Seems I'm a lot more hot-blooded than you are," I say and quickly show him the screen, placing his hand in front of the lens.

He chews on his lip briefly and then places his hand against my forehead. It feels cool.

"Well you're not hot..."

I shoot him a wry look.

"I mean, not internally hot. Outside is another matter." He winks at me.

"Are you flirting with me again, Mr. Foray?"

"Again? Whatever do you–"

He's interrupted by a wall of sound as all doors down the hallway suddenly swing open and bang against their walls. Simultaneously, the elevator behind us powers up with a thunderous whir, the doors closing quickly.

"It's go time," he says and we're off down the hallway to the first door.

Dex is just about to enter the room when the door slams shut in his face, almost smashing his nose back into his skull. He gives me a scared look I don't see on him too often. Probably the thought of having to get a nose job.

He goes for the handle and I'm right there at his side as he jangles it back and forth vigorously. It's locked.

We dash for the next door and the same thing happens. Same with the last door after that. All doors locked. Nothing to explore.

"Now what?" I mumble, feeling a familiar wave of cold snake around my feet and ankles. I point the infrared down at it, but it doesn't register anything out of the ordinary.

Dex doesn't say anything for a while so I look up at him. His eyes are focused above him, at a loose-looking vent on the ceiling.

"Perry," he says slowly, carefully.

I shake my head. "You've got to be kidding."

He looks back at me and shrugs. "What's the harm? I'll just boost you up there. If you crawl around for a bit, you'll probably end up in one of the other rooms and then you can open the door from the inside."

"I...don't even know what to say to that."

"No? You usually have some sort of witty one-liner."

"You go up there, Dex. There's no way in hell I'm going."

"You can't hold me up and it's too far for me to jump. Short man syndrome, remember?"

"You can't hold me up."

"Perry, for the last time, stop acting like you weigh one million pounds. You don't. You're as light as a feather."

I let out a laugh. I can't help myself.

"I'm not...anyway, even if you could push me up there, do you think I'd fit?"

"Again, Perry– "

"And if I do get up there, do you think that aging duct would hold me? I'd come crashing through like a bag of bricks."

"Stop using your non-existent weight problem as an excuse, just because you're too chickenshit," he challenges.

My mouth drops slightly. I am not chickentshit. And my weight problem isn't non-existent.

"Fine," I say and walk toward him. "If you don't think it's an issue, then away I go."

He steadies his gaze at me, sussing me out. I cross my arms and give him an impatient stare.

He nods quickly and lowers his hands joined together. I step on them unsteadily and before I can even question just what the hell I am doing, I'm boosted into the air, one hand on the camera, the other reaching for the vent.

Once Dex has me steadied and I can stand, albeit wobbly, on his hands, I climb to his shoulders and push the vent aside. It pops up and slides out to the side with an easy clatter that rattles down the hallway. Up close, it is big enough for me to fit through. But it's also black and fathomless and hides a wealth of things that could frighten me to death. It's a vent, for crying out loud. Since when did this show turn into Mission Impossible?

"You OK, kiddo?" he asks from beneath me, his voice shaking slightly, either from apprehension or from the strain.

"Not really. Have you ever been in a dark vent before?"

"Several times," he answers seamlessly. "Once you get up in there, I'll hand you the flashlight so you don't have to be in the dark."

"How thoughtful of you," I mutter and reach for my hands into the vent. It's cold and I fear it will be icky inside but the bottom of the duct feels mercifully dry.

"On the count of three," he says and once we count down, he pushes me up further and I'm waist deep. I feel his hands slip away and with a groan I pull myself forward until everything except my calves are inside the dark air duct.

I'm scared as hell. The sides of the duct have me unable to turn around and I can't see what's in front of me. For all I know, there could be a giant rat in front of my face, ready to gnaw it off, starting with the little tip of my nose. I am starting to panic and an attack in this tight of a spot would be a dangerous thing indeed.

"Uh, Perry," I hear Dex say. His voice is comforting but the tone isn't.

"What?" I say as quietly as I can. My words reverberate around me.

"I guess you can't turn around and reach for the flashlight…can you?"

I close my eyes and let my head thud against the cold bottom. "No."

"That's OK, I'm just going to stick the flashlight inside your boot. That way, when you get a chance to move around a bit more, you can grab it."

I feel him grab my leg, undo the laces on my left Doc Marten and shove the flashlight inside.

This has to be the stupidest idea ever. Some ghost hunters we are.

I sigh and then cough loudly from all the dust.

"Perry, I'm going to try and talk you through it. Just move forward until I tell you to stop. And when I tell you to stop, see if there's an opening off to your right. If there is, go down that way and it should place you in the laundry room. At least, I hope it's the laundry room."

"OK!" I yell, hoping my voice will scare off any hideous creatures that are waiting for me up ahead.

You can do this, I tell myself. One movement at a time, like a snake. Remember if you need to escape, you just need to back up and you'll be free.

I repeat this to myself as I slink forward, feeling more and more like Tom Cruise. Or Garth from Wayne's World when he keeps landing on his keys.

After what feels like a lifetime of wiggling and trying to refrain from vomiting on the infrared, Dex yells for me to look for a space going off to the right. I feel for it but though I still touch the same cold metal walls, there's a bit of a breeze up ahead, flowing down the right side of me.

I continue, hearing Dex's babbling from below becoming more and more muffled, until my hand doesn't slam against the side as normal. I found the opening.

I take it, maneuvering like a rat in a maze and wiggle down in a new direction. After a few beats, I can't hear Dex at all anymore and that realization fills me with dread. If I need to get out, I'll have to not only back up but make a turn going backwards as well. In the pitch dark, the idea is terrifying and disorienting.

But I continue because I'm determined to see this through. And soon enough, my eyes start to pick up something ahead of me. There's just a little difference of light up ahead and then my hands come across cool air and a vent covering.

My fingers wrap around the metallic grate and pull it up with ease. It rattles as I push it to the side and I stick my head down below, taking in deep breaths of fresher, non-contained air through my nose. I don't know what's below me, all I can see are a few red lights, which I guess are the on-off buttons of machines. There is some other light, though, spilling in from under a doorframe and with hope I realize that Dex and the hallway must be on the other side of that.

I carefully slide across the opening, distributing my weight on each side until I'm just past it, then I lower myself down, my legs dangling helplessly. I have no idea what the hell is below me but I'm just going to have to hope for the best. I take a deep breath, wiggle myself out until I'm hanging what must be a good few feet off the ground, and let go.

I land on solid ground, though the impact makes me stumble to the side and my body goes flying against a desk that makes an impression in my hip.

"Fuck!" I yell. That's going to leave a giant bruise.

"Perry?" I hear Dex call out from the hallway. I scurry over to the door, careful not to trip over anything in my way, and feel for the doorknob. I yank at it to open, but nothing happens. It appears to be locked from the inside and the outside.

"Are you OK?" he asks and I can hear the worry in his voice. He likes to surprise me by acting human from time to time.

"I'm fine," I say, rubbing my hip where the desk went into me. "But I can't open this fucking thing."

"Are you getting any reception on your phone?"

I tuck the infrared under my arm and bring my iPhone out of my jacket pocket, while reaching down for the flashlight in my boot. It works but the bars are gone. No service.

"No, are you?"

"No," he answers with a sigh. "Look, I've been trying the key she gave me and it won't open any of the doors here. I can't call her either. There are some stairs at the end beside the elevator. I'm just going to run up to the lobby and grab Pam."

"Dex, don't you dare leave me!" I yell and pound on the door for impact.

"Well what the hell do you suppose we do then? Hang out like this until a maid shows up? What if they are done for the night? Do you really want to spend a night locked in there?"

No. I don't. But I don't want him taking off and leaving me alone in this scary, dark room either.

"Look," he continues, "I'll be right back. And I mean, right back. I'm not going to let anything happen to you."

That's kind of hard to do when you aren't here, I think but I know I have no choice. Either he goes or I'm locked in here all night. That thought is too terrifying to fathom.

"OK," I say hesitantly.

He taps the door lightly. "I'll be right back."

I hear his feet scurry off and a door at the end of the hall open. And then silence again.

I put my back against the door and face the darkness of the foreign room. I flick the flashlight on and slowly graze it across the black.

In a creepy, fleeting light it illuminates a few laundry bins, laundry machines, a makeshift office consisting of a whiteboard, a file cabinet and the desk I ran into.

And a dead man hanging from the ceiling.

I scream bloody murder, dropping the flashlight and camera in the process.

They fall to my feet in an outburst as loud as my wail, and as I quickly fumble for them, the light in the room goes on.

I raise my hand to my eyes to shield them from the light and try to get a glimpse of what's going on. The image of that dead, bloated man hanging by his neck is seared into my brain.

The laundry hampers, machines and office are all still here.

The hanging man is gone.

There is an African-American woman who stands to my far left, her hand on a light fixture, giving me a quizzical stare. She's young and thin with large eyes and is wearing a plain grey dress with a white ruffled apron across it. A very classic-looking maid.

"Good heavens, child," she exclaims in a thick Southern accent. "What on earth are you doing in here?"

I blink hard, trying to make sense of the situation. The maid looks at my hands and what I'm holding.

"Are you filming me? Who are you? What is this?" she demands, her voice growing higher with each question.

"I...I'm Perry Palomino," I stammer, my voice squeaking.

"Am I supposed to know who you are?" she asks and puts her hands on her hips.

"Uh, no," I say and give her an awkward smile. "I'm here with my partner Dex. Dex Foray. We are, uh, we doing a project here. We have permission of the night manager. Pam...something. She said we could come down here and film."

"Just what are you filming. Charlie Chaplin?"

Hmmmm. How to explain the next part without seeming batshit crazy.

"Well..." I begin.

She cocks her brow at me and folds her arms. She's in no hurry.

I let out a burst of air through my nose and say, "We're ghost hunters."

She smiles, her teeth blindingly white. She doesn't sound as amused as she looks. "You're pulling my chain."

"No, no sadly I'm not. We have a show, Experiment in Terror. It's on the Internet."

"The Internet?"

"I know, it sounds lame but we've been doing quite well. I mean, we have advertisers and people actually tune into watch us. Well, watch me. Since I'm the host. Just not a very good one. Actually I think people tune into laugh at me, but whatever gets me a pay check." I'm rambling now.

"This is a radio show?" she asks.

"No, just on the web."

She frowns and walks toward me, eying my hands. "What kind of camera is that?"

Though there is nothing menacing at all in her voice, I flinch a little and back up into the door. She pauses and gives me another disbelieving look.

"You never seen a black woman before?"

"Huh?"

"I know we aren't too common out West here but you best be getting used to us."

Now it's my turn to frown. I study her more closely. She's at least in her early thirties, her pretty face is unlined but she has this authoritative air about her. Everything sounds like an accusation but one that's filled with a hint of doubt. Though she's trying hard to hide it, I can see she's as afraid of me as I am afraid of her.

I raise the infrared to her, slowly, as if she is a skittish cat, and show her the screen, flicking it on.

She looks at it and shakes her head, not getting it.

"It's infrared," I explain. "It picks up heat energy."

"Well my oh my," she says. "That's the dumbest thing I've ever heard. You trying to make a motion picture?"

"No m'am," I can't help but say. "Much less than that."

"And you what? You hunt ghosts?"

"It sounds ridiculous when you put it that way," I admit.

She snorts and turns around, heading back to the machines. "It sounds ridiculous anyway you put it, child."

"We've just been told the ghost of Parker Hayden is known to haunt this room."

She stops in mid-stride. Her whole body is tensed up. It makes me tense up too. I must have hit a nerve.

"Have you seen him?" I whisper, making sure the camera is running but not pointing it in her direction just yet. I don't want to scare her and just getting our dialog recorded would be more than enough for the show.

"Seen who?" she repeats slowly. She still doesn't turn around.

"Parker Hayden. The ship millionaire. He lost all of his money during the strike and then killed himself–"

"Don't you dare speak ill of him," she threatens in a low voice so raspy and ragged that it almost sounds demonic. "He would never kill himself."

I bite my lip, unsure of how to proceed. I have no idea what is going on but those hairs are standing up on the back of my neck again.

"Do you know who he was?" I ask carefully.

Finally, she turns around and looks at me with tear-filled eyes.

"He was...my friend."

I don't know what to make of that. "Pardon me?"

"He was...my lover. I haven't seen him for days, not since they threw him out."

Oh. Dear. God.

"He wouldn't have killed himself though," she continues, her voice warbling with emotion. A tear spills down her cheek, leaving a dark trail. "He has troubles but he wouldn't have done that. Not Parker. Not my Parker."

"Ummmm," is all I can say to that. I slowly raise the infrared camera and aim it at her.

"You're filming me now?"

Yes, I sure am, I think and look at the screen. My breath freezes in my throat. Through the infrared, I can see my own hand in front of me burning a deep red. The shape of the maid though is coming out a steely blue, like the blue I saw in the hotel room.

I look back at her. And I realize I'm talking to a ghost.

"I said, are you filming me? Answer me, child," she says, her voice angry. She wipes away a tear with a rough swipe of her hand.

"No," I say quickly and lower the camera. "Sorry, I...what did you say your name was?"

"I didn't. It's May," she answers. "I'd say I'm pleased to meet you Miss Perry Palomino, but I'm afraid I'm a victim of some terrible joke."

There's one thing I've learned about the dead: they don't like to learn they are dead. Things kind of go crazy when they do, like their entire existence is shattered and they go along with it. I mean, imagine you think you're alive and someone tells you you're dead. Then you start putting together all the pieces and BLAM! Your entire world is ripped apart. The very realization can make most ghosts simply disappear. The acceptance pushes them on into the afterlife, or whatever the next step is.

But for selfish reasons, I don't want to lose May. I don't want her to realize she's dead. Because while I've got her here, in this room, I can use her. I can use her to get to Parker.

"When was the last time you saw Parker?" I ask her innocently enough. I still keep the camera aimed at the floor.

"Five days ago," she says. "He said he'd come by the next day. I was here waiting. He never did. I reckoned...I don't know. I feared the worst. The very worst."

"Which was?"

"That he was dead, Miss Palomino. But not by his own hand. No, he that was murdered."

"By who?"

"The sharks. Who else?"

My face must have contorted into a look of pure confusion because she continues, her voice and demeanor more impassioned by the second.

"The sharks are the fellas who he owed money to. You just don't lose a boat without losing a few friends. These fellas meant business and I seen them threaten him more than a few times. Parker went and told the police but they do nothing. They don't have no control. Parker would tell me he was scared. So scared. He's a man who don't get scared, you hear that. So if he's scared, I reckon there's a reason for it. They are after his life."

The idea of Parker being murdered by men he owed money to is just as believable as suicide. I don't know what to believe but I choose to give the ghost the benefit of the doubt.

"Did Parker leave any proof, any records, that these men were after him?"

She closes her eyes for a second and it's then that I notice a strange transparency about her.

"There was his diary," she tells me. Her eyes open slowly. "It's his checkbook. But he would keep a log on the back of the checks he couldn't write anymore. Most of it doesn't make much sense to me...if I could talk to him, hear from him, he could tell you himself. I just need to talk to him. Can you find him for me? You said you knew the manager?"

"Yes...but I don't think it will make much difference."

"Why is that?"

"Do you know where he would have kept the checkbook?"

"On his person. Where else? What aren't you telling me? What are you really doing here?"

I look down at the screen and aim it at her. She glows a translucent blue. It's beautiful, for once, and not scary.

"What happened to Parker?" she goes on, her voice cracking over his name. I don't say anything but I meet her eye and I know, in one look, that she knows the truth. Maybe not that she's dead. But that he is.

Her face crumbles. She puts her hand to her head and stumbles backward.

Out of instinct, I go after her, my arms outstretched, hoping to reach her in time before she goes over.

I almost reach her when she smashes against the floor with a sickening thud. The world goes black. The lights go off and I find myself on my knees, my leggings ripping open on the cold hard floor.

"May?" I cry out and raise the camera, hoping to see her blue form through the darkness. I only read my own heat and no one else's.

I slowly get to my feet and try to flick on the flashlight with my own hand.

Cold fingers reach over my elbow in a stealthy grasp. I can feel the ice through my jacket.

I am yanked harshly to the side until I crash into a wheeled laundry bin and another hand grabs me by the face and pulls me over the side and into it.

All I can think about is the painful cold that comes from the grasp, as if permafrost is entering my veins and creating a sheet of ice on my face. And then I find myself face first in a laundry bin, smothered by a million towels and pulled deeper and deeper into them until I can't breathe and I can't scream and I can't move. I can only drown here.

The blackness behind my eyes grows darker somehow, as if the dark has a million different shades and nuances and I was only scratching the surface. It's a different kind of obsidian, one that signals the end, finality. I don't want to succumb to it, but all I can see is this blackness, and all I can feel are these hands that won't stop pulling me deeper, that won't let go, and my thoughts become less...and less...and less...

"Perry!"

I think I hear my name but it sounds too far away to be real. I think of May and wonder where she came from.

"Perry!"

My name again. It sounds familiar.

There is a rush of noise and light and commotion and I feel more hands grabbing me. Only these ones are warm and though they are strong, I can feel the care seeping through them.

I think of Dex. And remember where I am.

I put my hands at the bottom of the bin, and push myself off. As I do so, they come in contact with something beneath one of the towels. I'm afraid it's the remains of whoever was pulling me down before, but I still close my fingers around it as Dex yanks me out of the bin and into the harsh fluorescent light of the room.

I cough wildly, trying to find my breath as Dex keeps his hands on either side of my shoulders, steadying me. As the air hits my lungs and my wincing subsides, I notice Pam standing beside the door, a key in hand, her face in a look of absolute terror.

"Perry," Dex says. "Perry look at me."

I manage to look at him. His dark eyes are searching mine relentlessly, his brow furrowed, his stance tense.

"Are you OK?" he asks.

I nod, feeling relieved and embarrassed all at the same time.

"Was I sticking out of the laundry bin?" I ask with trepidation.

He nods and I see a hint of a smile tug at the corner of his mouth. It would have been a comical sight, my giant ass in the air and all.

"I leave you alone for five seconds..." His tone is light but he knows there is more to the story. And that I'll fill him in on it later.

"What's in your hands?" Pam asks, looking at them with curiosity.

I glance down and see I am holding a rectangular cover of well-worn leather. I open it carefully and see what I thought I would see. A checkbook filled with writing. The possible proof that Parker Hayden was murdered and not a victim of suicide.

I walk over to Pam and place the item in her hands. She looks up at me surprised and confused.

"You may want to run this by a historian. Or even the police," I say. "There's a chance that Parker

Hayden didn't commit suicide after all. It could be a cold case file. A very cold case."

I feel extremely cheesy as I tell Pam that. No surprise, Dex says, "Wow, I leave you for one minute and suddenly you're CSI: Portland."

I give him a tired smile. I'm ready to go home.

*****

A few days pass when I get a call from Dex. We're not at the point where we call each other just to talk, but every contact I have with him is still important and I still get stupid butterflies every time I see his name pop up on the call display. This time, he's calling to talk about our episode at The Benson.

"How's it all looking?" I ask as I sit on my bed, listening to my younger sister Ada argue with my dad downstairs.

"Oh it's looking fucking fantastic, kiddo," Dex says, his voice coming in low and smooth over the line. "I just want to hug you for keeping that camera rolling while May was talking. I'll have to run it over some other footage and do that little subtitle thing underneath but it really helps our case, especially when you get that blue shit on screen. That really is something."

"Best show ever?" I ask, amused at his praise.

"Well," he says slowly, "it probably would have helped had I been around but you did OK on your own."

"I'll take that as a compliment."

"There's something else, too, you should take as a compliment."

My eyes perk up and I sit up a bit straighter, putting down my Spin magazine. "What's that?"

"Pam just called me. She said she handed over the checkbook to the police who are having a division look into it or something. Anyway, the point is ever since our visit, all the haunting in the hotel has stopped."

"What do you mean, all hauntings?"

"Well she says she usually gets some sort of feedback each day. Since our shoot, there hasn't been any. I don't know what that means but she seems to think that whatever you did down in that laundry room...well, I guess you cleared the place."

"So I'm an exorcist now?"

"Don't flatter yourself, kiddo. You're miles away from being Father Merrin and for all we know the haunting could start up again. I'm just saying...next time you feel like being hard on yourself because we aren't making a difference and there's no point to any of this…I dunno. Don't. Because you did good here. You did good."

I let Dex ramble on a bit more to please my ego and then we hang up. Like the other times before, I still don't know what to make of my ghost hunting. I don't know how I got roped into doing the show, how I ended up being a magnet for the supernatural and what on earth it has in store for me. The only thing I do know is that it's dangerous and I'm compelled to keep doing it.

But I also know that even though someone is dead, is doesn't mean they're beyond help. And for every ten ghosts that try and kill me, if I end up saving one of them, it might be worth it after all.

Though you may want to remind me of that, next time I'm locked in a coffin or something.

OLD BLOOD

PROLOGUE

My dearest Declan and Perry. I don't know if you'll ever hear this. If these tapes are something you'll listen to again, if you'll keep listening to the end. I know everything is a mess right now and you're both hurting from what happened. Sometimes I may not be able to reach you but I can see you. You're with me – both of you – always, even if you aren't with each other.

Declan, if you do happen upon this one more time, you need to go after Perry. Swallow up your pain and pride and go to her. She needs your help more than ever and I don't know how much I can do for her. Here on the Otherside, I feel things...see things. Things that were once people who want to take her. Things that one day might come for you again. I'm afraid time is running out. So pick yourself up off the floor and go to her.

If you happen to hear this, bring this recording along with you. And when you save her, play it for her.

My story is her story too.

CHAPTER ONE

I don't know where to begin. Looking back on one's life is a daunting task, trying to recall every month, every year. Even here, in this Thin Veil, where my memories seem sharper, it's difficult to recall the many details of my life. All that stand out are the important moments, the moments, big and small, that shaped the path I chose. The same path that led me to my death. And led me to you both.

I never thought I'd tell a story that would end with the way I died. This won't be a pretty one. But it's the truth and someone needs to hear it. Especially someone like you and Perry. You both are so much like me. So much like each other. If anyone can learn from the mistakes I made it would be you.

I just hope that by the end, you'll find it in both your hearts to forgive me.

According to the records, I was born on a surprisingly cold day in May of 1925. There had been a rare snow storm that swept through the wooded valley where my father and mother lived in their tiny stone house and I was born under thick flannel sheets with the doctor coaxing me to breathe.

I regret that first breath.

My parents were particularly hardy Swedes. The woods encompassed a large lake, with the nearest town a two-hour walk away. My father was a Lutheran minister for a church that was on the other side of the lake. In the summer he'd row across the shallow waters, in the winter he'd skate. My mother was uneducated and liked to stay home and knit extra thick socks for the cold months. My earliest memory is of me itching away at the scratchy, coarse wool that covered my feet like abrasive boots.

We didn't have many possessions as my father was staunch in his belief that God gives us everything we need. To him, this also included love. I never saw an ounce of it from him, not to me, and not to my mother. To him his God was everything and we were just creatures of the night. Simple people. Sinners. He never said this outright, but you could see it in his eyes. The way he'd look down at his worshippers was the same way he'd look at us.

My mother was a quiet and well-mannered person who had been stripped of her backbone. I remember watching her at the stove in the mornings trying to heat the water to make coffee. She looked so small and frail, hunched over and defeated by life. Then there was I. Even at six, I was tall for my age and a bundle of energy that rattled my father's nerves. I'm fairly certain he saw me as a spawn of the Devil. He was never cruel in his beatings, but he made sure I felt them. He didn't like it when I made up stories about young girls lurking in our garden and wolves tearing babies apart. He said my imagination would be my demise one day, my ultimate sin, and if he didn't use his belt the way God told him to, I could never be saved.

I'm sure you realize that there *were* young girls hiding behind tomato plants and that the woods *were* full of hellhounds that ate abandoned children. I saw them, which makes it true. I never once doubted myself even when I should have. That's the main difference between you and me.

The first time it happened though, I did blame my mother. You wouldn't know it by looking at her, by watching the tight line that formed between her eyes as she knitted, the clipped and cautious way she talked around my father, but my mother was a wonderful storyteller with a surprising sense of humor. On Saturdays she would take me out into the woods and we'd follow this well-trodden trail through the birch trees until pine and rock took over and we could pass no more. We would stop at a ragged bolder and she'd hand me a piece of licorice. I'm sure she thought the salty sweet treat was the reason I looked forward to our walks, but that was only a bonus. I liked being with my mother as much as I liked being away from my father. She was like a different person all together. She still spoke in hushed tones, but her eyes would dance as she told me the legends of the land, about supernatural beasts that roamed the woods and lived in the lake and about clever trolls who waited for young girls like myself. The stories were half a warning – I see that now – to stay safe at home and never wander into the woods by myself, but I also knew it was a way for my mother to express herself. Maybe it was a way for her to feel like she was giving me something since we were allowed to have so little.

So, on one summer evening, when the light almost kissed midnight, I fell ill. I don't know what it was exactly, but it struck around dinner time, a terrible piercing at my temple that caused my arm to spasm and knock the smoked trout out of my plate. The pain was so bad that I could only curl up in a ball on the cool floor. My father was out at the church and my mother didn't know what to do. Back then we had no telephone, no radio, no anything. Not even a horse. My mother placed a cold compress on my head and got me into my bed, then she left for the closet neighbor, who was about a twenty-minute walk away.

The pain continued for a few moments until all I could see were black spots and waves and then as quickly as it had come on, it stopped. The pain had vanished and I felt fine. Perhaps better than fine. I listened hard as the ringing left my ears and was comforted by the rattle of woodpeckers outside and the silence of the house. For once, I was left all alone and I could do whatever I wanted.

I slowly got up and smiled at the sunshine that was pouring in the window. I remember a lake breeze blowing back the red and white muslin curtain and I smiled so wide it hurt my cheeks. This was freedom. My first taste of it.

I walked down our narrow staircase to the living room and kitchen and thought about what I could do in the next forty minutes or so. There was a chance that mama was running so I'd have to do it fast.

Unfortunately there wasn't I could do. As I said, we didn't have many possessions and the things I loved most were books that mama read to me when papa wasn't looking but I couldn't read yet. So I settled for licorice. I knew it was hidden in the washbasin on the highest shelf.

I brought out the chair from underneath the table and began to push it toward the shelf when I heard a peculiar sound. A giggle.

I stopped and looked around. I was alone in the house, I knew that. Yet there it was again. A light laugh. It was girlish and airy and sparkled in the breeze.

I forgot all about the sweets and walked over to the front door. I paused before I put my hand on the knob, listening again for the laugh. Now, there it was. It was definitely coming from outside, definitely not my mother. Nor a neighbor for I had never seen any children around except for the boy at the goat farm my mother was on her way to.

I felt a strange cool feeling travel down my spine. It made me wince and I began to second guess going outside to investigate but I still did. My hand turned the knob like it did every day and I stepped outside into our yard.

Our house may have been small but our yard was bigger. It stretched all the way down to the lake's edge where dull brown sand mixed with skinny weeds. Today the water lapped noisily at the shore in a hurried manner, like it was rushing to get somewhere. Perhaps the house. Perhaps me.

I shook such foolish thoughts out of my head and tried not to think about the giant fish woman my mother told me lived in the lake. I faced the trees that bordered the grassy yard and watched as they swayed against each other, their bright leaves glinting in the soft light.

The giggle resounded again. This time it was coming from behind the house where my mother kept a vegetable garden and a small root cellar for preserving over the winter.

I crept along the side of the house, grateful that my tiny leather shoes were worn and didn't squeak. When I reached the edge of the building, I slowly inched my head around and looked at the garden.

I didn't move but my breath left me.

In the garden, behind the tomato plants that were snaking up a knotted wood plank, was a girl. She was maybe a year older than me, about the same height. She had the blondest hair I had ever seen, a sharp contrast to my mass of dark waves. She was wearing a red dress that fell in a straight line, free of the bunching I was used to wearing, and shiny white shoes.

She was hiding behind that plant. And she was watching me.

There was no use in me ducking behind the wall. I had been seen and from the strange look in the girls aqua eyes, it looked like I had been expected.

I cleared my throat and tried to speak but all speech had left me. I tried again, worried that something bad would happen if I didn't say something and finally my tongue worked.

"I'm Pippa Lindstrom," I said, keeping most of my body out of her sight. "What's your name?"

I expected a response. Even for a little girl, it was a straight forward question. But the blonde one just lifted her finger to lips, a skinny pale thing I glimpsed through the tomatoes. Her eyes flashed wide and shot to a place over my head.

I followed her gaze.

Behind me, near the start of the path that led into the woods, was a tall, dark man. He was only darkness. I know this doesn't make much sense but I could barely make out any of his features, anything that made him human. Everything about him was shadows and black and emptiness. He was dressed in a black cloak, black shoes and pants and his bare skin, his neck and face, looked as if he was standing in the shade of a dense tree.

Only he wasn't. The sun was directly on him but it didn't...reach him. It was if the light couldn't even illuminate a single cell on his body.

My blood froze like a winter lake. I looked back at the girl behind the tomato plant and she was still there with her finger to her mouth, her eyes pleading with me not to say anything.

So I didn't. I didn't even nod in fear of giving her away. I just calmly looked back at the man as if he was the only person I saw outside my house.

The man stared at me. I don't know how I knew this because I couldn't see his eyes, even if he had eyes. But he was staring and in that way the owl does before he decides to bite the head off a mouse. It was predatory.

Then he turned and walked into the woods. Maybe he floated, my memory is a bit fuzzy. If I recall correctly, I think he just disappeared into the bark of the trees. But he was there one minute and the next he was gone.

Sure that the black man had vanished, I stepped around the house and walked toward the girl. She stumbled back a few feet, looking scared. I noticed how white her shoes stayed, despite the layer of mud in the garden from yesterday's rain. It was strange. But what wasn't?

"Who are you?" I asked, wanting an answer this time. "Where do you live?"

"I live in the lake," she said.

I giggled and put my hands on my hips. "You're a liar. No one lives in the lake."

Not even monsters, I thought. *That was make believe.*

She shook her head and began to walk through the mud. Her feet never left any footprints.

Was this make believe too?

"Where do you live?" I asked again as she skirted past me and walked faster, heading for the side of the house. I followed after her, my eyes glued to her feet that never got dirty, that never made a mark.

"I live in the lake," she said again, as if I didn't hear her.

As she reached the front and the lake loomed before us, the water calmed instantaneously. Like there was a switch that made the currents move and stop.

I knew the girl didn't live in the lake, but I also knew not to argue with her. She was the first girl my age that I had ever talked to. I wanted her to stay around and play with me. I wanted to give her licorice from the washbasin and ask her to stay for cake but I quickly realized the lake was the only thing she aware of now.

"Don't go," I cried out after her, my long legs catching up. "Please."

"I have to go home now. He'll find me here."

"Who?" I asked. I was walking beside her now and struggling to keep up. Though I was tall, she was a bit taller, older and more determined. Her fair hair bounced around her face and her aqua eyes were focused on the water. She didn't blink at all.

"Where are you going?" I asked, stopping just as my own shoes almost met the shoreline.

She didn't answer and she didn't stop. She walked straight into the lake, effortlessly, as if the water were just air. Her clothes didn't even soak in the liquid. The water slid around her like a shiny curtain and within seconds her head disappeared. She was in the lake.

I took off my shoes and tossed them onto the grass behind me, thinking not to get them wet for whatever reason, and then I went in the lake too. It was cold as January and deeper than anything, not the warm shallow water it should have been. Within seconds my body had seized up from the temperature and my feet couldn't find the muddy bottom. My head was above water, then my nose, then nothing at all. I sank and sank and sank until I found my blonde friend again.

At first I thought she was grabbing hold of my leg. Perhaps she was going to pull me up to the surface. My lungs hurt and my eyes were burning and I needed air more than anything.

But in the last moments before I lost consciousness I realized she wasn't grabbing me.

She was bumping into me.

She was upright, swaying in the murky water like a reed in the current. Her hair floated around her like a golden net. At her feet, at her white shoes that were now muddled with scuffs and dirt, were thick, rusted chains. They wrapped around her slender ankles and thin socks and kept her down, anchored to the bottom.

She looked dead until she raised her head at me.

My own face looked back.

I screamed and a rush of water filled my lungs within seconds. The watery world became shadows.

The next thing I remembered was waking up in my own bed, covered in a thick quilt, a mug of hot tea beside me.

I was in my tiny bedroom. It was nighttime, but I didn't know when. All I knew is that my mother was in the middle of speaking to me, as if I had been speaking to her too. It was boring stuff, something about a church and a minister.

Downstairs I heard cupboards slamming shut, a sure sign that papa was angry. Was he angry at me? What had happened?

My mother sensed my apprehension because she smoothed the hair off my head.

"You musn't talk about that girl anymore," she whispered. She leaned in close and I caught a whiff of the perfume she only wore on Sundays. Had I been sleeping for a couple of days now?

And the girl. The girl with the blonde hair and the boxy dress and the white shoes that wouldn't smudge until she was dead at the bottom of the lake. She had been real. She wasn't a dream. I had seen her, hiding behind that tomato plant.

"He's being good not using the belt," she continued. "You need to keep being good too."

I wanted to say so much, but I couldn't. I had no idea what I had been babbling about in my half-dead delirious state. There was no doubt my parents would have chalked any mentions of the girl to over-imagination, lies, and possibly the Devil's work.

A few days later, when my parents deemed me as normal and no longer a threat to myself, we heard news from a local woodcutter who was passing through. Greta Lund, the young daughter of one of papa's worshippers, had been found dead at the bottom of the lake. A man had been fishing and his hook got caught on her net of hair. There was no mention of chains but I knew what I had seen. I had seen her and I had seen what had really happened to her. She had been murdered. Was it the blackened man? I didn't know at the time. But I knew then that what I saw was real and not real all at once. I was special. And not in a fortunate way.

CHAPTER TWO

The second time this sort of thing happened to me, I was a few years older and could no longer blame my mother's stories for giving my gift fire. She had stopped telling them many years ago. It was the first time my special sight caused loss – I no longer had that closeness with my mother.

I had started going to school in Ullapa, the closest town and would get a ride in every morning with our neighbor Arstand and his son Stäva. As you may recall, Arstand was the goat farmer who found me, along with my mother, floating in the lake when I was six. That explained why Arstand was always a bit jumpy with me, as if I was going to pop up and say "boo!" at any moment.

But he tolerated me enough to fit me in his new vehicle and take me to school. My parents were still behind the times and my father shunned motor vehicles as being unnecessary idols and symbols of gluttony. I suppose he was right, but it was still a convenient way to get around.

Stäva had ended up being my only, and, by default, closest friend. He was a bit strange and funny to look at but strange suited me just fine. He was small for his age and had ears that stuck out. Arstand called him "elefant." It didn't seem to bother Stäva much though. He had a sunny personality and loved to listen to me prattle on about this and that. He was also quite the adventurer and when we first started playing together we would explore the farm he lived on, climbing up into the haylofts and jumping onto the piles below or feeding the baby goats (when we weren't chasing them around). My parents weren't too happy that I was spending so much of my time away from home, but I suppose my mother felt she was in debt to Arstand and after a while they didn't seem to mind. Perhaps it was a relief to them that someone else was taking care of me.

It was at Stäva's that I was introduced to more modern conveniences, aside from the car of course. Being a goat farmer was more profitable than being a minister and they had things such as a library and a radio. The library was a great place for me to sink my teeth, especially as I had learned to read at that point, but the radio trumped all. When I was there after school, his father, mother and two younger brothers would sit around the giant radio and listen to broadcasts coming out of Stockholm. I found the news to be boring, except when it touched on the troubles in Europe, but I lived for the plays and radio shows that played after. It was then that I fell in love with acting and the theatre. I couldn't see the show of course, and I had never seen a performance in my life as church singing didn't count to me, but I could envision it all in my head like I was there with the actors.

"I'm going to be on the radio one day," I remember whispering into Stäva's funny ear. We were sitting on the braided rug in his living room, a place that smelled like a mix of manure, sour milk and home baked bread. It doesn't sound like a winning combination but it's funny now how that smell makes me think of home, even though it wasn't my home. It's not that Stäva's parents were particularly nice to me. Like I noted, Arstand was always watching me carefully. His wife Else was a nice woman but she seemed lost in her head more often than not and spent most of her time working with the goat cheese or doting on Stäva's younger siblings. I wasn't a pest to them but I wasn't loved either. Yet I still had a sense of freedom and hope in their peculiar-smelling place.

With the idea of being an actress in my head, I focused solely on that. I mentioned it once to my parents and ended up getting a belt across my thigh. It didn't hurt. I was too angry for it to hurt. I was angry at my father for being so close-minded about his daughter's dreams (for what were we without dreams) and at my mother for never sticking up for me. Ever since the lake incident, when she stopped with her stories, she stopped being my friend as well. It hurt more than anything, more than all the belts, more than the feeling of drowning in that ice cold lake.

So I never mentioned it to my parents again but that did me no good. I should have known they'd investigate where the sinful idea came from and when they found out I'd be listening to the radio I was banned from going to Stäva's. They didn't care enough to ban me from seeing him in particular, just that I couldn't listen to the radio. My ears couldn't be polluted by foreign ideas. They even had a talk with his parents and to keep peace as neighbors, they agreed.

What was it to Stäva's parents anyway? They didn't care if I couldn't listen to the radio. One less child crowding their house.

It didn't break me, however. I merely became more resolved in my determination that I *would* be an actress one day. I'd find a way, somehow.

But since I wasn't allowed to spend too much time in Stäva's home anymore, we were left to our own devices in the great outdoors. Playing in the hay and harassing goats became tiresome by the time I was nine, so we started going on after school jaunts into the woods.

There was a part of me that was a little chicken over the tall trees and dark paths and I was forever on the lookout for a man with no face. He didn't show up. But something else did. Something much more horrific.

It was a cool, grey day in early fall. The leaves had just gone from crisp red to the color of soggy wood as they clung helplessly to the branches.

Stäva was walking ahead of me as he did, leaves crunching beneath him. He was two years older and only lately did he start to grow into his age. He often walked ahead, pretending he was a woodland hunter, or perhaps a wily prince, and kept me behind him. I didn't mind the protection, even if it was from an 11-year old.

I also didn't mind when he stopped on our walk at one point and took my hand in his. It was the first time I remember feeling the difference between us. He was a boy and I was a girl and that little thrill shot up my arm, the same feelings I imagined when I had listened to the more romantic parts of the radio shows.

I suppose I was so awed by the simple gesture of hand holding that I didn't hear the howl first. Suddenly Stäva's grasp tightened on mine and his bright eyes searched the greying woods.

"What is it?" I asked, not used to seeing panic on his face.

"Did you hear that?"

I tensed up and listened.

I heard it. A howl, like a wolf or a wild dog. It came from our left and seemed to fill the trees like a blanket.

I looked back at him with frightened eyes.

"We should head back," he said.

I nodded but just as we turned on the path I heard a child's cry mixed in with the canine's.

I stopped and pulled hard on Stäva's hand as he tried to keep walking.

"Listen!" I whispered hoarsely.

"We can't be out here with wolves!" he yelled back, struggling to keep his voice down. All Swedish children were likely to have been told tales of vicious wolves in the wild woods. I had heard mine from my mother. But the human sounds made this story different.

"There's a girl out there!" I told him as I heard another whimper coming from the same direction. I wasn't actually sure if it was a girl or not, but they were young like us and needed our help.

"I don't hear anything, come on," Stäva said pulling at me again.

"No!" I yelled and ripped my hand out of his sweaty grip. "Listen again, you can hear it."

The wolf howled first. Then fierce, drooling growls swarmed us. And finally, the child's cry.

"Daddy" I could hear the child yell.

But Stäva was immune.

"I don't hear anyone but wolves. We have to get out of here."

"You go!" I said and then I turned around and took off at a gallop into the darkening trees, toward the horrendous sound of snapping jaws.

I was aware of Stäva yelling behind me and perhaps for a bit he may have given chase. I certainly don't blame him for letting me go, or if it was a case of him not being able to catch up. He was older but I was the same height as him and my legs were born to run. Within a few minutes of tireless scampering through the birch trees and overgrown roots and berry patches, I was alone.

Alone and cursing myself with the only bad words I knew.

I waited with my hands on my knees, my socks splattered with mud, breathing heavily. I had lost the path at some point, so it didn't help that I was lost along with being completely alone.

Another howl and another human cry.

Of course I wasn't *completely* alone.

"You're an idiot, Pippa," I said aloud, hoping maybe Stäva would hear me. Hoping the wolves wouldn't. Just what was I thinking? I was tall but I was still nine and my survival skills consisted of picking berries and throwing stones. I was hardly a candidate for a rescue mission. And Stäva had never heard the child crying. Perhaps it was all in my head.

But now. There it was again.

"Someone help me!" the child cried and now I was certain it was a girl younger than me.

My fingers and toes ached with the cold that was steadily encroaching. Autumn in Sweden wasn't very kind. It would be blissfully warm one day and then a frozen wasteland the next. Being in the dark woods overnight could possibly kill me. Yet the fact remained that I had chosen to come out here and with that lay my fate. Knowing was better than not knowing, even if I wound up dead.

I know such thoughts don't make a lot of sense when you take into account how young I was. But there was a part of me that didn't fear things the way I should have. Though I was still afraid, the concept of death was one that never had much weight with me. It had nothing to do with my father and his religious ways, instead it was a matter of having experienced death before. I knew I died in some way when I found the girl in the lake. I don't know how I came back to life but I know that even though she was dead she still protected me. I felt safe knowing I could walk away from such a thing.

It was foolish of me to think that. I was young and, as I said to myself, an idiot. But that's the way it was. I'm sure you might think it noble that I would risk death to save a stranger, but I don't know if that's how I saw it. It was more a matter of something I had to do, than something I should do.

So even though every part of my body was cold and screaming for me to yell for Stäva, to at least try and find my way back before the real darkness set in, I didn't. I walked toward the noises like some child martyr, creeping silently as I could through the rough and dying foliage.

The darkness was dropping quickly and the forest began to take more ominous shapes. As the white bark of the birch gave way into rock and pine, my eyes played tricks on me. I saw shadows, shapes and faces everywhere I looked. It took all my nerve to keep it together and walk on.

Finally I came to a small clearing where the dying twilight penetrated enough for me to see.

I'll never forget it and I would pray every night that I could.

In the clearing, trampling down the long, wild grass were three dogs. I say dogs because they didn't look as sleek and lupine as wolves. They were bulkier, sloppier, and lacked any grace I would associate with them. Even while killing, wolves can look elegant. This was plain revolting.

The dogs were pulling at a young girl, maybe a few years younger than I. She had long brown hair that swung around her head as it lay limply to the side. One crocodile-toothed dog had one of her tiny feet in its mouth. Another had a hand and another the arm, teeth chomped down at the tender inside of the elbow.

They were tearing the girl apart and it took me a second to realize one of her legs was missing, ripped off somewhere underneath her bloodied skirt.

I froze, unable to move, to speak, to breathe. I don't even know how I existed in that moment except to say that I saw it all.

The dogs never looked at me, they just continued to pull and tear until the one dog ripped the hand away at the wrist. With a wet, red tear she slumped unevenly to the ground as the remaining dogs played tug of war from opposite sides.

Then she lifted her head up and looked at me.

She was still alive. Her face was white as snow, her eyes pink and puffy.

"Why did he leave me?" she cried out, her voice barely heard above the dog's snarls, their sick, chomping jaws.

I couldn't speak, I couldn't say anything. I was foolish. Helpless. Useless.

The girl kept her dark eyes on mine, almost oblivious to the horror which was happening.

"Why did he tell me to go?" she asked, expecting an answer from me. I could only shake my head slowly from side to side, not even sure if what I was watching was real, though I knew it was.

The dog at her foot gave a throaty growl and took a large bite near her knee. With one sickening solid chomp it tore it off. Not cleanly. It was messy, bloody, a gruesome mix of bone and stringy tendons.

The girl finally stopped looking at me. She closed her mouth. She closed her eyes.

In my head I heard her.

Go Pippa, run now!

I couldn't explain how she was able to get inside me but she was. I didn't waste any time either. The spell-like haze I was under lifted and pure panic filled my able joints.

I took off into the woods like a shot, not looking behind me once. Her cries had stopped but the snarls of the monsters carried on and followed me until I was coming out of the woods just outside of Stäva's place. I ran until the warm lights of his house welcomed me home and I told his worried family what had happened. I left the part about the girl talking to me in case they didn't believe it, but I told them everything else. At least Stäva could attest for the dogs being out there.

In my hysterical state I was driven home and sent to my bed with a strong cup of vodka and tea that mama made me drink in a few gulps. My parents were worried about me, how could they not when I saw what I did. But from the glances I caught between them, I knew they were worried about more than dogs. I just didn't know what.

That had happened on a Friday, so I didn't get a chance to see Stäva and his family until the weekend was over. I had spent my days inside, my mother terrified of another dog or wolf attack. When I finally got into Arstand's car on Monday morning, he told me that a few hunters had scoured the woods over the last few days. They found evidence of wild dogs in the area, perhaps a pack that had been tormenting chickens the next town over and they found traces of girl's clothing. But the clothing had been decaying and out in the woods for many, many years. Whatever the dogs were fighting over wasn't a young girl.

But I knew what I saw. The fact that there had been clothing found only gave me the proof I needed. The girl I saw wasn't alive, just as the girl in the lake wasn't either. She was probably a victim of neglect. You see, in the old days when families had sick children or were unable to care for them, they would take them out to the woods and let them be eaten by wild animals. That practice had stopped a long time ago, but I believed I saw the remains of it. One last cry for help...directed at me.

I thought about that for many years to come. Thankfully nothing that terrible haunted me in the years following. I never saw any more wild dogs or girls in the garden or men of shadows. I concentrated on my acting now that I was taking part in the program at school (somewhat secretly) and tried to forge my way forward the best I could.

Only on some days would I stop and wonder, why me? Why did they choose me when they could have anyone else?

I still don't really know.

CHAPTER THREE

When I said that nothing that terrible haunted me, I meant it. I was still haunted but by less terrible things.

There was the time I saw twin boys appear behind me when I was walking home from Stäva's. They never said anything, they just stood there with their pale faces and stared at me. It made me uneasy, to put it mildly, and they followed me down the road. It was only near my house that they ceased to exist, literally shimmering away like the air above hot pavement.

Another time I was serving detention after English Language class. I can't remember what for but I was a particularly rambunctious student and had a hard time sitting still. To my teacher we were alone however I was very much aware of an older boy in the corner of the room. At first he tried to get my attention by calling my name over and over again. The teacher never noticed so I had to assume he was a spirit of some kind. It helped that his eyes were bright purple with no pupils to mar the blank slate. Very unnatural.

When I continued to ignore him, he worked his way up to spitballs, flinging them in my hair. It was curious because the spitballs were real and stayed in my hair until I found some of them later that night. Finally, the boy gave up and left the room, a trail of shiny blood following him out the door. I watched my teacher carefully to see if he saw anything at all. He only shivered as the boy passed him by and didn't even bat an eye when the door opened and the bloody nuisance stepped out.

Little incidents like this happened all the time and I went on ignoring them. I didn't know what they wanted but when I was in public, it was wrong to ask them. Small town mentality existed back then and I did not want to be branded as the minister's crazy daughter.

At any rate, I had the theatre to keep me company. I joined the tiny drama club with the aim of putting on A Midsummer's Night's Dream by the year end. With my perseverance I won the role of Helena and wouldn't you know it but Stäva got the part of Demetrius. We were sixteen now and he had grown into quite the handsome young man, something I had never noticed until I was in the play with him. Surely I had noticed the way some of the girls my age would drool over him, but to me he was always the boy next door, the goat boy, my closest and dearest friend.

That all changed when we decided to go for a walk after school to discuss the play. We stayed clear of the woods as we usually did and strolled along the edge of the lake until our path turned upward into rolling hills of rye that waved in the breeze.

It was October and very cold but the sun was strong and heated my skin that wasn't wrapped in shawls and wool. The sky was as wide as a dome with that surreal blue that contrasted with yellow fields, just like the country's flag.

"Pippa," Stäva said, his voice low and his brow knotted. I stopped and looked at him, not used to seeing him look so grave.

He reached out for my hand and grasped it tightly. My mouth opened and a tiny "oh" came out, though I wasn't really sure what was going on. Were we rehearsing?

"We have to be young lovers," Stäva continued. I nodded. His eyes were filled with fear and something else I had never seen before. I had never seen lust on a man. It was so very different from the big doe-eyes the girls would give him.

"Yes. For the play," I told him.

His eyes narrowed slightly but were tempered by a lazy smile. "Yes, for the play."

"Are you nervous?" I asked. I suddenly was. My eyes dropped from his strange expression and focused on his long fingers curling around my own.

"Very," he whispered. I still didn't look up. The dynamic between us, between best friends who shared everything and were as comfortable around each other as worn socks, had changed. I didn't like to feel nervous because of Stäva and I didn't want him to be nervous because of me.

"We can act. We are actors," I said quietly. I took my eyes away from our hands and looked at the yellow grass at my feet.

"We don't have to," he said and he took his other hand under my chin and tipped it up so I was forced to meet his eyes. Before I could process what was happening, his lips were on mine. It wasn't easy –

it was both our first kiss. Our teeth knocked against each other and his nose pressed uncomfortably against my cheek.

I wish I could say that the kisses improved after that. They didn't. But I had figured that was the way things were. I had no frame of reference, after all. Oh, I didn't mind when Stäva kissed me or touched me but I didn't feel the way he felt. I didn't have the girly deer eyes and I didn't have that lustful look that was always on his face.

Nor did I feel anything the first time we made love. I say made love because I truly did love Stäva with all my heart, but it was a different kind of love. It was more brotherly than anything else. Though sex had been ingrained my head as morally wrong by my father, I broke the rules and decided to bed Stäva in his hayloft one balmy summer night. I hoped by doing so, the way I felt about him would change, that I would awaken some sexual being in my 17-year old soul.

All it ended up doing was awakening my fertility.

I ended up pregnant.

I figured it out after missing my monthly red visit and being sick for days on end. I didn't tell my parents, knowing how they'd feel about it. I didn't tell Stäva either. I knew there would be no point.

Children were something that I eventually wanted. But there were so many more things I wanted before then. I wanted to live. I wanted to spread my wings and get out of this small, dead place. I wanted to move to Stockholm and experience the city life. I wanted to take my acting and apply to somewhere that counted; not a tiny school but a theatre with paying patrons and lavish seating. I wanted that life first. Then I would work on what was expected of me. It's not that I didn't want to fall in love and start a family. I just wanted the choice of when.

If I told Stäva I was pregnant, he would make me go through with it and I loved him enough to do so. He already talked about us getting married. If I wanted that life, being a farmer's wife in a small town, maybe doing the occasional play in between pregnancies, then I would have been thrilled. Any girl would be so lucky to have Stäva as a husband and the father of their children. But I wasn't any girl. Far, far from it.

I got rid of the seed inside me by paying a visit to the local witch. This sounds fantastic, I know, but there is no way to describe her. Some said she was just the local whore, others said she made potions and powders when she practiced witchcraft, others said she was a holistic, natural doctor. All I knew was that she lived alone in a cottage in the high woods, where tall trees climbed upward into rocky outcrops and that no one said her name in public. They just called her "häxa" or The Witch.

There was a single dirt path that led the way, the age-old grooves in the dirt from hundreds of years of horse and donkey-drawn carts. I was frightened to death of going to see her but the prospect of having a child and being tied to the town was even more frightening.

The woman's name was actually Maria and even though she was intimidating with her wild white hair and rough mannerisms, she was rather nice. She made me up a tonic to put into tea, a combination of local sage, leaves and other herbs. She warned me against the pain and the bleeding but didn't pass any judgment on me for asking for it. It was like she understood where I was coming from and an expression of pride passed through her tired eyes when I told her my plans for the future. I was glad my secret was safe with her and hers – that she probably was a whore, judging by the man who came knocking on her door while I was there – was safe with me.

The next month was a blur. I passed the seed in the lake on a clear evening. The sun had just gone down enough past midnight that no one would see me if they were looking. I didn't like the idea of being in the water still, but as soon as the bleeding became nonstop, I felt it was the cleanest choice. I was afraid of what the smell of all that blood would attract from deep inside the woods. I suffered through the pain I deserved.

After that, it was time to go back to school. I had other plans. The abortion ravaged me with guilt daily and the longer I stayed where I was, living with my parents, going to school, going steady with Stäva, the more I felt guilty for what I had done. If I was going to go through such a selfish event, I had better follow through with my reasoning. Otherwise what was the point?

And so I dropped out of school just as we came into the last year and decided to head to Stockholm to pursue my dream. Maybe then the guilt would stop clawing at me.

My decision came as a shock to everyone I knew. Stäva wouldn't come with me and didn't understand how I could leave him. Neither did any of my classmates or teachers – to them, we were the perfect couple. My parents were livid. They told me that if I left I would not have a home to come back to when I returned. In other words, they disowned me. I expected as much from my father and didn't really care what he thought but my mother's actions surprised me. I suppose she was so hurt that I would leave them that I didn't deserve to be her daughter. I am still not sure if that's true or not. On good days I think my mother was wrong to shun me like that. On bad days, I couldn't really blame her. At least it prepared me for a pattern that would endure for the rest of my life. Looking back, I wonder where my "karma" began to fester. Was it when I had the abortion? Or was it when I selfishly abandoned my only love and family?

I left the place of my childhood with nothing on my back but a small sack full of belongings. I can still tell you what was in there: Two dresses, one fancier than the other. A tube of red lipstick for "acting" purposes. A clip for my hair. My nightgown, corset, stockings and two pairs of bloomers. A copy of Dante's Inferno in English to help my language skills (I nicked it from the school library). A tiny notebook and pencil. A handful of licorice.

I didn't have any money and was planning to hitch rides to the big city, but Stäva surprised me and borrowed his father's car to drive me to nearest train station. It was about an hour away and together we had our last ride together. He didn't say much to me but I could see how I was breaking his poor heart. It absolutely tore me up inside and I when he hugged me goodbye – slipping a wad of kronas in my pocket for the train and a few nights in a hotel – I broke down in tears. As emotional as I was on the inside, my steely reserve finally collapsed and in his arms.

"I don't understand you," he whispered into my ear as I choked back the tears that wouldn't stop coming. "But I hope you find what you're looking for."

And with that ringing in my ears, I got on the train and left my old life behind for good.

CHAPTER FOUR

In some ways, I did find what I was looking for. When I arrived in Stockholm two days later, dirty and tired, I was immediately enthralled by the big city. There was a pulse here with bright buildings as high as I've ever seen them and so many people it was like I was swimming in a sea of them. Speaking of the sea, the water stretched onward dotted by hundreds of tiny islands. This wasn't a lake but a moving and breathing sea that stretched to faraway lands. It was a gorgeous and bustling metropolis to this country girl and I probably stood on the streets for hours, just gazing at everyone and everything.

Eventually I had to fix myself up, eat and sleep so I found a nearby boarding house by enquiring into local shops. It took a few tries and a lot of my patience until I found one that was willing to take me in. The war was going on and though Sweden was a neutral country, there was a surplus of people from Norway, Denmark and Finland hiding out in Stockholm until the war was over.

The place I ended up finding was a bit run-down but it was for women only, and that made me feel safe. No one was very talkative and they kept to themselves, but the owner helped me with finding a job. I worked as a maid at the house for two weeks, my work for my keep in return, before I found my dream job – or the closest thing to it.

A community theatre had an opening for an "all hands" type woman. They wanted someone with experience in the theatre, particularly in either makeup or wardrobe, and who would also be able to clean-up the theatre after the performances and rehearsals.

As you can imagine, I jumped at that listing. At school, I had done the makeup for the plays as well, and though I didn't have experience with wardrobe, I knew I had a flair for it regardless. In my mind, I was perfect for the job and I was determined to get it.

The theatre was downtown but near a rather derelict area. I was scared out of my wits going there to meet the manager, just as I had been when I met with Maria in the woods. In my town, I was never leered at by strange men, I never had vagabonds shout rude words at me. Part of me wondered if it was some kind of test that I'd have to go through, to see if I wanted this life badly enough.

By the time I made it to the theatre, I was a pile of nerves. It didn't look like much from the outside, just a grey stone building with chipped pillars and slippery steps, and I started to think if I had perhaps made a mistake.

But the door flung open and a rush of warm light bathed me from the inside. Before me stood Lisbeth, the theatre manager. She was taller than I and in her late thirties, wearing men's trousers and a short, curled do. Her lips were smeared with red lipstick that matched my own (later we would simultaneously compliment each other on it) and a smile that lifted my weary heart.

"You must be Pippa," she said, holding out her hand.

I nodded, feeling shy for the first time in a while and shook her hand back. Hers was strong and vibrant.

She ushered me into the building and it was then that I knew I had passed the test. I was meant to come here.

Though falling apart on the outside, inside the theatre was opulent in a museum-type way. The halls had plush, dark green carpeting, creaky chandeliers hung from the ceiling, and tapestry paintings of classic performances and plays, from Roman theatre to Shakespeare, hung from the walls, competing for space with fading posters of shows long past. There was a staircase leading to the balcony level that had gold-glazed railings, that even though they were old and chipped, still gleamed like the heavens. The theater itself had rows of velvet and gold-trimmed seats in a deep, wood brown.

Then there was the stage. It wasn't a big theatre but it was big enough for me. The red curtains were embroidered with metallic swirls and hung from the edges of the stage while ornate fixtures framed it from above. The stage was a worn wood that had seen decades of dancing feet. I immediately saw myself up there too, receiving red roses that were chucked from the crowd.

At that moment I knew I'd do anything to get the position but as fate would have it, I didn't have to. I guess Lisbeth liked me or saw potential in me or perhaps took pity on me, but I was more or less hired on the spot. I would be starting in two days and would be in charge of makeup, wardrobe and cleaning on performance and rehearsal nights. I would also attend any cast and crew meetings that she would arrange. The pay wasn't very much considering some days I'd be working every night and others I'd barley be working, but it was something and I would have been a fool to turn it down.

My luck improved later that night when one of the main actresses, Anne Todalen, made an appearance.

Anne was 22-years old and had been acting with the company since she was my age. She told me she finally worked her way up and this was the first year she was a featured player. She also told me that she was looking for a new roommate. Anne was renting a small apartment not far from my boarding house and said her previous roommate got married, leaving her unable to take care of the rent on her own. I assured her that I wouldn't be getting married anytime soon.

"Sure, but look at you," Anne said to me after we said our goodbyes to Lisbeth. "You're beautiful.

Once our actors get a glance at you, they'll all be fighting for your hand."

I laughed and blushed at the compliment as we made our way out of the theatre and into the September night. Being with Anne made me feel safe in the seedy area and what she had said tickled my fancy. Perhaps I would finally meet a man who I'd love in more than one way.

Anne wasn't bad-looking herself. She had a face and body that was made for performing. She was tall and not reed thin, which was good for being seen on stage. She had a pretty face with a wide mouth and nose that was slightly too large, but paired with her sparkling eyes and high cheekbones, her parts created a sum that was just as intoxicating as her personality.

The next day I moved out of the boarding house and settled into a place that would become my home for the next five years.

Anne's apartment was on the top floor of a white-washed building which was a real drag when you came home from shows absolutely exhausted but it was a place I loved to pieces. It was a tiny one-bedroom apartment with a shoebox bathroom and a balcony that only fit two chairs and no table. Some of my best memories were sitting on that tiny space during the summer and smoking cigarettes over beer and vodka as Anne and I watched the city wind down from another long day.

Because Anne had the bedroom to herself, I got the sofa in the living room. These were pre-Ikea times but us Swedes still knew about the "futon" before the rest of the world. It was comfortable enough and though I lacked privacy, I didn't have to pay as much in rent. My salary barely allowed me to live as it was but Anne was paid more and was always generous with her budget. She would often cook on the days we had off and would make too much, so I had no choice but to help eat it. I knew she did this on purpose, so I didn't feel bad about her charity, but the food was so good that I didn't care. Besides, I knew it made her feel good to do things for me. Like me, she didn't have the best upbringing either and we both leaned on each to replace that.

At first my job was extremely nerve-wracking. Back in the country, I never had a problem being loud and outspoken but in the theatre, I was in constant awe of everyone around me and constantly aware of how I didn't measure up. From Anne, Marianne and Henri, to Frederick, our star player, to the supporting cast of Paula, Johanne, Vala and Peter, each actor was larger than life.

It should be noted that not everyone was as lovely as Anne, either. Frederick was a menace to me and to everyone around him. He was relatively famous in Sweden for his good "dark" looks (though to be honest, I think he resembled a monkey in a tuxedo) and over-the-top acting style and he never let anyone forget it, especially someone like me, who, as a cleaner was the lowest of the low. Every time I would do his makeup before a performance he'd ask if I had washed my hands and even when I said yes, he would make some comment on how no dirty housekeeper should be allowed to touch his face.

I wanted to slap him in his ape face, but of course I never did. I held in my feelings and harsh words and dealt with it. And with time I began to see how he would grate on everyone else's nerves. He once refused a kissing scene with Anne because she smelled of herring. The remark was ridiculous because everyone in Sweden smells like herring.

Eventually though, my work got better as I settled into the role. I became less nervous about putting makeup on the actors and after a while, when we branched out onto more fantastical plays, I was able to do some really creative artwork with my makeup. Clowns, fairies, witches, starlets – I was able to do a range of looks from just my own imagination. The clothes became more interesting too and I quickly taught myself how to sew in my spare time. Before I knew it, I was making clothes for the cast - as well as myself. Another way your frugal Pippa was able to pinch pennies.

It was as my career was getting more fluid and comfortable though, that other parts of my life were getting...strange.

One night I was cleaning up after a performance. It had been a particularly tiring night with everything going wrong. The stage scenery had fallen during a scene, Paula fell and hurt her ankle during a dance routine and had to be replaced by Anne's understudy. There was a snowstorm outside and only half the theatre was full. By the time everyone was done, they just wanted to go home. I told Anne to go on right ahead and not wait for me. She was exhausted from performing five days in a row and in pain and I had at least an hour of cleaning up to do. I told her I'd take a cab home, a necessary expense sometimes and especially when the weather was foul.

I was sweeping the floor in between the seats when I heard a peculiar laugh fill the theatre. My heart stopped and I listened with my ear cocked. Everyone had gone home, hadn't they? Perhaps one of the actors was still hanging about.

I looked around but couldn't see anyone.

"Hello?" I called out. I waited for a few tense moments then shook my head and resumed sweeping. Sometimes, when I particularly tired, my eyes and ears played tricks on me.

Then I heard the laugh again, followed by a thump-thump of wood. I flung my head in the direction of the stage and gasped.

There was a teenage boy sitting on the edge of the stage, his long legs kicking up and down against the side.

Thump-thump.

Thump-thump.

"Can I help you?" I called out, squinting at him to get a better look.

He wasn't one of the actors but he could have been a patron who fell asleep on the balcony or something of that nature. He was wiry and tall with a shock of red hair and a freckled face. He wore a huge grin, like he was enjoying himself as he watched me clean, like that was the greatest entertainment on the planet.

He didn't answer but I wasn't about to be intimidated by someone who looked at least a couple of years younger than me. Still, I clutched the broom hard in my hand as I walked over to the aisle and slowly made my way toward him.

I noticed then that he was holding an apple in his hands. Its shiny red color flashed as he quickly spun it around. He had on leather shoes, shortened pants and suspenders over a dirty white shirt. A newsboy cap sat on his head. It was not the style of our times. He looked like he had just come out of an orphanage with only used clothes from yesteryear on his back.

Still, he continued to grin at me. It began to unsettle me.

"Who are you?" I asked.

He tossed the apple up in the air and caught it just as he jumped off the stage. I staggered a few steps back, not wanting him to get too close to me. Up close he wasn't as tall as I thought, just long-legged, but I felt uneasy around the stranger and probably because he *was* a stranger.

"Jakob," he said, holding out one hand for me. "Pleased to meet you."

I eyed his hand, wondering if I should shake it or not. I then looked to his eyes. They were a strange grey color, as if they had no color at all and there was no discernible ring around his iris. The grey just sort of bled out into the white of the eye, creating a marble statue effect.

Somehow, as I was lost in those strange eyes, I found my hand in his. He pumped it twice, firmly, then dropped it to his side.

"I'm..." I said, then stopped myself. Was it safe to reveal my name?

"You're Pippa," he said. He smiled and took a huge bite of his apple.

"How did you know my name?" I asked, startled.

He shrugged and looked around him. "I know a lot of things. Not a very good gig, is it?"

I was still wondering about my name, so it took me a second to realize he was pitying me.

"It is what it is," I said haughtily and the grip on my broom tightened.

He shrugged again, chomped on the apple and walked past me, sauntering up the aisle to where I was earlier.

"Well I won't keep you," he said over his shoulder.

I hurried on after him. "Where did you come from? How did you get in here?"

He raised his shoulder, about to shrug once more, but I took my broom and poked him square in the back. Hard.

"Ow," he cried out and turned around. A piece of apple shot out of his mouth and landed at my feet. I hated knowing I'd clean it up later.

"Tell me how you got in here or I'll report you to the police!" I kept the broom in front of him, wielding it like a sword.

"I'm always here Pippa. You're not very observant, you know. Your head is in dreamland."

What on earth did that mean?

He read the confused expression my face and put his hand out, lowering the broom. He had this way about him that was almost hypnotic, like he had some spell over me that went in and out of range.

"I'm here to help you. And calling the police would do no good."

"Help me?" This was starting to feel as outlandish as one of the plays we put on.

"You'll see. When you're ready."

And then he walked out into the foyer and through the front door. A gust of white snow blew in and danced in the air as the door closed behind him.

I stood there, leaning on that broom, for a very long time.

CHAPTER FIVE

Jakob was on my mind for the next couple of days. He was right about my head always being in a dreamland, only this dream was about him. I couldn't figure him out, who he was or where he came from. Why was he so cryptic, so vague? What did he mean when he said he would help me?

My memories of the girl in the lake and those tearing wolves came flooding back and that was the sole reason I never told anyone about Jakob. I knew there was a slight chance that it was all in my head, or perhaps I'd seen something that was only meant for me. I also knew that Jakob could have also been a living, breathing boy who came in off the street searching for warmth. He could have been any of those things and it was the not knowing that anguished me.

Finally, after the last performance of The Importance of Being Earnest, I saw Jakob again. The snow was building throughout the day, but the evening still went well. Anne was swept away on a date by one of her new suitors, and I had no problems taking another cab home.

After I was done cleaning up, I locked up the theatre and bundled a scarf around my neck, preparing for the cold walk to find the nearest cab. It was lucky that when the snows came, the derelicts in the neighborhood were inside, hiding from the minus temperature and I felt a lot safer walking short distances.

I was just coming off the last step and onto the snow-dusted sidewalk when my boot slipped and I began to pitch forward. I knew I'd hit the snow hard but hopefully it would be soft enough to break my fall.

I never did hit the ground. A hand shot out from behind me and grabbed hold of me, lifting me up to my feet.

I gasped. It was Jakob. He grinned at me in his boyish glee and stepped back.

"You almost fell."

"Where did you come from?" I gasped. Never mind the fact that he just saved me from possibly hurting myself – I knew when I walked down the steps there was not a single soul in sight. There was no earthly way that he could have been hanging about to save me.

"Around," was his answer.

"That is not an answer, young man," I said, taking a step toward him. I was no longer afraid. "Where did you come from?"

He watched me carefully for a few seconds, a bit of the sparkle leaving his eyes. Then he shrugged at some internal dialogue he was having with himself and pointed to an area at the side of the theatre, between the building and snow-covered bush.

"From the bushes?" I asked dubiously.

"No, look closer," he said.

I squinted my eyes, unsure what he was saying. He took my hand in his and raised it so I was pointing at the area.

"Do you see the waves?"

I didn't know what on earth he was getting at. What did he mean by waves? All I could perceive was a building, a bush and snowfall.

And then, as if my eyes adjusted themselves, I saw it. I saw the waves. The air in front of the bush danced and jostled, like I was looking at the reflection of the scene on the surface of a waving pool of water.

"That's where I come from."

"What is it?" I whispered, sure that I wasn't supposed to be seeing this magical thing.

"The Otherside."

I took my eyes away from the hypnotic dance and looked at him. His grey eyes glowed in the light of a yellow streetlamp.

"Can I go there?" I breathed.

He chuckled and turned his back to me and started to walk along the sidewalk into the city.

I ran after him. "I was serious."

"Pippa," he said, but didn't say anything else.

"Who are you? How do you know me?" So many questions were begging to tumble out of my lips.

"I told you, I'm Jakob. I'm from the Otherside. From the Thin Veil. And I know you because I've been watching you your whole life." He said all of this like he was listing off his favorite comic books.

"The Thin Veil?" I stammered and stopped walking. The words sounded familiar but I had no idea why or how.

He stopped too, the snow whirling around his slight frame. He didn't seem the slightest bit cold.

"You'll freeze if we don't keep walking. Don't worry, I'll keep you safe until you get a cab."

"How?"

He walked off and I followed again, my boots kicking up the snow. My legs were starting to go numb.

"How what?"

"How...everything," I said. "What are you?"

He looked at me over his shoulder and smiled. "Jakob. Pay attention."

"Are you dead?"

"It doesn't feel like it."

"When were you born?"

"A long time ago."

"Can I go to the Thin Veil?"

Now it was his time to stop. He placed his ungloved hands on my shoulders and shook me ever so slightly. His grey eyes looked deep in mine. It was odd sometimes how boyish he looked, just like any 14-year old kid, then in the next minute it's like he would grow a million years inside.

"You can but you shouldn't."

"What's there?"

"Others like me. But they aren't all like me."

I paused to wipe rogue snowflakes out of my face. "Ghosts?"

He wiggled his thin lips around and his eyes roamed in the empty space above my hat.

"Something like that." He tugged at my arm. "Come on, let's keep walking, it's not safe."

I was eager to get out of the cold but I looked around at the empty streets. "But there's no one here."

"That you can see," he said just as the lights of a car flashed in our eyes. Jakob raised his hand and for a second I thought how foolish that gesture was. How could the car see him if he was a ghost?

But the car stopped and it was indeed a cab. The door opened and a man stuck his head out. "Excuse me miss, do you need a ride?"

I looked at Jakob who whispered. "He can't see me."

"But-"

"Don't talk to me, he'll think you're a nutcase."

I nodded, shocked and walked toward the cab driver.

"Y-yes please," I said. The driver gave me a wave to come over.

I looked behind me at Jakob.

He was gone.

~~~

After that incident with Jakob, I didn't see him for a very long time. I didn't see him until my life took an entirely different direction. I didn't see him until after I fell in love.

The following Spring, when the cool winds swept in from warming climates and pushed the snow away, Frederick announced he was leaving the company. I knew Lisbeth was concerned at his departure because even though he was a pain to work with, his name did draw in the crowds. Everyone else was overjoyed, including me and even Lisbeth admitted it would be good to have some fresh, younger blood in the company. Because Frederick was at least ten years older than Anne, their pairings on stage were always a bit off.

One day I came into work for an impromptu meeting with the cast and crew. Lisbeth had settled on a more-or-less unknown actor by the name of Ludwig Ericsson. I was unprepared for the sight before my eyes.

Ludwig was tall, well over six-feet, with shiny honey-colored hair that dazzled under the lights. His skin was a smooth, tan-color that was only a shade lighter than his hair. Against the glow, his teeth shone white and his eyes were a beautiful clear blue.

I was speechless and could only smile like a fool when he shook my hand. His skin on mine made my nerves jump inside and it felt like we were the only people in the room. Of course, we were surrounded by everyone else in the theatre and he had to introduce himself to all of them. Still, it sounds silly now, but I felt his attention, even when he wasn't looking at me. Something had just happened between us and I couldn't quite articulate it.

Anne did though. Anne knew men like the back of her hand and she was always with a different one. Some of our friends would call Anne a "loose woman" behind her back, but I lived with her and I never saw any of her male friends stay the night (although she would sometimes stay out until the wee hours). Besides, it didn't matter what Anne did as long as she was happy and I was more than happy to talk about Ludwig when she brought him up later that night. I wanted her expertise and advice for this new endeavor.

"He likes you," she said with a smirk as she piled some boiled dill potatoes onto my plate. It was a late dinner, as was usually the case for us. The balcony door was open a little, shuffling a bit of cool air into the apartment but I felt all warm inside. The brandy I was slowly swilling also helped.

I blushed. I couldn't help myself.

"Who?" I asked more coy than I normally dared.

"You know who. Ludie."

I raised a brow. "Is that his name?"

"Ludwig is a horrible name," she said between bites. "So Ludie it is. And you know he fancies you. I saw the way he held your eyes earlier."

I brushed it off, not wanting to get my hopes up. I had noticed though, the way he kept looking at me throughout the night and was giddy that she had noticed it too.

"Well I am sure I just reminded him of someone."

"Yes. A beautiful young woman. You be sure to watch out for him."

Now I felt a bit concerned. "Watch out?"

She winked at me. "You might fall in love, Pippa."

And I did. I think I was in love with him the moment his hand grasped mine. All these years later and I still feel that way. Some love doesn't die, even when you do.

Naturally, I was not sure what Ludie really thought of me. Our first time together was fraught with nerves and embarrassment on my behalf.

It was before the rehearsal of Hamlet and the cast had to be in costume, which meant I was dressing them up and doing a light dusting of makeup.

I was as anxious as anything when I knocked on Ludie's dressing room door. He and Anne were the only ones with private ones, while everyone else shared the men's and women's rooms. I probably would have preferred to have done him up in a more public setting as the idea of being alone with him was nerve-wracking but that was not the case.

"Come in," he said. His voice was deep and rich and carried through the door with ease. The placard on the front still said Frederick. I was surprised he hadn't taken it with him when he traded us in for a larger, more prestigious theatre deeper into the city.

I took in a deep breath and pushed my hair behind my ears. I had paid extra attention to my face that morning, making sure my lipstick was on neatly and not half off my lips as usual. I knew I wasn't bad to look at and that I often had the attention of young men, but there had never really been any reason for me to look good. I had kept my head down and focused on work until I met the one man who made me focus on him.

I opened the door and stood awkwardly in the doorway until Ludie turned in his seat and grinned. Amazing how the parting of teeth and lips and the scrunching of eyes can act like a wave. It welcomed me and made me blush from the tops of my head to my toes. Oh, I was certainly a goner.

"Pippa," he said warmly, keeping his eyes locked on mine.

I looked away as I closed the door gently behind me, feeling quite unnerved and hot. My chest began to steam under my dress. I kept my eyes on the floor, feeling scrutinized like a bug under a microscope as I walked over to him. I purposely wore flat shoes that day, not wanting to add extra height to me, even though he was much taller, but that did not prevent me from wobbling like a drunkard.

I stopped beside him and looked into the mirror across from us, lit up by high wattage bulbs. It felt safer to look at him there, direct but indirect.

My, how his face belonged there, framed by the lights. Never you mind my pale one with my dark hair, how I contrasted horribly with him. He was such a delight to look at. He knew it too, I could see the way he lifted his chin as if he was used to being admired so.

"So," he began, then smiled again instead of saying anything.

I knew I had to start talking even though my tongue was tied.

"I'm just going to put some powder on your face," I said, sounding unintelligent and completely young.

"You're not going to put me in my clothes first?" he asked. "What if you decide the green robe would better go with green shadow on my eyes?"

"Oh, you're right," I said stupidly even though he was joking. I put my makeup kit down on the counter and made my way to the racks where I had put his costume the other day. I had his measurements given to me, but this would be the only time he'd be fitted.

Fitting men in costume wasn't something I particularly minded (with the exception of Frederick) but now I felt uncomfortable, not professional by any means. I was very much reminded that he was a man and I was a woman.

Ludie, however, gave no hint of anything except unending ease and charm. I took in another deep breath and brought his Prince Hamlet costume off of the rack and walked it over to him.

"Here you go," I told him. I held it up and he eyed it carefully.

"You won't help me?" I searched his face for sincerity and found none.

"How old are you?" I asked.

He finally looked surprised about something. "I'm 25-years old. Why?"

"Well, then I guess you know how to dress yourself."

I placed the costume in his hands and headed for the door.

"Call me when you are properly attired," I said and stepped out into the hallway, shutting the door behind me.

I let out the breath I was holding and shook out my arms and legs. He was already doing a number on me. Still, I showed him I wasn't going to fall for any lothario type advances. This was my job and I had to treat it as such.

That didn't stop me from grinning to myself until I heard him call me back in.

He looked rather ridiculous in the costume. It was all green. The velvet robe, the high-waisted pants, the shirt. Even the pointy shoes.

"How is it?" he asked as he eyed himself suspiciously in the mirror.

"You look like a tree," the words escaped my lips.

I thought he would take offense to that. If it had been Frederick, I would have never heard the end of it and he would have probably demanded some other woman work on him, one who didn't compare him to plants. But Ludie wasn't like that.

Ludie laughed. It was loud and calming at the same time. Uninhibited.

"You're quite right Pippa, I do look like a tree," he twirled around so we could get the full effect of the cape. He paused and pondered his reflection. "But what kind of tree? That is the most important question. What kind of tree would Hamlet be...or not to be?"

I couldn't help but laugh at his corny joke. "That *is* the question."

After that, things got easier between us. I should say it got easier *after* I poked him in the eye with my makeup brush. I felt so terrible about it but Ludie said the only way he wouldn't tell Lisbeth that the makeup artist tried to blind him was if I agreed to go out for dinner with him the next night, before the round of shows began.

You know I said yes.

I won't go into too much detail for the sake of you both. I know the last things you want to hear about are the sordid thoughts and actions of this woman in love. Yet, I also want you to understand just what Ludie did to me – and why our affair would affect me for the rest my life.

CHAPTER SIX

Needless to say, I was fretting about the apartment all of the next day. I hadn't been with a man in years and part of me was afraid that it would be just like the time with Stäva. That I would feel nothing and, because of that, there would be something very wrong with me.

The other part of me was excited, a feeling that was scary in its own right. What if I fell for this man? What if he broke my heart? What if the date went wrong and he never wanted to see me again and I'd have to spend the rest of my career working under him?

Luckily, Anne was around to talk me down and make sure I had enough to eat. She dressed me up in the finest dress I had, one I had snatched from the theatre, and for once I had my own hair and make-up done. I wanted to wear my hair down – it was long and shiny– but she put it up with curls which highlighted my cheekbones and eyes. She nixed my usual red lipstick in favor of something more "kissable."

Then she gave me a round of advice on how to be a lady. Let the man open doors for you. Laugh at his jokes. Try not to drool over him like a fool. Don't talk down to him or poke fun of him.

Also, when she thought I wasn't looking, she slipped a condom into my dainty purse. I was shocked and a bit abhorred by her actions. Condoms were for sailors and dirty prostitutes. They weren't for young ladies like myself and Anne.

I could tell from the look in her eyes though, she was just trying to prevent another pregnancy with me. I had broken down drunk with cognac one night and told her everything that had happened. I was dying of shame still and it helped to have someone else know what I had been through. Anne was looking out for me and far ahead of her time when she whispered, "The man may rule the date, but don't count on him for everything."

Truer words had never been spoken.

Ludie rang the buzzer five minutes early, cutting into my preparedness time. I slammed back a shot of vodka hoping to relax myself in a hurry and danced on pins and needles until he arrived at the door.

He looked absolutely gorgeous, wearing a dashing dark blue suit that illuminated the golden tones in his hair.

"Ladies," he said as he took off his sharp fedora and did a slight bow from the waist. "I am here for the beautiful Pippa Lindstrom."

Forget about the vodka – just being in his presence made me feel drunk. Thank goodness for Anne who put my coat on my back, my purse in my hands and led me to the door like an invalid.

"I expect you'll return her at a reasonable hour," Anne said. Her voice was hard but her eyes were good-humored.

"A reasonable hour by my standards or by your standards?"

Anne pursed her lips. "Well, I'm going to guess they are the same."

He winked at her, happy with that response and held his arm out for me. I had enough sense and power to oblige and together we stepped out of the apartment. I looked back one last time at Anne but the door was closed and I was alone with Ludie once again, about to embark on an evening that was very much on the table. This wasn't about work. I wasn't with him because I had to be. I was with him because he wanted me to be.

Outside, Ludie's car was waiting. It wasn't new but it was shiny and sleek like it had been painted with a million pounds of chrome. It was also sky blue and extremely eye-catching in a time where decadence and frivolity was frowned upon. Ludie didn't care though and as I stepped into the car, he informed me that he had bought it after his first big theatre gig. It cost more than his living expenses, so at first he was sleeping in it until he could afford an apartment again. But to him, he worked hard and he deserved it and it was a sign he was living his dream.

That was always Ludie's philosophy in life. There was much to be admired about that, taking what you knew was yours and enjoying the finer things. Later on I would realize how selfish that way of thinking could be. Everything was always owed to him and there never were any consequences, at least not for him. If he thought he deserved something, he went for it, even if it meant trampling over other people.

But I will get to that later. For now, I was enthralled with him and his dashing looks and mannerisms. He took me to a fine seafood restaurant on one of the upper class streets I never walked down because it inspired too much envy in me. He wasn't recognizable yet, not the way Frederick was, but women stopped to stare at him just the same.

They also stared at me and unlike the doe-eyed girls that fawned over Stäva in school, these were full-grown women with hearts full of jealously and hate. I was their enemy just for being on the young man's arm and though I knew I wasn't too bad looking myself, it brought upon feelings of being inadequate.

Ludie did his best, however, in making me feel like I was the only one in the restaurant. He asked me many questions about myself and always kept his bright eyes tuned to mine. Oh, he wasn't mysterious either and would gladly answer any questions I had about him. I learned about his upbringing (in Gotland), his family (father died when he was young, he was still close with his mother and two younger sisters), his love for performing arts (he was a dancer before he moved into acting). The night flew by in a whir of clinking cutlery, smoke, coffee and brandy. Our talk was easy, the flow between us was effortless. As first dates go, this one could not be topped.

I am sure you don't want to know how the night continued but I can tell you that I was very much a lady and I was home at a reasonable hour – even by my own watch. I burned inside for Ludie, feeling flames that I had never felt before but that night I had listened to the caution in my heart, that feeling that I had to approach things slowly and carefully.

If only I kept on listening to the whisper inside, the one that knew of things to come. The next time Ludie and I were together we made love. Love, right in his dressing room, a ferocious and consuming sort of love making that both surprised and scared me. It turns out my fears were unfounded and there was nothing wrong with me at all. I had found the one I was meant to spend the rest of my life with and my body responded in kind.

And so began our very messy, passionate affair. Things were easy at first. We couldn't get enough of each other and were intimate every chance we got. As we would emerge from the back looking rather untidy, it soon spread like wildfire that we were an "item." Lisbeth had a few words for me, mainly not to get too close to a man like Ludie and to be aware of our working situation, but I was reckless and stupid and didn't listen. What did Lisbeth know about men anyway? I knew Ludie and he was mine.

But Lisbeth was right. Ludie was a performer, an actor, and as such he not only attracted a great deal of attention from the opposite sex (indeed, the looks he got on our first date were nothing compared to the ones he received while reciting Shakespeare on stage), he was moody, selfish and insecure by nature. He demanded time and attention, not just from me, but from everyone. He was jealous of every man who talked to me, including the other actors, yet he enjoyed the flirtations of other women. He would be in a joyous, generous mood one night, and depending on how much he drank or how well his performance was perceived, he would turn angry and cynical the next.

I wasn't the sort of woman to take things lying down, either. Despite the rules that Anne had told me, I did often poke fun at him and I often talked down to him. It was hard not to when he was behaving like a child. What resulted were nights of constant fighting – fighting that would eventually combust when we found ourselves in each other's arms again.

It was push and pull, give and take, love and hate for a number of years. Despite how bad we would get on each other's nerves, how vicious we could be with our insults, how miserable we could make each other, it never dampened the unending, all-consuming love I felt for him. The fire that roared in my loins, my heart, my soul. I believed that he felt the same way too, why else would Ludie stick around if he didn't love me the way I loved him? I was so naïve and blind that I never really considered any other reasons.

I discovered the reason in person one fateful summer day between shows. Her name was Hanna and she was Anne's new understudy. I was cleaning up around the theatre, believing Ludie to have gone to a café with Peter and Lisbeth, when I heard some noises coming from his dressing room.

To his credit, Ludie had locked the door. It was my curiosity and concern that kicked the door in anyway, especially after hearing a female's high pitched giggles from inside.

What I saw…I can't even describe. I don't even want to think about it, it still destroys me, burns my heart to this day. All these decades later and I can't…well, all you should know is that I found Ludie with his pants down around his tanned ankles, with blonde and vivacious Hanna attending to him.

The rest was a blur, thank the Lord. Instead of cleaning up his dressing room, I messed it up, throwing chairs, tossing about clothes and makeup. I slapped Ludie repeatedly until Hanna tried to intervene, then I hit her right in the lip. I was livid, beyond this plane of existence, I was somewhere else trying to breathe and hold onto the belief that I had love on my side. In one second it was all over. Everything I had, that was important to me, was gone. Ludie was my life and the reason my heart kept beating, the reason my soul kept soaring.

Sadly, even after all that, even after finding out that he had been carrying on with Hanna and a few other women from time to time, he still continued to be my all. I was doomed by my love.

I called in sick the next day and the next day after that. Anne took care of me when she could but she had to go to work – she wasn't going to let that horrible woman take her place on stage, not after all of that. In fact, Anne was just as mad as I was, also feeling duped by Ludie and she made a vow to make his life and Hanna's life a living hell.

I never figured out if she did or not. Oh, Anne would tell me how she tripped up Hanna one day after rehearsal, or she openly mocked Ludie during one of their scenes. But I never saw it for myself because I quit my job. My wonderful, promising job. Oh, it wasn't my dream of all dreams – it hadn't got me up on the stage yet. But it kept money in my pocket and hope in my life, and I was good at it, damn it all. I was good at my job and I had to go and fall in love with a self-centered actor and spoil the whole thing.

For the second time in my life, love had ruined me, only this time it was my own love that was at fault.

I am more than aware of how dramatic I sound. Let's face facts, Ludie was not the only actor here. I wasn't on stage but I had all the desires of the craft and unfortunately the same tendencies as he did. I am sure I was as much to blame for the end of our relationship as he was. But it was a terrible ordeal nonetheless.

Because I quit the theatre and the life I had built up steadily over the years, I had to find work elsewhere. I stayed with Anne because I had no other choice: she was my best friend and confidant and let me live with her rent free until I found a new position.

At first I applied to other theatres, not even caring if I ended up putting makeup on Frederick again, but soon the search proved to be fruitless. It was after the war and money was still tight. Businesses were closing and people were learning how to prioritize in the wake of global turmoil. I eventually found work at a coffee shop near the ferry terminal, serving pastries, cake and caffeine to passengers bound for Finland or Denmark.

It was thankless work but with tips it brought in more money than the theatre position, particularly as tourists would ditch their remaining kronas with me. But despite the steady income, it did nothing to fill the void in my heart.

I worked there, feeling empty and joyless, for a few years. A year can feel like such a long time when you are young and living it, but looking back, I don't remember a single event or day of my life during that period. Just occasional evening with Anne, listening to her talk about the newest man in her life, as we both drank more than we should. All my work days blurred into each other, an endless sea of hot brown coffee and faceless people. Such a waste of my life. Life is such a precious commodity when you're done living it.

Then I met Karl. Karl who was kind and warm and gentle. Karl who was tall and built like a small bear. Karl who had a dark beard and dark eyes but possessed the sunniest, lightest disposition in Sweden.

Karl was a frequent customer to the café as he was often taking the ferry over to Tampere, Finland, to do business. He would sit at the counter and make small talk with me, always tipping generously, and when he would return from his voyages, no matter how early in the morning or late at night it was, he would bring me a Finnish Moomin toy as a present.

As I didn't have much going for me, I started looking forward to those visits from Karl. And I started to find Karl more and more attractive each day. It wasn't the burning desire I felt for Ludie, nor was it the brotherly indifference I felt with Stäva. It was somewhere in between and that was finally sounding smart to me.

Karl's intentions were pure, honest and obvious. We started courting each other with the caution I should have taken with Ludie and soon we were an agreeable and happy pair. Karl had his own business importing caviar to other European countries and he did quite well for himself. I quit my job as he took care of me and eventually I moved out of Anne's and into his house on the outskirts of town. We were married shortly after.

The wedding was a very small, civil ceremony in a courthouse. Anne was my maid of honor, Lisbeth was there too and so was Peter. Karl had his older sister Lulu and a few of his employees and army buddies. I wore a simple white gown that matched the ease of the event and for our honeymoon we sunned ourselves for a week on the beaches of Spain.

We frantically tried for a baby. I felt that because my career was a now distant dream and I had security and a reliable sense of love, that having children would be the most logical step. I felt ready for them, more than I ever had before.

But though Karl and I were intimate as much as possible, nothing ever "stuck." I was left feeling useless and ashamed. I worried that the abortion I had all those years ago had done some permanent damage to my body and I blamed myself day in and day out as my monthly redness kept coming like clockwork.

Being the good man that Karl was, he never blamed me. He was over ten years older than I and often made remarks that perhaps he was too old to become a father. I told him it was nonsense – he was older but he was a still a man and in fine shape and health. I knew it was because of me, because of the horrible choices I had made when I was younger.

We kept trying though, year after year. The goal eventually became less important as we got older and we focused on other things in our life – for me it was watching films and sewing skirts in the latest fashions, for him it was sailing his new sailboat around the archipelago. But the urge to have a child kept building and building inside me, like tiny flames that would never fully go out.

Eventually though, I had to give up on that like I had given up on so many things in my life. Oh, I know I sound selfish complaining about a life that most women would have been happy to have. I had a husband who loved me, whom I loved too, I didn't have to work ever again and spent most of my days toiling around our house in the countryside or on the sailboat. But I was lonely and loneliness can do so much damage to even the hardiest individuals. Anne had married a film director and had moved to Hamburg, Germany and I had lost touch with my other friends. Only Karl's sister Lulu would come by but even though she was pleasant company, she was too plain for my liking. There was still that part of me that craved the drama and excitement that life used to have.

To tell you the truth, there were some days where I would pray to see Jakob again. My meetings with him had happened so long ago but there was excitement and adventure in the ghostly boy and it saddened me to think that might all be over too.

As it was, in 1959, when I was 34 years old, my past finally came back to haunt me. Only it wasn't Jakob. Not at first.

CHAPTER SEVEN

I was strolling through the open air market down by the docks, perusing the stands for the freshest shrimp for that night's dinner when I heard someone call my name. It was a male voice, deep and rich but ripe with uncertainty.

There was no guessing whose voice that was. I could tell from the way the hairs on my arms stood up, from the hot, pooling feeling in my stomach, from the way my heart skipped a beat and staggered on.

Despite feeling frozen to the ground, I turned on the spot and saw Ludie through the maze of shoppers.

He was pushing forty now and looked even more handsome than he did when he was younger. His hair had thinned out a little bit and had lost a bit of the sheen but it was still colored like gold and honey and his eyes were that sharp, calculating blue.

I didn't know what to do or what to say. All those feelings of betrayal and heartache came rolling back just as if it were yesterday. A part of me wanted to hug him in the joy of seeing an old friend. Another part wished I could have taken the nearest fish and battered him over the head with it then kicked him over the side of the docks until he hit the water below and drowned.

Ludie didn't seem to be too concerned with how I was going to react. As soon as he saw my face, he raised his hand in a slight wave and his lips parted to show those show business teeth of his.

I wish I could tell you that I told Ludie to go straight to hell and that he wouldn't deserve anything more than that, but I didn't. I was a fool, again. A weak, sad woman.

I returned the shy wave and within minutes we were walking together out of the market and to a nearby park, the sun sparkling off of his hair and the buildings and his smile and the light in my heart.

"Listen, Pippa," he said taking hold of my hand in his, adjusting himself on the park bench to face me. "I was a terrible fool."

I gave him a slight smile, not disagreeing with him at all. "You were. But so was I."

"No, my darling," he said, reaching up for my cheek. "You were magnificent. You were the love of my life and I threw you away. I was young, stupid and out of my mind. I didn't know how to handle my feelings or my fame or anything of that nature. I spent the last few years regretting what I did to you, wondering if I'd ever get the chance to redeem myself in your eyes."

"It has been almost fifteen years," I told him, trying to take my hand back. "A lot has changed since then. You can't blame yourself for your past."

"But I can and I do," he said. His eyes explored my own and I was shocked how little they had changed. It made me wonder that if the eyes were windows to the soul and his reflected the soul of the selfish boy I once knew, was that person still inside of him?

"I'm married now." I flashed him my ring.

"Are you happily married?"

I sucked in my breath through my teeth. He was so bold with his questioning, asking me things I didn't want to think about.

"I think so," I answered and looked down at my thighs.

"Are you happy in life?"

I bit my lip and slowly shook my head, no. I wasn't happy in my life.

"I'm not either," he said. "I never have been since I hurt you. Since I lost you. I want to feel that happiness again and I need you."

He continued on like this for a while, saying his promises and declarations of love and other lovely things. If I were a stronger woman, a good and righteous woman, I would have told him to forget it. I would have left him in that park and I would have gone right home to my loving husband and I would have continued living the life I carved out for myself.

Alas, I did not do that and I am sure you knew that was coming.

I didn't go home to Karl. I went with Ludie to the hotel room where he was staying (as he had been performing in England until a few days ago) and we made passionate love until I absolutely had to go home.

It wasn't a so-called "one night fling" either. This lasted for the next year. I was out of the house every other day, pretending I was going to fabric stores or meeting new friends or just exploring and all the while I would meet Ludie at the hotel, and eventually, as he found theatre work again in the city, his house. I was a woman living two lives and though I was happier in Ludie's arms, I still felt miserable in both. I was the opposite of an honest woman. I had no idea if my parents were alive anymore but if they weren't, they'd be rolling in their graves.

It was amazing what fifteen years of growth and life would do to a person, however. Though he was still self-centered and short-tempered, I detected a sense of peace in him that I hadn't seen before.

"You're amazing, you know that," he told me one night as we lay sprawled across the sheets of his bed.

I blushed as he still had the ability to bring color and heat to my face and smacked him lightly with my hand. "Oh, stop that."

"I'm serious," he went on, reaching for my hair and brushing it out of my face. "You are. I've never met anyone like you in my entire life."

I wasn't sure what he was talking about since I was as ordinary as everyone else.

"You have this...way about you. I can feel you from across the way, like you give off this energy. It's...a sadness."

I looked at him sharply. Sadness?

"It's a like you have so much life and potential somewhere deep inside, some greater purpose that is dying to come out. But you don't know what it is or how to reach it. So it festers in this blue pool. I think of blue when I think of you Pippa. Blue, cooling, calming, like the sea, like your eyes. It soothes me to be with you."

"What do you think I'm meant to do?" I asked quietly. It felt foolish to even humor his ramblings. What could I, at 35-years old, offer the world anymore? What was my purpose if it wasn't to be a great actress, if it wasn't to have children?

"I think you're meant to save people," he said. His eyes flashed with something like pity. "Let's start with me."

That night I cried for the first time during our love making. It was like the damn burst in my soul and I wept for the love I felt and the life I never had.

A week later I was leaving the public library with a stack of books about makeup and fashion design, feeling strangely inspired for the first time in years. Ludie had gone to Gotland to see his sister and I spent the last few days keeping busy, waiting for his return. It was winter and dark out at three in the afternoon, so I was acceptably cautious as I left the library and made my way to the nearest tram station.

This is why when I sensed someone walking behind me, I didn't turn to look. I kept my eyes forward, my head high. There were a few people on the street but they were hunched to the cold and it was dark as anything. I was paranoid but in this situation I thought it would suit me well.

Wherever I walked though, the presence followed me, until finally I had to spin around and glare at whomever had appointed themselves my stalker.

I saw a shimmer of wavering air and then before my eyes, it became Jakob.

My books went crashing to my feet, sending the snow everywhere.

Jakob was a few paces away and staring at me hard. He looked exactly as he did all those years ago, still a teenage boy, but the expression on his face had changed. His eyes were cold, his smile, what was left of it, was tight.

"Jakob," I said. I looked around to see if anyone was about, anyone who would catch me talking to myself.

"Follow me, Miss Lindstrom," he commanded with a soft voice. He walked past me and headed in the direction of a nearby alley. I picked up the books and followed him, feeling as if I had no choice. I was scared but enthralled and let myself go with the strange pull he had over me.

We entered the alley. It smelled of urine and snow and cold pipes. It was dirty and narrow and a dead end and the flakes that fell from the sky disappeared quickly into the darkness. Only a rusted fire escape filled the area, hanging a few feet off the ground.

This would be the perfect place to lose your life, I thought to myself and eyed Jakob carefully. I never thought the boy could or would hurt me but the grim expression on his face didn't do anything to dissuade my fears.

He didn't say anything any first, he just stopped in the middle of the alleyway and let his eyes roam all over the bricks, his head cocked slightly as if he was listening. I knew better than to interrupt him, so I kept my mouth shut and licked my dry lips anxiously.

Finally he looked at me and that hard gleam returned to his eyes. "I'm sorry I didn't come by sooner."

I was caught off guard by that understated remark. "I..."

"I don't have too much time to explain Pippa," he said. He took my hands in his and I was amazed at the strength and warmth of his touch. He looked past my shoulder and nodded. I turned my head and saw the end of the alley ripple and pulse, the door to the Thin Veil, the Otherside.

"I have to go back there soon, and it's not safe to take you there right now. Not in your state."

"My state?" I asked, my heart slowing down by a few beats.

His hands squeezed mine and he kept his eyes on me, serious and grave.

"Pippa, you're pregnant," he said. His words sounded colder than ice and as impossible as it was, I knew it was true.

I could barely form words so my lips moved soundlessly. I was pregnant. Most likely by Ludie, my one true love. I was finally going to have a child. His child. The notion should have filled my heart with joy, but though it was beating faster, wanting to drum in the possibility, the look on Jakob's face made me pause, made me stifle the expanding feelings.

"What's wrong?" I asked him. "Shouldn't you be happy for me?"

He smiled and his eyes crinkled at the corners, but they weren't happy at all. Once again he looked years older than fourteen and I had a feeling I was about to receive some very bad news.

"You are a special woman," Jakob said and I was instantly reminded of what Ludie told me in bed. "And being special makes you at great risk for others who want to use you."

I brought my coat in closer and stamped my foot impatiently. "I haven't seen you in sixteen years. When I last did, you were talking about this Otherside. You told me you weren't alive. I don't even know who you really are or what you are. Please, don't think you'll get away this time without explain absolutely everything that you know. I deserve that much."

"That could take some time and I don't have time."

"You have the time to tell me I'm pregnant!" I said, raising my gloved finger at him. "Now you're going to finish telling me why I'm special, why I'm at risk. Why does it matter if I'm pregnant? It's what I've always wanted."

Jakob placed his hand at my stomach and a blanched at his touch. "The baby is not safe."

My heart sank. Could this all be over before it has even begun?

"What do you mean?"

"You need to get rid of it."

I was dumbstruck by his cruel words and searched his face for some sort of answer. He was not joking with me, his grey eyes were glinting like steel and his face was robbed of all its color.

"I will do no such thing," I said quietly and made my gaze match the intensity of his.

"Please," he said and his eyes darted quickly over to the Thin Veil and back. "I don't wish to show you so you just have to believe me."

"If you think I will give up this child growing newly inside me because you said so, you must be as crazy as you are dead."

"You're the one who will end up crazy," he hissed at me. "Or dead!"

He let out a sigh, his breath failing to create steam in the frigid air and grabbed my arm. "Come on."

He began to lead me toward the shimmering air. Panic bubbled up in my throat and I stopped my legs, keeping them locked to the ground. Jakob tugged again.

"You told me it wasn't safe to go there," I said. I started to shake all over, from the cold, from the fear, from the unknown.

"It isn't," he said, his grip tightening. "But you aren't giving me much choice. I can explain things better over there than I can here. The ones that are looking for you are already on this side."

For the second time that night, I was speechless. And scared out of my wits. But Jakob pulled at my arm again and I let him lead me toward the air.

It was fantastic up close. I felt like I was looking through a cool pond and instead of seeing the bottom, I saw the rest of the street, the snowy sheen of Stockholm, albeit filtered as if it were tinted with grey gauze. The air was constantly moving, rippling back and forth, and it sparkled too.

"What will happen to me?" I whispered, my eyes hypnotized by the sight that danced before me.

"Hopefully, nothing," Jackob said. "But if you want the whole truth, you have to come with me."

Then he walked forward into the air, which shimmied and stretched around him. He looked faded now, half transparent, as if he was close to disappearing completely. His hand reached through toward me, into my world again, and became solid. The snow fell and collected on his sleeve as he went for my hand. I took it gingerly in mine and then I was yanked forward into a shimmering wall of pressure.

The first things I noticed were a distinct lack of sound and smell and sight, like everything around me ceased. Then my eyes adjusted and sound filtered back in and my nostrils flinched with a vague scent of burning. It looked like I was back where I was, on the street, except it was completely empty, the snow had stopped falling and lay undisturbed at my feet. Colors were dull and de-saturated.

Jakob cleared his throat and I whirled around to see him standing behind me. His red hair was now a very dull shade of grey. His eyes remained the same.

"What do you think?" he asked and I saw that flash of little boy hopefulness in him. He wanted me to like this place, his home.

"It's different," I said simply and looked around. It was different. It was like an unpopulated version of my world.

"We are in another layer," he said and walked toward a bunch of crates that were stacked up at the entrance of the alley. He sat on one and patted the other.

"Sit down and I will tell you what you need to know. And many things you'll wish I didn't."

I did as he said, noticing that my feet made no marks in the snow as I walked, feeling no chill in the air at all.

"All right," I said. I adjusted my position on the crate so I was facing him and waited patiently for him to continue.

"This place, the Thin Veil, the Otherside, the Black Sunshine, is a parallel world for the dead. It is a place of transition, the world where souls first step into before they travel above or below or to the other places I have not seen yet. My name is Jakob but it wasn't always Jakob, that is just my name when I am here. All us guides are called Jakob. We help souls cross over to where they need to go and some of us, some of us are guardians. We keep this place free from monsters and special people such as yourself."

That was an awful lot for my uneducated brain to take in.

"You keep this place...free from...people like me? Monsters? How..."

His voice dropped to a lower register. "Monsters are real, Pippa. I know you've seen them when they cross over. Sometimes they look like ordinary people. At other times, they look like the demons they are. Or faceless shadows. They come from the underworld, a place of blood and sorrow. The Thin Veil is the closest point for them to break through. They look for souls to possess, for bodies to have, for lives to devour. They are very, very dangerous. And they tend to go after people like you. That is one reason why people like you are a threat to this place."

"Well, my goodness. You know I would have never come here had you not dragged me here. It's not like I can step into this place anytime I want."

"Oh, but dear Miss Lindstrom, you can. You can come here anytime you want, now that you know. And if you're really powerful, which I suspect you are, you can create doors whenever you wish."

I was powerful enough to create doors to another world? It was too unbelievable for my ears, despite the fact I was sitting with a spirit guide in what appeared to be another dimension.

"So they want me..."

"They want you because you possess this power. It is very attractive to them. You also attract other beings, not just monsters and demons. You attract ghosts, spirits who remain here because they are unable to move on. They can see the world they left behind and roam among it but others do not see them. Except for you. Can you imagine an eternity of loneliness, of being ignored, and then finally being seen, being listened to?"

Oh, I didn't have to imagine that feeling. I had experienced it many times before.

"So why am I safe here? Why am I not safe on the other side?"

He looked around him. "The guardians are out doing their job, keeping the demons at bay. They can't do anything for the spirits who spend their time here and in your world, but the demons they can control.

However, if they slip past, and it does happen, they are free to cause destruction. The guardians cannot come to the other world, and even guides shouldn't."

"Will you get in trouble for coming to see me?" I asked, wondering who exactly Jakob answered to.

He shrugged. "I might. But I'm pretty stealthy. This world is as vast as yours and they can't be everywhere at once."

"And in my world?"

He chewed on his lip before speaking. "In your world, it's...easier to be watched. From here, you can conjure up doors or windows that will open up anywhere you please. It's how I've been able to watch you while you were a child, then watch you now. When I'm in your world – the living world – I am aware that at any moment one of the guides or guardians, or even demons, can find out where I am or what I'm saying. It's like a mental and physical leash that keeps me tethered to the Otherside."

I rubbed at my temples, feeling a bout of pressure on them.

"You're in pain," he said and began to get off the box.

"No, no." I waved at him to sit back down. "It's just a lot to handle."

"That's why no one should ever know. You knowing you're special was always enough, you never needed to know it all, to come here. That's why I tried to keep it from you. That's why we aren't allowed to tell."

I pinched the bridge of my nose and the pain subsided a bit. "You said there are others like me out there...people who can see ghosts. Are they in danger too?"

He nodded. "Some more than others. You have this ability, this light inside you that promises power that few have. A power that will only worsen from here on in."

I gave him a sharp look. "What? Why?"

He pulled anxiously at the cap on his head and didn't say anything. I put my hand on his leg and squeezed. Hard.

"Is this about the baby?" I asked, my voice trembling.

He sucked in his breath and nodded. "I know I won't succeed in preventing the child from being born. I can see that you'd never let that happen. But I will tell you this much, that child will bring pain to your life and to others."

"How could you say that about an unborn child!" I shrieked, the words coming out of my mouth in a hot fury. "About my child!"

Jakob remained nonplussed. "Any woman who carries life carries a great power within her. You already have a power, a life force that others want, need, crave even. With a child growing inside of you, you will be more susceptible to...other forces. You're putting yourself in great danger. Not to mention your child. If she manages to emerge unscathed, untainted by dark spirits, you may be subjecting her to a life just like your own. A life that will end in pain and misery."

For all the frightening and horrible things that he had just told me, my brain froze and fixated on the little, minor detail he let slip: It was a she. I was carrying a baby girl.

"Yes, it's a girl," Jakob admitted, quite literally reading my mind. "And maybe you won't pass your powers onto her. Maybe it will skip a generation. But you're dooming someone to a life just like yours."

I felt weak and was glad to be sitting down. I shook my head lightly, feeling tears creeping up behind my tired eyes. "My life isn't so bad. I have Ludie. I have a child. I have a home and I have money. I have what I've always wanted."

I didn't know if I was trying to prove something to Jakob or to myself.

"But those things won't last, Pippa, and you know it," he pointed out with a gentle tone, as if that could soften the blow. "Ludie is just an ordinary man."

"He's more than ordinary," I spat at him.

"But he's not like you."

"So you're saying I can't love him because he doesn't have this wretched power, this disease?"

"I am not saying that. You will continue to love him, no matter what happens. But he isn't like you, he won't ever understand the real you – this you - and when things get hard in the future, he will run. He will always run."

I looked down at my gloves and absently picked at them. I felt low and ashamed. "He thinks I'm special too."

"Of course he does. But Ludie is just a man, Pippa. He's a perceptive man and more in touch with his feelings than others, he is more open-minded and he can feel that energy you give off. It attracts him like all other living and non-living things. But his heart isn't drawn to yours like yours is to his. Very few people with these abilities can find each other in all the worlds. When it happens, you know. It's a magnet affect, a sense of finding your missing half, someone who gives off what you do and draws you in like they do to you."

"Let me get this straight. I'm doomed to be alone until I find someone like me?"

"I can't answer that," he said.

I glowered at him. "You seem to know my future very well. I'm going to assume my heart won't be acting like a magnet with another anytime soon." When he didn't say anything to that I continued, "And my daughter. What's to come of her since nothing looks very rosy anymore?"

"I do not know," he said. "In my vision, you wouldn't have the daughter at all."

"Because you told me to?"

"Because it's not your husband's. It belongs to another man who will leave you as soon as he gets word of your pregnancy. Because it's dangerous and you are not in the best health and are getting old."

The nerve of him. I was not *that* old.

"Why are you telling me all of this, Jakob? Why didn't you just let me be? You didn't have to follow me today. You could have stayed away like you had been doing all this time. I would have never known any of this. Why did you do it?"

He looked sheepish as he stepped off the crate and walked away.

"Because I'm selfish. I'm lonely."

I was caught off guard by the honesty of his answer. He stopped and shot me a shy look.

"It's true. This is probably why we aren't allowed to interact like this. You draw me to you just like everything else is drawn to you. I like watching you. I like talking to you. And I have reason to believe it will be easier for us to converse now."

I squinted at him. "How?"

He raised his hands to sky. "Now that you've seen this place, you'll be able to come here whenever you like. You can see me or choose not to. You'll step out of this and feel changed. You might notice other abilities about you that you hadn't noticed before."

"Like what?"

He strolled back over to me and held his hand out for mine. "I do not know that Pippa. But I am certain you will once you leave this place."

I placed my hand in his and let him raise me up.

"You say that by choosing to have my baby, I've chosen a path different from the one you saw," I told him. "So how do you know that everything I am supposedly doomed for will still happen. You don't know, do you? I could find someone else like me. Ludie could stay by my side. I might divorce Karl, maybe Ludie and

I will get married and live somewhere wonderful. You don't know anymore."

His smile was small. "I do hope you prove me wrong, Pippa."

He kissed my hand and then gestured back to the darkened alley.

"Now, we shall see what you can do already. Concentrate on that air, on that space, and imagine a door opening. Will it to be true."

I looked to the grey, stale air above the alley and tried to focus my eyes on the nothingness that was there. I thought of the shimmer, I thought about walking through a portal, a door, and stepping back into a land of noise and color and people and life.

It took a few seconds of silence and concentration but before I knew it, there it was. The way out of the Thin Veil. The way back into the world I belonged.

I looked at Jakob.

"Are you coming with me?"

He shook his head. "I don't want to press my luck. But I'll see you again."

"Anytime I want?" I asked.

He pursed his lips in concern. "I'll let you know first, how about that?"

He sounded uneasy, like there was something he wasn't telling me, but I was so tired from getting all the other information out of him. There had to be some secrets left and I was OK with that.

I was OK with everything now. I was pregnant after all.

With a small wave, I held my breath as a precaution and stepped through the pressured air until I was engulfed by cold and snow and exhaust and colorful books that lay at my feet.

I turned around to see a car putter past the alley. That was it.

CHAPTER EIGHT

Jakob ended up being right about everything he warned me about. It started with the increased abilities, these changes in myself. Before visiting the Otherside, I was vaguely aware of the world around me. Oh, I paid attention all right, but never enough attention it seemed, for now I was seeing ghosts everywhere. But perhaps it wasn't a matter of my eyes opening, maybe I was giving off a stronger energy now that I had been to their world and back.

Either way, it didn't matter. There were ghosts where there weren't ghosts before. No longer did I contend with random boys in my classroom or drowned girls, but people, all the time, from all walks of life. They never approached me or talked to me, but they watched me. They always watched me.

I don't have to tell you both how god damn unnerving that is. It was no wonder that my sanity would crumble one day and crumble it did. Another point for Jakob's perceptiveness.

But I'm getting ahead of myself here, as we all know how that story ends. The visit to the Otherside brought about seeing ghosts but it also brought about a strange...I don't know the term for it. Kinetic ability? I found that under periods of extreme duress, I was able to manipulate objects by my emotions. One day, after a particularly rough fight with Ludie, I thought about smashing the plates in my kitchen. I was so unbelievably mad. The next thing I knew, the plates in the good China cabinet came crashing down. At first the actions were uncontrollable and random but as the years went on, I began to assert some aspect of power over them. They were still unpredictable when my emotions were high, but when I was calm I could do minor things like move chairs and make books float in the air. It was a rather pointless ability to me, but it was mine now.

Of course, the other things that Jakob was right about were more life-altering. I could handle ghosts and rattling pans, but I couldn't handle Ludie when he skipped out on our life together.

I know I shouldn't have been surprised, but there was a part of me that wanted to prove Jakob wrong, and desperately so. I wanted Ludie to love me like I had him, but his heart was no magnet at all. When I told Ludie I was pregnant and that I was going to keep the baby, he withdrew from me. At first he told me that he would be there for me, support me emotionally as he assumed I would still be with Karl and raising it with him. But when I said to Ludie that I was going to admit to our affair and request a divorce from dear Karl, he panicked. Ludie loved me but only in that noncommittal way that suited his lifestyle just fine.

When I was seven months pregnant, Ludie sent a letter to my house. I cried and cried as I read it at the kitchen table, grateful that Karl wasn't home. Ludie told me he had found work in a popular off-Broadway play in New York and that he was going. In fact, as I read the letter, I realized he was already there. He signed off by saying he'd think of me always and our child, but that he was doing the right thing.

He would go and make more money, get famous, and come back for us one day.

I don't need to tell you that the one day never came.

The only thing that kept me going during this time, this second round of heartbreak, was looking after the baby and waiting for her to be born. I had decided to call her Ingrid, after Karl's mother. It was the least I could do, considering she wouldn't ever be his child.

Did Karl ever suspect? I am sure he did. Looking back, he had to have known I was having an affair. Near the end I was quite careless and on the days when I had been with Ludie, I noticed Karl could barely look me in the eyes. And of course when Ingrid was born, that was another sign right there. Ingrid had pale blonde hair and bright blue eyes, just like Ludie. She was a gorgeous, lithe-like creature and grew to have no resemblance to Karl at all.

But Karl, good, sweet Karl, he never said anything to me and he loved Ingrid as if she was his own. When he was around, he would dote on her as often as he could.

However, because there was an extra mouth in the family to feed now and caviar wasn't what it used to be, especially when a company such as IKEA opened up, Karl had to start another business (marine instruments) and spent the majority of his time working. He felt bad for never being around and told me we could hire a nanny, but I didn't want to do that. Ingrid was all I had and I wanted to spend every minute with her, doing everything for her that I could.

Oh, I loved that girl so much. She was so beautiful that people would stop on the streets and stare at her. I couldn't help but marvel at her big sapphire eyes, her perfect nose, heart-shaped face and high cheekbones. Her hair was white blonde and stick straight with just the right amount of thickness and shine. She was stunning, just as her father was, and I dressed her in outfits I created myself, indulging in my wardrobe cravings again.

Ingrid was the belle of the ball and fairly smart too. But there was something about her that was slightly off-putting. I felt just the tiniest bit afraid of her. It was completely irrational, but there were times that Ingrid would look at me, even at four years old, and I felt...judged. It was as if she was looking down at me, at her own mother. At other times, it's like I wouldn't even show up on her radar and she was looking through me, as if I were a ghost.

Sometimes I would lie in bed at night and wonder why I never saw any love from her eyes. Ingrid seemed to take interest and delight in other things. She liked fashion and must have gotten that from me. She liked being on her father's knee and pretending she was riding a pony. She had friends, she giggled over boys and laughed at cartoons. But when it came to me, it was like a switch went off. Smiles disappeared, laughter stopped. Oh, she was a polite girl because I raised her to be and she would talk with me about her day and tell me stories. But she was missing something crucial. She was missing the mother/daughter connection.

Because of this, I often wondered if something *had* gone wrong with her. I thought about accessing the Thin Veil and seeking out Jakob, asking what he knew. The pregnancy had been fine, Ingrid seemed like a normal girl with everyone except me. Just because I hadn't experienced the dangers, I never saw any demons or monsters coming for her, did it mean she emerged unscathed? Or was she cursed in some way to never love me?

Perhaps it was none of those things and I was just unlovable. I never did find out. I just had to accept it was the way it was. Some girls never had a close relationship with their mother and that seemed to be the case with Ingrid and I.

As she grew up and became a young lady, I wondered if perhaps did have some things in common.

One day when she was eleven, we were strolling down a busy shopping street and enjoying the sunshine. I spoiled Ingrid rotten and gave her everything she asked for. On this particular day, she wanted to get new headbands because there was some boy in her class she wanted to impress.

I obliged, of course, and as we were coming out of a store, I decided to test something on her.

"Ingrid," I said and pointed across the street to where an old man was leaning against a shop window. He had blank eyes with no pupils and was absently twirling a pocketwatch. "Do you see that man over there?"

She looked, squinted, then shook her head. "What man?"

My heart sank. "The man twirling the pocketwatch, leaning against the window."

She gave me a funny look. "Are you drunk mama?"

"Ingrid," I admonished her. "Of course not."

"But there's no one there," she said smartly. "So you must be drunk or crazy."

I narrowed my eyes at her and looked back at the man. I was foolish to test my theory. Of course there was someone there, but he was dead. Ingrid couldn't see him. She wasn't special like me.

That should have made me feel better, but it only made me feel alone.

"Never mind," I said to her and pulled her along to keep walking.

"You're often drunk and crazy," she said in a sing-songy voice.

I stopped, my breath paused, placed my hands on her slight shoulders and turned her to face me.

"Why do you say that?" I asked uneasily, leaning over a bit so I was more at her level.

She rolled her eyes, a gesture I found infuriating. "Because you are. I hear you all the time, telling people to go away, or acting like things are coming after you. There's never anything there."

A flush crept on to my cheeks and I straightened up. "Don't lie, sweetie."

"I'm not lying!" She pouted. "You scare me mama, you always do. You see things that aren't there. You're like those people in the crazy places. Perhaps we should lock you up there one day."

To hear those words coming out of my daughter's mouth hurt me more than anything in the world. She said them with such venom, such hatred. I wondered what I ever did wrong, why I deserved to be treated like this by someone whom I did nothing but love.

"You will do no such thing, Ingrid," I whispered, straightening out my dress. "You will love me as I love you."

"You love me too much," she replied under her breath. It surprised me. I opened my mouth to say something but her eyes lit up at the sight of another clothing store. "Oooh, I must go in there! I saw a darling dress that Erika was wearing the other day and I need one much better."

She took off for the store and I was left on the street. It took all of my strength to not collapse into a heap of tears.

CHAPTER NINE

As much as it hurt to hear my little darling daughter tell me those things, she was right. I was losing it. The ghosts became more and more frequent and whereas they used to just watch me, now they were stalking me. Talking to me. Touching me.

I tried to ignore them but it often made things worse. There was an old Asian lady with bound feet who would appear in my bathroom while I was in the tub and she would take all my items off the shelves and the medicine cabinet and throw them in the bath with me. I would scream and I'd hear Ingrid telling me to shut up, or Karl would pound on the door and demand to know what was going on.

Sometimes there was a little boy of about five or six who had half his face blown off by a shotgun accident. He would appear before me during my morning coffee, often sitting in the chair across from me and whining about how his brother knew where their father had hidden the gun and that he wanted to play with it.

One time I was felt up by a greasy-haired man in tight pants. He smelt like sewage, had coal black eyes and freezing cold fingers that rammed themselves up my skirt during a ferry voyage to the Åland Islands. It took all my self-control not to scream but even then I could tell the people around me were getting concerned.

Karl was especially worried and would insist I needed to go to a doctor. I told him I was fine, that it was just stress and being an older mother instead of a younger one. Ingrid, on the other hand, used my relapses as an excuse to further push me away.

At fifteen she had started modeling for local catalogs and magazines and began to pull in some money. She was gorgeous and she knew it and so did everyone else. Eventually her career picked up speed and she was soon offered a contract with a big modeling agency in New York City. At sixteen she decided to drop out of school and do it.

Now, I say she decided because although Karl and I were her parents and in legal control, we had a hard time saying no to her. We agreed to her following her dream, provided she only went for a year and that I would go along.

Naturally Ingrid balked at the idea. She was adamant that I not be there, convinced I would further embarrass her with my "kooky" ways and that I'd ruin her "best chance at happiness."

That was the way it was though and Karl had a business to run. He was getting much older too and had hip problems and wasn't one for long distance traveling.

So despite Ingrid's protests, I made up my mind to go with her to New York.

She wasn't the only one who protested, however.

A week before we were set to fly over, I was sitting in the back garden enjoying my last days there in the evening sun with a cup of tea. I felt a familiar chill brush across my skin and knew that I wasn't alone. Jakob came up behind me and took a seat at the table.

As usual, he hadn't changed. But I sure had.

"Do you only come every sixteen years or so?" I asked, my hand shaking slightly as it grasped the porcelain cup. I was nervous and excited to see him.

His smile was quick. "I only come when you're about to embark on something you shouldn't."

"Oh really?" I asked wryly and leaned back in my chair. My bones ached a little and I was reminded of how much older I was now, almost 51. "No dropping by just to say hello."

"You could have said hello to me," he said, leaning forward on his elbows, the same old white shirt he always wore.

"You told me to not visit, to wait for you first."

"I said that so you wouldn't start going into the Thin Veil and attracting attention to yourself. You saw what happened when you came back out. The abilities."

"Yes," I said, taking a sip of tea. It had cooled rapidly in his company. "How wonderful it is to make the room shake when I'm angry, how gratifying it is to be harassed by ghosts all day long."

"Don't say I didn't warn you."

"You didn't warn me!" I hissed at him and a bit of the tea spilled over the side of the cup. The saucer on the table rattled by itself ever so slightly.

I placed the cup down and composed myself. "You didn't warn me. You brought me to that side knowing that things would get worse for me."

"You wanted to know the truth and that's the only way I could tell it to you."

"I don't know," I mused angrily. "I think maybe you were testing me, to see what I was capable of."

"Perhaps I was curious," he said fidgeting with this shirt. "But that's not why I'm here."

"No, you're here to warn me about something else, I'm sure. What is it this time, boogie man is coming after me? Perhaps there are some trolls who are going to pay me a visit."

"Don't go to New York, Pippa," he said in a grave voice.

I studied his face, his sincerity. It rankled me to know that whatever he was about to tell me would end up being true.

"And why not?" I asked, too tired to protest.

"Because it will not end well for you. Because Ingrid needs to stay here. And you need someone who loves you, Karl, you need him to protect you from her."

His words iced my veins. "Protect me from her? What do you know about Ingrid? What is she?"

He raised his red brows. "What is she?"

"She's not right," I said awkwardly.

"You're not right either. Neither of you are. And if you go to New York, she will turn against you and fall in love with a man. She will leave you to your own devices, cast you aside like a sick dog and you will have no one."

I looked down into the tea and managed a smile. "Oh, but I'll have you still, won't I boy. In spirit, of course, till another event threatens my life so."

"I am being serious here."

I glanced at him and saw that he was. Still, I shrugged. "I've made up my mind and I'm going. I'm doing this for Ingrid you know."

"Not to see Ludie?"

I gasped even though it was partly acting on my behalf. I couldn't pretend I hadn't thought about tracking down Ludie while I was there. "No, not Ludie. This is for my daughter, not for me. I want her to be happy and it sounds like she will be."

"This is about more than Ingrid. She may not have your abilities but it doesn't mean her children won't."

"Children?" I asked with reluctant interest.

When he didn't say anything, I continued, feeling more annoyed by his presence by the second. "So now this is about Ingrid marrying some man and bearing me grandchildren that will be cursed with this as I am. What am I supposed to do about that?"

"Don't go."

I stood up in a fury, knocking my chair back onto the lawn. "You are giving me too much credit. Too much...power! This is ridiculous, to put this responsibility into my hands. This is Ingrid's life too and I am not about to ruin it because some guide for the dead thinks my future grandchildren are in danger. This is too much, can't you see?"

I shook my head and walked away from him, my arms waving at my sides, not caring if anyone in the house was watching. "No, I won't do it. I won't manipulate lives around for something that should be beyond my control. If she wants to fall in love let her. Fate has a way of finding people anyway, doesn't it?"

"You're right about that one, Pippa," he said, getting to his feet. "Fate will always find you."

He walked himself over to the garden gate and disappeared into a faint shimmer that appeared and disappeared in a blink.

He didn't even say good-bye.

~~~

My meeting with Jakob, the uncomfortable predictions he presented me, had me in a funk until my feet touched American soil. Suddenly that was all swept under the rug as I drank in the new country, the hot dog stands, the smell of butter and sweat, the sound of a million cars honking and jackhammers firing away.

New York City was like a tonic to me, and to Ingrid as well. Her face was constantly lit up by the vibrant pulse and life that the streets offered her. I could see the possibilities sink into her brain and I lived through that, that something I had only once, when I was young and Stockholm had been my oyster. My, that felt so very long ago.

Karl was constantly wiring over money into my bank account, so we were able to get Ingrid a small apartment on 53rd street next to a smelly Chinese food restaurant. We spent the first few weeks with me on the pull-out couch, living out of my suitcase, eating Chinese food until we burst. At the time, Ingrid was still very thin and didn't give too much thought to what she ate, providing she remained the same size. That would soon change however, as the industry got a hold of her. Soon, everything changed.

It started with the modeling. I went with her on a few bookings, just to get the feel for things, but I knew I was making Ingrid uncomfortable and I stopped. It didn't help that the ghosts were back in large numbers. The city had so many of them, it was overwhelming at times and I had to do everything I could to keep them at bay.

Ingrid got a lot of work and soon she was hanging out with the wrong crowd. They were on drugs, no doubt, skinny little trainwrecks. She began to party, she stopped eating, her weight dropped off and she began to change. Her ability to tolerate me disappeared and one day I came home to find all of my belongings packed. Her boyfriend, Stew or Drew or something, was moving in and I was moving out. I had no say in the matter, either. She was making money now and the rent was pretty much being covered by her earnings.

I knew better than to argue. She was seventeen and unstoppable. I had no power over her, I never really had.

So with an extremely heavy, helpless heart, I let Stew or Drew move in with his ripped jeans and scaly leather jacket and I put myself up into a roach-covered motel until I figured out what to do with myself.

The answer came in the form of a Help Wanted ad in the paper. A family on the upper west side was looking for a nanny to look after their two young boys, aged six and nine, and in exchange the nanny would receive room and board.

I had a fluttery feeling in my stomach about this, like it was a good idea. Being in another family would make me feel safe when I felt very much forgotten and alone. I knew I could have gone back to Sweden, to Karl and perhaps I should have. But even though I couldn't live with Ingrid, I couldn't leave her either. I would stay in the city and try and keep an eye on her when I could, be there for her if she should ever need me, as unlikely as it was.

The next day I took a cab from the hotel to the posh surroundings of a neighborhood on the rise and found myself in front of a narrow but tastefully decorated brownstone duplex. This was the home of the O'Shea's.

It had been a long time since I had a job interview and being in my fifties with a heap of unwanted life experience did nothing to squelch my nerves. I watched the cab drive off with butterflies in my heart and took a deep breath before I climbed the steps of the brownstone.

I rang the doorbell and waited, admiring the good shape of the small porch area they had outside, the relative calm and ease that the eloquent but tightly packed neighborhood gave off.

At first I heard nothing but the echo of the bell, then silence. No children laughing or crying, no stampede of feet. I checked my watch to ensure it was the right time and the right date and just before I pushed the bell again, the door swung open.

On the other side stood a man well over six feet, with the darkest brown eyes I'd ever seen and though he was around my age, his hair was remarkably thick and free from grey hairs. His posture was straight, his clothes neatly pressed and immaculate, and even though he gave me a very winning smile, there was something closed-off and strained about him.

"You must be Pippa," he said and offered his hand. "I'm Curtis O'Shea."

His accent was 100% Irish though he worked hard to make it more Americanized. I shook his hand in return and found it firm and quick.

I greeted him and he ushered me inside.

The house was very bare and tidy at the area around the door. There weren't any signs of children, no shoes or toys scattered about. Even the walls had pastoral scenes of Ireland mixed with modern art, but there were no pictures of the family or a child's art work proudly displayed.

"Thank you for agreeing to see me so quickly, we only put the ad out yesterday," he said, walking past me and down the hall. He looked over his shoulder to make sure I was following.

I quickly took off my shoes, not wanting to disturb the austerity of the area, and walked quietly after him. It felt like a house you couldn't be loud in, a heavy feeling of tension sat in the air above our heads.

"Were there any other applicants?" I asked.

"A few. Come, let's sit in the living room."

He went through an opening to his left and I came after. As I neared, I snuck a look into the kitchen across the way. It was an utter disaster with pots and pans piled high in the sink, army trucks and dinosaurs scattered about the floor and dripping stains coming off the high-gloss counters.

Curtis caught me looking and I averted my eyes quickly. It was obviously something I wasn't supposed to see, but then I suppose it would be my job to deal with messes like that.

"I'm not a very good caretaker," he explained as I came in the room and he indicated I sit in on the sofa across from him. "You can see why we need a nanny."

I nodded, sitting down on the slick leather and folded my hands in my lap. I could see he was embarrassed. "Are you a single parent?"

He gave me a quick smile, still handsome and still strained. "No. I am not. I have a wife, Régine. But..." He trailed off and did a quick sweep around the room with his eyes. "I'm an investment banker. I work very long hours and I'm not home often. Your job would be to take care of the children, cook their meals, clean the house...essentially do the job that Régine currently cannot."

I didn't want to pry, but I had to know. "Is there something wrong with your wife?"

He let out a sharp puff of air and tugged a bit at his hair. I opened my mouth to apologize for my bold question but he spoke, "She's ill. Mentally. We don't know what's wrong with her. And she drinks too much. She's...she's been steadily going downhill and it's coming to the point that I can't even deal with my own family. I need someone else to deal with it for me."

"Someone like me?" I asked. I was starting to wonder if I had applied for something that was well beyond my abilities. Certainly I was no spring chicken and had a hard enough time chasing after Ingrid all those years ago. Would I be able to handle two young boys and their alcoholic, mentally ill mother? It seemed like it was a bit too much for me.

Curtis caught the look on my face and as he twirled his wedding band around his finger, said, "I know I am not painting the best picture here but I want to be honest up front. My dignity means a lot to me and I need someone who will keep the image I have built up for myself. I am a good provider to my family and give them everything they wish to have. The boys, well the oldest anyway, are well-cultured and well-groomed. I work very hard to give them this life but I cannot be their mother. I don't expect you to be their mother either, but the help would be more than appreciated. It would be better than what we currently have: A deadbeat."

I flinched at hearing him speak about his wife like that but he didn't seem to notice. "I must say, I don't know if I am the right candidate. I am in my fifties and have seen better days. Are you sure you wouldn't want someone fresh and new?"

He shook his head. "No. No, I saw quite a few fresh and new women this morning and I'm afraid they aren't cut out for the job. It is not about the energy here. I doubt my boys will run you ragged, as I said they are, for the most part, very well-behaved. I need someone with the mental maturity to handle the situation with grace and class. For first impressions, you seem to have that."

Curtis tugged at his hair again, a gesture that I realized was a nervous tick. I wondered how he still had such nice hair with such a habit. He looked up at me, his face very serious. "I'll pay you handsomely you know."

I didn't want to assume as much, so I just smiled at him and ran things over in my mind, not really sure what to do. I didn't know if such a household would be the right place for me, considering all I had gone through with my life. I certainly did not want to live it all over again. The fact that he would pay me well didn't even factor into it.

"Jesus Christ," he suddenly swore and I jumped in my seat. He got up and marched over to area between an armchair and the fireplace. He bent over and when he emerged he was holding a broken glass trophy in his hands. His eyes were wild with anger and I could feel it flowing off of him like it was steam. He looked to the mantel above the fireplace where I assumed the trophy once stood.

"That son of a bitch," he said, his voice lowered, the full brogue coming out. As if I didn't exist, he stormed past me and stuck his head out into the hallway.

"Declan Pierre O'Shea!" he bellowed, his voice echoing throughout the house. "You get your arse right down here this instant!"

I turned in my seat and watched Curtis. He was clutching the trophy so hard, I was surprised he wasn't drawing blood.

"Is everything alright?" I asked him.

He shook his head, the anger never leaving his eyes, and waited by the doorway. I heard a shuffling and a small boy reluctantly appeared in front of his father.

He was the youngest, the six-year old, skinny as anything, with a tuft of messy black hair that matched his father's. His eyes were downcast, staring at the floor, but I would have bet they would be the same mahogany brown too.

"Did you break Michael's lacrosse trophy!?" Curtis yelled at him.

The child, Declan, didn't move or say anything. I could see he was frigid with fear. I felt the same fear myself and my heart was catching in my chest.

"Look at me when I'm speaking to you," Curtis growled. He grabbed Declan's small arm and pulled him roughly toward him. "Answer me! Did you?"

He was right in the boys face now, the power of his words causing his hair to fly. Slowly Declan raised his eyes to his father's. They were surprisingly hard. I had expected him to be crying but that was not the case.

"Yes," the boy said in a flat voice. "I'm sorry."

"Sorry doesn't cut it," Curtis said venomously. Declan tried to move out of his father's grasp but Curtis tightened his grip to the point where it looked as if he'd break his own child's bones and he pulled Declan in front of me. I gasped at the act, I couldn't help it.

"This is Declan. He's the only one who might give you trouble."

Curtis shoved him toward me. The boy kept his eyes to the ground.

"Declan, promise me you won't be a bother to this nice woman as you are to me and your mother."

"Oh, he's just a young boy," I began to say, but Curtis cut me off.

"It doesn't matter. He knows how to behave and breaking his brother's trophy is out of the question. Just because he's jealous it doesn't give him the right. You hear me Declan?"

"It was an accident!" Declan wailed, finally showing some emotion. I felt extraordinarily bad for the child. "I was throwing the ball and-"

"You know not to throw anything in this house!" Curtis's face was now turning an ugly shade of crimson. "We have rules."

Declan looked back at the ground and mumbled, "Mikey wouldn't play with me and mum said I was giving her a headache. She told me to go away, to play inside."

"Enough with the excuses." He tugged at his hair again and sighed. Then he quickly patted Declan on the head, his face contorted slightly, as if he was petting a lizard instead of his own son. "You go get your brother. I'll deal with you later."

Declan nodded. Before he left, he looked up at me and in his big, dark eyes I saw a plea for help. That's all it could have been. It was almost as if he shouted "Help me" inside my own head.

I nodded back, dumbstruck and frightened, and Declan left the room, shoulders slumped and head down. Defeated.

Moments later Michael, the nine-year old, came into the room. He was tall for his age and had similar good looks to his father, perhaps with less of an olive complexion than Declan had. His hair was lighter and cut short and he was wearing a neat shirt and khakis. There was no question that Michael was the favorite son. I could almost see him wearing that fact like a badge of honor.

After the meeting, Curtis quickly showed me around the rest of the house, except for the master bedroom where Régine was apparently sleeping. I got a glimpse, however, of the tastefully appointed room that would be my own.

"This will be your room, if you're to take the job. Pippa, I really hope you do. We need you here," Curtis had said. He had calmed down and though he wasn't quite jovial, he was more pleasant to be around and was back to trying to win me over.

I wasn't sold on the idea, so told him I would need a day to think about it, especially since he wanted me to start right away.

I got in the cab and gave him a short wave. Just as the cab was pulling away I caught a hint of movement on the second floor. My eyes traveled up to the window to see small, little Declan standing there. Not waving, but watching me leave. He was too far away to see clearly, but I felt a wealth of desperation and sadness in his eyes.

I didn't know the full dynamic of the O'Sheas. I knew that my job would be a difficult one. But if I couldn't be a mother to Ingrid, perhaps I could be to a little boy who desperately needed one.

Two hours later I called Curtis from the roach motel's crackly phone line and told him I would take the job.

A day later, I was moved into the O'Sheas as Pippa Lindstrom, their new nanny.

CHAPTER TEN

I never regretted my decision to become Declan and Michael's nanny. I hope you realize this Declan, no matter how hard it is to hear me rehash those troubled times. I never ever regretted a thing.

That said, as far as jobs go, I doubt you could find one more difficult. Especially at first as there was a large learning curve.

Curtis, as he had said, was rarely ever home. It wasn't my business to ask where he was, even when I wondered how he could be doing business when he left at dawn and came home at 11 o'clock at night. I also didn't ask where he went when he wouldn't come home at all and for several days at that. He was either a workaholic or he was having an affair. Perhaps several affairs. Sometimes I would catch perfume on him and I could tell it wasn't from Régine. The two of them never spoke, except in yells and slurs.

Oh, Régine. It's difficult for me to summarize the way I felt about your mother Declan. I certainly know how you feel about her. I can understand your shame and anger at having such a woman for a mother. But though Régine frightened me, disgusted me and angered me, I could see she was a victim of her own mind and uncontrollable circumstances. There must have been a normal, good-hearted person somewhere in her soul, it was just a pity that by the time I came to the family, she wasn't there anymore. In her place was an absolute monster.

Régine had two problems, the very ones that Curtis had warned me about, and they were so intertwined it was hard to see what problem came first. Was she mentally ill because she drank all the time or did she drink all the time because she was mentally ill? I suppose the same question could be said about us, too. Are we mentally different because we see ghosts or do we see ghosts because we are mentally different?

Notice I called her ill and us different. Maybe later the ill part could have been applied to me, but Régine was in fact a very sick woman. She couldn't function or she didn't want to. She spent most of the time sleeping in an alcohol-induced coma. She would then crawl out of her room around noon, wearing the same clothes she'd been for days, smelling like something awful. She'd walk unsteadily over to the kitchen and pour herself a small bowl of cereal and several cups of black coffee. This was the only thing she'd put down, other than booze. She rarely spoke when she was sober or sobering up. She would just mumble and shake.

Occasionally she would look at me and be confused, like she didn't know who I was. One time she asked me if I was a ghost who kept following her around. I wanted to make something of that remark, but I couldn't. She was just so lost in that head of hers and I was so desperate to find someone like myself.

She wasn't mean, however, when she was sober. She was just distant. Michael and Declan both competed for those rare slots of attention, but she never gave it to them. Her eyes would glaze over, her face would go slack, and the boys would have to busy themselves. Luckily, Curtis was adamant they be involved in a lot of activities as possible, so there was sailing, hockey, lacrosse and a whole range of sports to keep the boys busy and distracted.

When Régine was drunk it was a whole other story and unfortunately she was drunk more often than she was sober. As the years went on, her violence and depravity worsened.

I won't go into many details because I don't think it would do Declan any good to remember them, but to give you an idea what a night at the O'Shea's was like, here's an example:

Declan was eight years old at the time and I was looking after him alone one weekend. Curtis was who knows where and Michael had gone to a science fair that was being held out of state. I normally would have gone with him and taken Declan with me but he was paired up with one of his classmates and his family wanted to look after him. I could see how much Michael wanted a weekend away from Declan and I. He wasn't overly fond of his little brother and at times I think he might have even resented me. Maybe it's because Declan had taken a shine to me and naturally I was overprotective of him. For whatever reason, Declan was the one his parent's rage would always be directed at, a living, loving target.

It was a warm spring and Declan and I were out in their small back yard until the sun went down and the early mosquitoes came out to play. I was enjoying a small cup of espresso and the new lights we had installed over the garden while Declan was reading a book with a flashlight. It was a mystery novel, I remember that well, and I asked him if he'd rather go inside to read as it was getting so dark.

He looked up and shook his head. I recognized the fear in his eyes, exaggerated by the flashlight's eerie glow.

"What is it?" I whispered.

"She's in my room again," he whispered back.

I got off my seat and kneeled on the cool grass beside him. I smoothed the hair off of his forehead, thinking he was due for another haircut.

"Who is in your room?" I asked.

"Mum. She's tearing it apart."

I looked over at the house. I couldn't see his room from the back but all the lights in the house were off.

"How do you know that?"

He shrugged. "I just know. I get a feeling sometimes."

He resumed looking at his book for a few seconds. Then he put it down and his eyes were watering.

Even in the worst situations, when Curtis would spank him, or yell at him, or Régine would call him names, nasty, terrible names, I never saw Declan cry. To see those brown eyes filling with tears brought my heart to my knees.

"Oh, Declan boy," I said soothingly. "What's wrong?"

He tried hard to keep those tears back but his voice wavered. "She's ruining my stuff, I know it. I don't want her in my room, Pippa. It's my room. It's supposed to be safe from her."

I was breaking inside for him, filled with sorrow and building anger at having seen up close just what his family was doing to him over the years.

"You know what we'll do then? You and I will go together and we will make her stop."

He shook his head adamantly. "No, she'll hurt you. She'll hurt me."

"Your mother seems scary at times, but I've been through more than she has and I'm stronger. Mentally and physically. We will put a stop to this. I don't want you to ever be afraid. And I won't let her put a finger on you."

He wiped away at the lone tear that spilled down his cheek, seeming to think things over. There was something so old and mature about that wee little boy. He then said, "OK" with all the determinedness of a soldier going off into battle.

He gripped my hand, his palms already sweaty and we made our way into the house. I flicked on all the lights, steadied my nerves which weren't as calm as the front I had put up, and we made our way up the stairs. Nearing the top, I could hear growls and little screams coming from Declan's room.

The door was closed but there was no doubt Régine was in there. I heard her movements, her French mutterings and a strange droning sound. I kept Declan behind me and knocked at the door. I hoped his mother would respond to reason. I was stronger but I was still fifty-five and she was in her early thirties.

A spewing of swears and curse words came out from behind the door. I could only pick out half of them, the rest were buried in slurs.

I gave Declan's hand a squeeze and whispered, "Stay here" to him and opened the door.

He was right. She was tearing apart his room. His mother was on her hands and knees in the middle of the floor, ripping the head off one of the few plush toys that Declan had left. The room smelled like urine and feces and I saw brown stains smeared on the walls and damp spots on the carpet. Régine looked like a wild, rabid animal, wearing a vomit-covered white nightgown that was half torn off. Her fingers were brown and red, her arms were scratched and dripped blood. Everything around her lay in ruins, including his bed which had a slit down the middle and stuffing spilling out of it.

She smiled at me, then quickly chucked the toy at my head. I ducked as it sailed past, even though it wouldn't have done much damage, but it didn't help that the headless, bloodied thing came to a stop by poor Declan's feet.

"Get out!" she roared in her accented voice, staggering to her knees.

I was too stunned to move, I could only say, "I'm calling the police."

"But I haven't given my son his present! A wonderful present pour mon beau fils!"

I did not want Declan to receive anything from her so I found my strength and quickly shut the door on her. Then I scooped Declan up in my arms, and as hard as it was on my body, I carried him down the stairs, going as fast as I could. We were almost at the bottom when I heard the door to his room open and Declan gasp.

I turned around just in time to see Régine holding a beehive in her hands. It was a young hive that

Curtis had taken down a few days earlier when he found it growing on the side of the house. The droning sound emanated from inside the white, papery exterior and before I could comprehend what was going, why she even had it to begin with, she threw it down the stairs and it bounced after us like heatseeking missile before it hit the back of my legs and then the tiled foyer. It cracked open and thank the Lord there were barely any bees or wasps left in the thing otherwise we might have been in big trouble.

I made it to the front door and out onto the street with only one sting at my ankle. Declan, with his allergy, was traumatized but fortunately unscathed. I headed to a house across the street where I knew the couple and used their phone to call the cops.

This wasn't the first time I had called the cops on Régine and it wouldn't be the last. There were many incidents similar to this one and I was powerless to stop it. I had expressed concern for my safety and the children's many times to Curtis but he didn't want word to get out that his wife was a drunk. He was against sending her to a treatment center and would get angry when he found out the police had gotten involved.

After that incident, Declan slept in my room. I wanted to sleep on the couch, but he was too afraid to be alone, so I took to sleeping on a cot beside him. He had become more withdrawn and irritable. His grades at school went down, he was disinterested in the activities he once liked, he had a hard time concentrating and the differences between him and his do-good brother became more and more apparent. He was also becoming increasingly agitated by what I could only assume were ghosts. You see, to add to the horrors of his daily life, it turns out my dear boy was just like me.

A year earlier, Declan and I had taken the bus to Central Park as we often did. I invited Michael too, of course, but he said he'd be spending the day at a friend's. I didn't blame Michael for spending as much time as possible away from the house, from his family. Unfortunately Declan was still young and at the time, curiously friendless, so I took up most of his attention.

We were strolling along the path, the trees just sprouting new, fresh green leaves and I noticed Declan staring curiously at a woman who was standing out on the Great Lawn. I had seen her many times before. In fact, the woman in her 1920's attire, was always there, standing in the same spot and staring at the ground, never moving. I knew she was a ghost of course, but this was the first time I could see Declan noticing her.

"Declan," I said. "Do you know where people go when they die?"

He didn't seem too concerned over my odd question and ate a piece of caramel corn from the box he was cradling in his arms. "To heaven or hell."

"That is true, though no one can be sure for certain," I told him. "But I do."

"Where do they go?' he asked, his eyes glistening with new curiosity.

"Some don't go anywhere," I said. I kept my eyes on the woman in the field. "Some stay where you and I can see them."

"They do?"

I stopped walking and pointed his body towards the wide green lawn.

"Yes, Declan. Do you see that woman over there, standing in the middle of the lawn?"

He nodded. A surge of pride ran through my old blood.

"I see her every time I come here," I continued, so happy to be able to talk about it. "It doesn't matter what time of day it is, or what season it is, but I see her. And now that I know you see her too, it means we share the same gift."

"A gift?" His dark brow furrowed in comic confusion.

"Yes." I pointed over at a nearby bench where an old chap was feeding pigeons. "Go over to that man there, don't be shy, and ask him if he sees her too."

Declan looked even more puzzled but there was a side of him that was brazen and bold with strangers. He nodded and walked over to the man who peered away from his cooing birds with annoyance.

"Yes son?" the old man said.

Declan pointed to the woman. "Excuse me sir, I have to ask you a question. Do you see a lady standing right there?"

The old man followed his finger and gaze and then looked back to him with squinty eyes. "You pulling my leg?"

Declan sniffed and peered back at the woman. Satisfied, he said to the man, "No sir. But do you really not see the lady?"

"There's no one there," the man said gruffly after he sneaked another peek.

"But that's not true, she's right there, my nanny and I can see her!" Declan's voice was raising a few octaves and he bit his lip, getting anxious.

"Your nanny is either a nut or she's lying."

"But I see her too."

The man waved at him dismissively and turned away, looking back to the pigeons. "Then you're both nuts or maybe having a bit of fun. Now scram, you're scaring my birds."

At that, Declan moved his little legs over to me.

"Well?" I asked.

He was wide-eyed as he spoke. "He says you are a nut and I am a nut."

I crouched down and brought him close into me and looked deep into his eyes. "And that is why we must never tell people about the things we see. They can't see it and they won't understand. It's not safe."

"But she's standing right there. Why can't he see her? Is he blind?"

"In a way, Declan. In a way. You see, she's dead."

He jumped at that.

"Dead?" he asked incredulously and looked back over at her, his eyes filled with fear and wonder.

"She's a ghost," I said simply, trying my hardest not to scare him.

"But...ghosts are only in books and movies."

"And in Central Park," I said and ruffled up his hair. "Would you like to go talk to her?"

"Can we?" he asked.

I smiled at his bravery and took his hand. "Why not? It's what we are meant to do."

Together we walked across the lawn toward the woman. I could feel the eyes of the old man watching us as he threw seeds at the pigeons and knew he'd soon see us talking to no one, but I didn't care.

As we got closer to the woman, I saw that she was in her late twenties and pretty with a short, curled bob. Her dress hung off her in the Flapper-esque way that was so popular back then and she had on dainty white gloves that lay clasped in front of her. Her eyes continued to stare at the ground, lost in sadness, and she didn't acknowledge our presence until we stood right in front of her. She looked up at us, tired and confused, and then looked away.

"Hey lady," Declan said.

She was startled.

"Me?" she asked with a shaking voice.

"Yes, you."

"Don't be rude, Declan," I chided him.

The woman looked back and forth between us.

"You can see me?"

"Of course we can," I told her. "Why do you ask that?"

"Why, most folks ignore me like I'm not here. Even when I ask them for the time."

Ah, that explained a lot. Normally all ghosts that I saw were very well aware of me. After all, I was attractive to them and gave off the attention and energy they craved. However, this woman did not know she was dead. That was a first for me.

"Do you want to know the time?" I asked.

She nodded. "Please. I'm supposed to meet my boyfriend here and I'm new to the city. I'm a bit worried, I shouldn't be out here so late. The park is scary at night."

Something told me it was this late night jaunt into the park that killed her.

"It's not nighttime," Declan said, looking at her strangely.

I patted his head and gave the woman a soft smile.

"Well, I hope your boyfriend comes around soon," I told her. "You shouldn't be out here by yourself."

The woman returned a weak smile back and resumed staring at the ground.

I put my arm around Declan and led him away.

He looked over his shoulder at her. "Why did she think it was nighttime?"

"Perhaps that was when she died and it's forever dark in her mind."

"Why didn't you tell her the truth?"

"I will, someday, but not now. We've both had a lot to comprehend for one afternoon, don't you think?"

And I did end up telling the woman. I wanted to come back, without Declan, as I did not know how well she would take it. I thought perhaps telling a ghost they were dead was akin to waking up a sleepwalker.

I was partially right. When I returned to the park and to the woman, it took a lot of denial and yelling on her behalf. Had anyone else been able to see her, she would have created quite the scene. Then, as the truth finally sunk in after all these years, she broke down in tears, weeping for the life she once had, the people she once loved.

I wasn't sure what I would do with the bawling ghost, but the Otherside answered that question. For the first time in a few years, the air warped and shimmied. My heart leaped, thinking I might see Jakob again, realizing at that moment how fondly I thought of my guide, but what appeared was a somewhat heavy man in a suit. Really, I wondered just where these guides came from.

"Are you Jakob? One of the Jakobs?" I asked.

The man nodded at me and turned his attention to the woman. He held out his hand to her.

"Lorraine, come with me please. I can help you."

I expected this Lorraine to balk at the idea of going off with a stranger, especially one who came out of thin air. However she took his hand without hesitation and at his touch, a smile and glow came over her face. My Jakob never brought me peace while I was alive, but Lorraine's Jakob brought her peace in death.

And just like that, she was gone. It was a strangely beautiful and touching moment, one that I would think of often as my life started to disintegrate before my eyes.

CHAPTER ELEVEN

Knowing that Declan had the same ability as I did, made me feel much less alone. However, though I would often confide in the young boy about the ghosts I saw, he never did the same with me. I would ask him but he wouldn't say or he'd avoid the question. He liked to hear about it without acknowledging that it happened to him. Who knows, Declan, perhaps you never saw things the way I did. After all, my ability never really worsened until I went to the Thin Veil and back.

Regardless of Declan's input, it helped to share with him as he was the only one who would and could listen to me without threatening to drag me away to the loony bin. Things were getting worse for me, with the ghosts and with my own family.

No, I hadn't forgotten my dear daughter, or Karl, but my relationship with both grew more and more strained. I admit, it was also I who was pulling back, devoting more of my time and energy into Declan and Michael, and in my increasingly fragile and paranoid state, I was afraid to talk to Karl and Ingrid.

Ingrid managed to pull herself out of the wrong crowd because she met Perry's father, Daniel. I met him a few times for lunch and found him to be far better than Stew or Drew or whatever new man Ingrid was shacking up with. I would never have pegged my daughter to be with someone like Daniel. It was almost a comical sight to see his short stocky demeanor beside her tall and willowy one. But Daniel was smart, driven and passionate and was spending a year at the Holy Trinity Roman Catholic Church as part of his graduate thesis. For whatever reason, Ingrid was drawn to him and he to her. He pulled out grace and goodness from Ingrid that I very rarely saw.

I suppose that's why I withdrew from them as I did. Before, I would have been adamant about spending time with both of them, but there were some days I was too afraid to leave the house for fear of the reaction I would cause. The dead kept coming for me, multiplying year by year, all wanting a peace of me, whether it was my ear to listen to their sob story, or, at times, my soul.

There was one particular ghoul whom I remembered from my past. The man with the shadowy face who I saw tormenting the girl in my garden, all those years ago in the Swedish countryside. At first I saw him prowling the backyard, then the streets outside the house. He would just stare, watching me. One night as I got up to use the washroom, I had a weird sensation I was being watched. With my nerves on fire, I crept through the house and felt this malevolent intensity rolling out from Declan's door. He was about twelve now and was a strong kid, back to sleeping in his own room. Some nights the door was locked but tonight it wasn't and as I quietly opened it, I saw the shadowy black figure standing above his bed. It was just for a second though and when I turned on the light, awaking the poor boy, the man was gone. Declan fell back to sleep unaware of what had been there.

The fact that I could feel the evil from the figure, who was constantly watching me in a most predatory way, made me believe that this was no ghost. No human. This was a demon, a creature. And as the years went on and the creature appeared more frequently, I knew it was true. Jakob had mentioned as much.

There came a point where the day-to-day fear of never knowing what this demon might do to me, or the ones I loved, finally took its toll on my sanity. I began to talk to myself and to the demons, to the ghosts, not caring who saw. Curtis and the boys became increasingly concerned about me. With Michael and Declan I knew the concern came from the worry in their heart but with Curtis I could see his disappointment and annoyance in finding a nanny who acted just as crazy as his wife.

I started to fear I'd be let go. But that didn't happen. No, it was Curtis who left. One day and without much warning.

Declan was thirteen and Michael was sixteen when Curtis pulled me aside in the kitchen and told me that he recently completed a huge transaction of sorts and that he was putting a large sum of money in a trust for the boys when they both turned eighteen. I never knew how much it was, but I assume it was a lot. Curtis then told me he wanted to thank me for all my hard work (*oh, here it comes, I'm being let go*, I thought) and that he arranged a trip for me and the boys to Atlantic City for the weekend. They'd both be allowed to bring a friend and that we were free to spend his money as we liked.

Naturally the boys were ecstatic. At this point, Declan was in a band with a few friends and invited his drummer, Joey, to come along. Michael had a beautiful girlfriend, Marguerite, and even though I had been quite strict with the amount of time they spent together alone (no young lady was getting pregnant on my watch), I relented and told him he could bring her, knowing the young ones would all be sharing the same suite.

That was one of the best weekends of my life. Even the ghosts and demons were kept at bay and I was free to enjoy the sweet salty air of the boardwalk, such a nice change from the harshness of the city. It was wonderful to see Declan truly smiling and enjoying himself. At this age he dressed in loose pants and flannel shirts, his hair was shoulder-length, wonderfully wavy and streaked with red. He begged me to let him get his eyebrow pierced with Joey at one of the beachside tattoo parlors but I had to put my foot down somewhere and said no. Ever the rebel, he and Joey pretended to go to a movie later that night and wasn't I surprised in the slightest when they came back and I saw matching rings on both their faces.

I knew Curtis would kill him for it (indeed, he would publicly lament Declan's long hair and grunge attire even though the boy was passed the point of caring), and he would most likely reprimand me as well. But I decided not to worry about it until Sunday night. For now, this time and peace and sunshine was all we had and needed.

I am ever so grateful I let the boys be boys, even if it ended up with piercings and Michael and Marguerite sneaking away to the beach at night to canoodle. When we returned, no one would ever be the same.

The house was empty, save for Régine who was quietly weeping at the kitchen table. She was drunk, but not dangerously so, though she could not tell us why she was crying. The sight shocked us since Régine rarely showed any sadness, it was always anger.

On a hunch, I went upstairs to the master bedroom and found the room to be emptied. Everything that belonged to Curtis was gone. His clothes, his shoes, his books.

I ran down to his study and it was emptied too. His degrees and certificates, his computer and files, everything had vanished. There was no note, no anything. He just up and left that day and that was the end of it.

Suddenly I knew I was faced with a problem larger than myself. I had inherited a family but I had no money to support them as the breadwinner was gone.

I never knew the reasons why your father left, Declan. I guess we will never know. One can only assume that his image and pride was worth more to him than his family and rather than trying to maintain the cover up, he left it all behind. Maybe he ran away with a mistress, perhaps he was evading the police, loan sharks or taxes. It doesn't matter. The fact is he was a coward and he left a giant mess behind him.

I reached out to the O'Shea's family friends, those who had been pushed aside over the years. With their help we got Régine into a treatment center and while she was there, I took care of Michael and Declan off of my own savings. Eventually I called Karl and he agreed to help me, then pleaded for me to go back home. I should have listened and I didn't.

The truth was, I needed the boys as much as they needed me. But there came to be a time when I couldn't look after them anymore. The shadowy demon was tormenting me. The pleas and touches in the dark never stopped. Even Declan was affected my actions - I could tell he was sometimes afraid of me and that hurt.

But how silly it sounds to say that for it was foolish of me to worry about my own feelings when it came to the boys. Michael handled it as well as he could and continued to excel at school and football. Declan started getting in fights after class, failing exams and fooling around with older girls from the wrong side of the tracks. He devoted all of his time to music and penning shocking poems that I found scattered about in his room, stuff I wasn't allowed to see. Though Declan feared his father and was never once close with him, he took Curtis's abandonment hard. He was an angry, frustrated young man and I could not fault him for it.

Finally, Régine emerged from the treatment center a somewhat new woman. She was prickly, skinny and stern but she was sober. For the time being, at least. She was able to get a job at a call center, which meant not only would my services cease to be needed, but she couldn't afford me anyway on her new salary. They ended up having the bank foreclose on the house and she and the boys moved to a tiny two bedroom apartment in Brooklyn. Michael was close to graduating so he was able to stay at his school in Manhattan but Declan had to start all over again.

Sadly, this is where my story and Declan's story part ways. Even after they moved, I still came and visited Declan when I could. I lived in Queens, renting the basement of a young family, surviving on Karl's generosity, and the journey wasn't very far. But after some time, as I deteriorated, Ingrid and Daniel came swooping into my life.

~~~

It was to my surprise when Ingrid and Daniel paid me a visit one day, showing up at my door unannounced. My small suite was a mess and I knew how it made me look. The dishes weren't done, there was garbage on the floor and all my favorite books were scattered about, their pages spread open and covers torn off. The dishes and garbage were because I was too tired and depressed to help myself anymore. The tossed books were the actions of a poltergeist that wouldn't leave me alone, however try explaining that to people.

Oh, maybe I'm kidding myself here. It has been a long time and there are some parts of my life that remain a haze. I am sure my apartment and the way I looked was far worse than I am describing to you. It was bad enough that Daniel insisted they would take care of me. They were now living in his small rented condo in the city and they were engaged to be married.

The next while was a blur. I fell into tough times. I'd react to things no one else could see. I was living in fear, too afraid to let my guard down for one minute, too paranoid to bathe, to eat, to sleep. The lack of sleep was the worst of all and it toyed with my health and sanity. But I couldn't sleep unless I was forced too – my dreams felt all too real and I was unprotected. I had begun to dream about things that were yet to happen, dreams about being locked away, dreams about being raped by faceless figures, dreams about smashing open a makeup kit, dreams of blood.

I didn't improve, even with their care, and Ingrid ended up having to give up her modeling job to take care of me. As if that child could not resent me more.

Finally, they had to call Karl and ask for his opinion on what to do with dear old Pippa. He couldn't come to me, so he insisted I was to go home where I could be given proper medical care. He would be there to love and take care of me while the Swedish mental health system would ensure I was treated properly and respectfully.

That never happened, despite all of our best intentions. We were close; I had the ticket bought for me and had some things packed in my small suitcase. I calmed down in the last few days leading up to my flight, enough that I could feel the overwhelming sense of relief at getting help. Maybe with the right medication, the right people, I would be able to keep the ghosts solely in my nightmares. I was going to miss visiting my dear Declan though and hoped he wouldn't forget about me.

As such, I couldn't leave the country for good without saying goodbye to him and perhaps imparting some of the wisdom I had gleaned from Jakob and it was Régine's I was heading to on the day I fell apart.

I was going to catch the subway and was just about to head down the dirty stairs when I saw a familiar blonde head coming out of a ritzy restaurant.

It was no one other than Ludie and time stood still. I dropped the newspaper I was holding and let it fall absently to my feet. I stared at him enthralled, enraged.

He was finally showing some age, looking refined but tired. His smile was charming and aimed at a young redhead on his arm, but the sparkle was gone in his faded baby blues and his hair was greying and thin.

I can't tell you what happened exactly, but I lost it right there on the street. I approached him with boiling breath, asking why he hadn't shown any interest in our daughter.

He recognized me. I know he did from the fear and surprise that flashed briefly across his face. But, ever the actor, he covered it up and flat-out ignored me. He acted like he'd never seen me before and told me I didn't know what I was talking about. I ended up spitting in his face, attacking the innocent redhead much like I did to the understudy back in the theatre days.

I needed to be restrained. I was violent, hollering nonsense. Out of my sorry mind and out of control.

I broke apart from the crowd that had gathered around us and in my blind despair I ran down the subway stairs. I fought my way past the greasy turnstiles like a panicked bird and in an unrelenting urge to leave my sad life behind, I ran for the nearest tracks, to the train that was just about to hit me head on.

I don't know who saved me from throwing myself in front of that train and ending my life, but I know someone did for the next thing I remembered was waking up in a psychiatric hospital, the very place I would spend my last years before I died.

CHAPTER TWELVE

I think if there was a hell on earth, it would be inside a state-run psychiatric ward. It is a hopeless place filled with people who are either empty shells of what they used to be or monsters of another making.

I never knew what I was. I felt like a shell of the woman I was and I felt like a monster too. All I did know was I was left alone and afraid and never saw my family again, not in the ten years I was locked up there.

To be fair, I was shown pictures of my family. Karl wrote to me often, which was nice when I was in the right frame of mind to read and not tear the paper up. He wished he was well enough to come visit since he was having hip problems still, but I figured it was all a lie and that he had moved on with his life and found other people to love. And Ingrid. My daughter, who once swore – with Daniel – that they'd never lock me up, my daughter who went and did the opposite. She lied for she was the one who put me away. She also wrote to me, first to show me her wedding photos, then her pregnancy photos, and then photos of her and Daniel smiling above a beautiful dark-haired child they named Perry.

I am ashamed to admit that I tore up those first photos too. I was wildly jealous that Ingrid got to have the husband she wanted, a child she loved, and I ended up here, with nothing. I hated Perry at first for no other reason than that.

Then, on my days when my delusions calmed down and I had enough strength to push through the medication (which, Declan, as you know, did help a bit), I realized that Perry needed me. Everything that Jakob said about my grandchildren being cursed with my gift ran through my ears. What if Perry were to grow up as I did, and with Ingrid of all people as her mother?

I felt utterly helpless and spent most of my time feeling sorry for myself. I should have listened to Jakob when he had warned me, I was just too selfish to listen. Then I realized Jakob might have the answers. Jakob might be able to help. Perhaps he could do for Perry what he did for me.

I tried to access the Thin Veil, to make the portal appear in thin air, but nothing worked. I was probably just some crazy old lady waving her hands about like some wizard. I almost gave up hope until I skipped on taking my medication for a few days. I had been a calm and pleasant patient most of the time, so the nurses weren't as watchful over me as they were over others.

It was then, on one rainy night with water and wind battering the tiny window of my room, that the air around me moved and glistened and I stepped inside.

That familiar pressure pressed down on my head and made my eyeballs feel as if they were about to burst. It lasted longer than last time but soon enough the pain subsided and I was in a grey zone, the parallel world. Here, Jakob was in the room with me, sitting on the uncomfortable stool in the corner.

"Pippa," he said with a jovial nod.

Tears sprung to my eyes.

"Jakob," I cried out. I got to my feet and found them to be sturdy and willing. Here in the Thin Veil I was more able, stronger and I used this change to embrace the young guide in my arms and sobbed all over him.

When my tears finally subsided, I begged Jakob to go after Perry and to help her.

"She might have someone at some point," he said. "There is no need for it to be you."

"But can I help her? Can I use this place to reach her?"

He didn't say anything for a long time, weighing his options in his mind. But I could see the truth in his eyes and he knew it.

After a minute he said, "You can use this place for many things, but it doesn't mean that you should. The most you can do, the most you should do, is just watch over her like I have watched over you."

"I'll never get a chance to meet my granddaughter."

"That might be for the best."

I nodded at that, a sinking feeling in my heart.

"I should have listened to you," I admitted softly.

"Yes. But what is done is done. I can only guide you, I can't make your choices for you. You made the decisions which you thought were best at the time, and I don't blame you for doing so. And you shouldn't blame yourself, either. Perry and Ada-"

"Ada?" My head snapped up.

He gave me a wry smile. "Yes, I had said grand-*children*. Perry and Ada will have to make their own choices in life too and it'll be up to them to handle the cards they have been dealt. There's not much you can do or say to change that."

I mulled it over. There seemed to be a loophole somewhere in what he was saying. I could do anything I wanted in the Thin Veil, including watching over people. What more could I do. Could I actually use it like a mode of transportation?

Jakob watched me carefully and I was afraid he was reading my thoughts. If he had though, he gave me no indication of it.

"Would you like to see her, Pippa?"

I nodded eagerly.

He put his hands together. "Very well, just do as you once did before. But instead of creating a portal, create a window and concentrate on that image of Perry you have in your mind."

"But the picture I saw is a few years old now."

"It doesn't matter."

I did as he said and concentrated hard on a window, willing myself to see a young toddler, one with giant stone blue eyes and long black hair, on the other side of it. I kept this rate of thought and power going until I felt more pressure inside my skull and before I gave into the pain and blinked, the air parted like the Red Sea and a glassy window was in place. On the other side of it, the real side of real life, was Perry. Now she was at least six years old, a little round thing but still so very beautiful. She had a type of beauty that was unique from her mother's and Ludie's and I cherished that I could look at her without feeling guilt or shame.

Perry was sitting in her room, surrounded by toys and reading a picture book filled with dragons. She chewed at her fingernails, more out of an anxious, excited gesture than one of worry. She was so young and so innocent and I knew it would be hard for me to stay away.

"Can I always come in here and do this?" I whispered even though I knew Perry couldn't hear me...she couldn't, could she?

The girl in the image shivered a little but that was it.

Jakob said, "You can...but..."

"But what?" I was afraid to take my eyes off of her.

"Time outside the Veil doesn't stand still. You are not in your room at the hospital right now. If a nurse were to come in, you would see them but they would not see you. You must never give people reason to suspect the veil exists. Even though most wouldn't believe it, it would be dangerous if the knowledge got into the wrong hands. It's dangerous for you too. Not only would you cause attention to yourself but every time you visit, you will bring a different...disability back with you."

I managed to look at him, only for a second, only to see how serious his pale grey face was.

"I'm not following...seeing ghosts? How can it get any worse for me?" I asked bitterly. "You've seen where I am. What I've become!"

"Things can always get worse," he said. "I just know that a normal human body is not meant to continuously visit this world. One time might be enough to increase telekinesis or telepathy. It might be enough to create more energy within yourself, or attract others from the Veil. Or it might start to ravage your body and your mind, leaving you a little bit weaker. Maybe a lot weaker."

I forgot about watching Perry for a moment. "You're saying when I go back to my world, I may be in rougher shape than I already am?"

"It is possible. Pippa, I can only warn you."

"Yes. And you have and I thank you."

My attention went back to Perry who was now scribbling into a coloring book, her tongue sticking out of her mouth in concentration.

"I will be leaving you now," he said.

"Where are you going?"

"I'll be around. I have other people to help, you know."

He started walking to the door.

"Wait," I called out after him. He stopped and looked at me from over his shoulder. "I met a boy..."

"Declan," he said. He saw the wonder on my face. "As I said, I have been watching you."

"What is to become of him?"

He shrugged. "I do not know."

"But is he going to have a guide too, someone to look after him?"

"Not everyone gets someone like me. Your power has never been latent. Perry and Declan's is and will most likely remain that way."

"Most likely?"

"People make their own choices," he replied rather ominously. "Declan is closed off to our world. Perry is just a young girl. Neither possess the power that you have, therefore neither of them would warrant it."

"But how do you know that? What if their gifts develop and they end up just like me?"

"Just try and worry about yourself, Pippa," he said. He smiled, waved then opened the door to the hallway and stepped out.

I was alone in the Veil version of my room, grey and stale-smelling. But I wasn't alone was I? No, I could see young Perry through the window in a lavender haze. I could see her. But was that all? Could I make her see me?

We all make poor choices from time to time and I believe they shape who we are. The Lord knows I have made so many in my long life. Standing in that hazy, dull room, in a world parallel to the one I was born in, I made a decision that I would regret ever since. It was a selfish decision that I masked as selfless one. I wanted to reach out to Perry to warn her of the difficulties to come, to let her know that I would be there for her, no matter what. And that was the truth. But the larger part, the selfish part, was that I didn't want to be alone anymore and I wanted her to know who her grandmother was, to love me like I loved her mother.

So, I concentrated, made the window into a door, reached into Perry's room and pulled her into the Otherside.

The shock of it working knocked me backward onto the floor, but sure enough there was little Perry beside me, her blue eyes grey. I wasn't sure how to make it look like she was in the Thin Veil version of her room and from her confused and frightened face, I knew she had no idea where she was.

"Mom!" she wailed, looking around her frantically, her long hair whipping past her. I quickly put both my hands on her shoulders, careful not to scare her any further.

"Perry, don't be afraid, it's me, it's your grandmother, Pippa," I told her in hushed, soothing tones. "I'm your grandmother, Perry."

It didn't matter what I said, Perry struggled to get out of my grasp and then the tears began to spill down her round cheeks.

I really had not thought any of it through. Just what was I hoping to do with a six-year old girl? Did I think she would have a notion of where she was or, more importantly, who I was?

I bit my lip and looked at the portal I had just pulled her out of. I could still make out her room there, although it was fading and getting hard to see. The thought of never returning her to her family made my heart skip a beat.

"Perry!" I said to her. "I'm sorry, do you want to go home?"

She looked at me and nodded through the tears.

"Ok darling," I told her and reached for her with my hand. "Don't be afraid of me. I'll take you back. You'll go back to your room OK? You'll go back and it will be like none of this ever happened."

I didn't know if I had the ability to control someone's mind like that, to erase memories. It's obvious that Perry never remembered the incident, even with her therapy sessions and regression. Either it had worked or Perry naturally blocked the traumatic event out of her head.

Perry wiped her tears on the sleeve of her plaid dress and gingerly put her hand in my outstretched one. My skin looked so papery thin and faded with dark grey smudges of age spots. By contrast, hers was as smooth as cream. I grasped it tightly and looked at her little face, thinking it would not only be the first time I saw her but the last. A tear spilled out of my own eye, which seemed to calm Perry down.

"Why are you crying?" she asked. The concern in her face was genuine and graceful.

"Because I love you and I have to give you back," I said, choking on the words. For the first time I felt the blood of myself in another. It felt like I had known Perry for all her life.

Then, she did the sweetest, most wonderful thing. She took a few small steps toward me and wrapped her arms around my neck.

"If you don't cry, I won't cry," she whispered into my hair. I was so shocked at her affection that I couldn't move my lips at first.

"It's a deal," I said breathlessly. I squeezed her back and then composed myself. "Let's put you back where you belong."

So, with a gentle nudge I pushed Perry through the portal and back into her room. She stumbled a bit, falling to the softly carpeted floor but she seemed OK. I couldn't bear to watch anymore so I closed my eyes until the portal faded and its place was the one back into my room.

I stepped through, succumbed to the horrible pressure, and everything went black.

CHAPTER THIRTEEN

I woke up days later in the medical ward. Apparently the nurse had found me passed out the next morning and completely unconscious. However, even when I came to, nothing was the same. Jakob was right once more. I was so far gone that there was no hope for me. My body was weakened, my mind was gone further than it had ever gone before and I saw demons everywhere I looked. Everywhere. Even in my reflection. I started acting out again, attacking nurses and other patients, until they had to put me on the strongest drugs they had.

It's how I spent the next five years of my life. The last five years of my life. I don't remember any of it, except for brief flashes until the end. It skips around like an old roll of film. I see myself laughing alone. I see myself dressed up in drapes and funny clothes, and putting outlandish makeup on myself and on others. The nurses indulged me with that, letting me relive my times in the theatre, so long as I took my medication and did what I was told like a good girl.

There was no hope for me. No respite. Memories of my other life, of Karl and Ingrid, of Declan and Perry, of Sweden, even of Ludie...they all faded and became inconsequential in my haze. There was no way out but death.

One night, I smuggled some of the makeup back to my room. I took my chair and as quietly as I could I crunched an eye pencil sharpener underneath its heavy leg. The sharpener shattered, spitting out the shiny puzzle piece I lusted over.

The blade.

I picked up the tiny danger between my shaking fingers, and before I could give it any more thought, I sliced it up both my wrists.

I felt no pain – not physically. The blood ran a shiny dark red down my failing arms and I marveled at it with an eerie sense of detachment. It felt peaceful.

At first.

Then, as I lay down on the floor and the life began to drain out of me in a stream of silken crimson, I felt immeasurable pain. They say your life flashes before your eyes but mine didn't flash. It crept along slowly and I was forced to relive all the pain and the few fleeting moments of glory. I clung to those moments with Declan and Michael in Atlantic City, to me and Ludie making love in the theatre, to giving birth to Ingrid, to having my granddaughter's arms around me despite the impossible odds. I tried to let them live in my mind, to win out over the pain and sorrow that was oh so present and oh so persistent. And I don't know what side won. Was it the brief happiness I felt in the small things, the simple joys in my life? An accepting look or forgiving touch or sunshine in the backyard? Or was it the feeling of being deserted, abandoned, unknown and unloved?

Either way, I died with an aching heart for the things I suffered through and the things I loved. In the end, it's all the same.

In the end.

~~~

Oh, but my story doesn't end there, does it? I don't think anyone's does, I'm just one of the first people to tell you so.

Death seemed like an eternity of blackness but who knows how long the moment of emptiness and shadows really was. I opened my eyes and I was no longer on the floor of my room. I was no longer bleeding. I was standing beside the lake back in Sweden, back at my old house. It was grey here, it was dull and grainy but it was still home. I had gone home again.

I heard a throat clear from behind me so I took my eyes off of the shiny, beautiful lake and looked to the forest. Jakob was standing at the edge of it, leaning against a birch tree.

He smiled at me and held out his hand.

"Come with me, Pippa," he said gently. "You're not home yet."

I grinned at him in return, pleased to see that I was no longer my incoherent self, but younger and able-bodied. I walked toward him up the slight grassy embankment that ran up the side of the house. My house where I grew up with its stone and wood and silence.

I was happy to see him, happy to go. But...

I stopped a few feet away and looked back at the lake. There in the middle of it, the water shimmered more than normal. A portal!

"Pippa," he said in a warning tone.

I shook my head and looked at him apologetically.

"I can't go yet."

"There's nothing you can do for them. They have their own lives to live." He knew I was thinking about Declan and Perry. "You have yours to continue living. In another place. In your home."

"No," I told him, the lake holding my full attention. "If I can help them, at least help them find each other..."

"Fate will bring them together if it's supposed to be that way."

"Curse you and your fate!" I sneered at him, my anger surprising me. How had it followed me from one plane of existence to another?

His boyish face, forever young, showed no sign of annoyance. It's like he expected it all along. Maybe he knew this to be my fate no matter what I said to him, no matter what I did. Fate would find me.

I looked down at the ground, at my feet that were no longer in the hospital slippers but in glossy, beautiful dancing shoes, ones I only dreamed of owning once upon a time. The sight of them made me smile again and I willed the anger to disappear.

I must remember these little joys, I thought to myself. *Even in death.*

"You're not coming then?" he asked.

Somehow, even in the Thin Veil, I heard the call of birds across the water.

"No. I will not go. Not yet. I've made some mistakes that I'd like to make up for."

I glanced quickly at Jakob. I could see he knew that I brought Perry across into this side all those years ago. I wasn't sure if I ruined her life by doing so, if I made her see ghosts where there were no ghosts before, and I had to help her if I did. I had to help her anyway, because I cursed her to this life. As for Declan, I knew the potential he had and the life that knocked him around. He'd need me too. I just wasn't sure how I'd make a difference at all.

But I had to try.

Jakob gave me a salute and walked into the woods. I knew I'd see him again. Until then, I wouldn't move on.

I had to keep trying.

I'm still trying.

THE DEX-FILES

PROLOGUE

I was six years old when I got my first taste of hell.

I woke up to a horrible howling noise, like a dog caught in the throes of deep emotional pain, agony that went beyond the physical. It was chilling. Terrifying. Like, make your balls shrivel up into pricks of ice sort of terror. It quickly plucked away whatever ignorance my sleep had thrust on me and slapped me in my young face. This wasn't a dream. This was as real as all hell. There was a monster in my house, the kind that preyed on little boys, but it wasn't under my bed or in my closet. It was next door. Or, as it seemed to be, the floor below, scratching and howling its way from the kitchen.

It was my mother. And from the sounds of glass breaking and furniture scuffling, my dad had found her. The howling intermixed with his booming voice, his threats, his pathetic cries that betrayed the collected man he was always trying to be. It sounded ugly. It always sounded ugly but tonight I was especially scared. When a vicious cry was followed by the sound of someone being shoved into a wall, I'm not ashamed to say I promptly wet myself. Pissing your pants seemed like the only thing to do when the monster was loose and I made a silent, naïve prayer to the man upstairs, praying that it was my mother who was thrown against the wall. I'm callous, maybe. I've been called worse. But if it were my father, and he was out cold, she'd come looking for me next.

I thought about pulling the covers over my head and hiding from it all like a coward, but that never worked. I would pretend all I could that my blanket was my invisible cloak and it would shelter me from everything bad in the world, but I learned at a very young age that there was no such thing as shelter. Maybe I would have been safer if I didn't care. Maybe indifference could have been my protector. But I still loved – and feared – my parents. That love is what scared me. It gave them the upper hand. They sure as fuck didn't love me.

I heard a shuffling from outside my door, slow and light. It was only Michael, though it rattled my wee body to think things were bad enough that *he* got out of bed. Michael was just three years older but he might have well been another decade. He was the golden boy, the child of light. I was the runt, the child of dark. I feared. Michael didn't.

I quickly jumped out of bed and scurried across to the door, purposely missing the part of the floor that I knew squeaked. I turned the knob silently and saw Michael's shadow just down the hall, heading toward the stairs. Half of him was lit up by a dying night light.

He stopped as soon as he heard me and though I could barely see it, I could *feel* the look. It said *go back to bed, you'll get us in trouble*. Only I could get us in trouble just by being awake. I still don't know why my mother had it in for me. Sometimes I think she saw a lot of herself in me, even at such an age. That's a fucking terrifying thought. I'd be lying if I said that, and other things, didn't keep me up at night.

That look though from Michael, that was the most I'd ever seen him scared. It felt good, selfishly good, to know he wasn't inhuman, that he feared things too. Maybe not the way I did, but hell if I hadn't been wondering if my brother was born without a soul.

Now I knew he was just older and better at hiding it than me.

I opened my mouth to say something but he placed his finger to his lips. We listened. The wailing had stopped. There was no more noise.

The fresh piss felt cold against my legs and I was suddenly, acutely embarrassed of what I had done. It's damn funny how Michael had that effect on me.

Even funnier was how I remember reaching out for his hand, looking for some sort of pathetic comfort in my blood relative, my Mikey. He jumped as if my very touch startled him or scathed his skin. Yet he let me hold his hand, even though it was tiny and clammy and I grasped him hard, until bone rubbed against bone. I never felt as grateful to my brother as I did at that moment, for not letting go. Yeah the asswipe would let go later. Fuck, he'd order up my own execution if he could (don't think he wouldn't try). But at that moment, I wasn't alone.

We made our way down the stairs, holding hands. You'd think it would be less scary without the yelling and the damn woman howls, but the silence was hazed with suspense and unheard threats. And forget the smell of urine emanating from me, I was *this* close to shitting myself.

When we reached the floor we heard a very slight tinkling of glass. We both froze and Michael's grip on mine intensified. Just for a second. But it was enough.

The sound was followed by a groan. Then a flopping sound of body and skin against shiny tiled floors. This wasn't good. This was very, very bad.

I wanted to turn and run. I think I may have tried. But Michael held me there and we both watched as a dark figure came crawling out of the door to the kitchen. She moved on the floor like a drunk snake. That's what she was, after all. A fucking drunk snake out to eat us alive.

She didn't get far. Her arms were outstretched and reaching for us but she got two feet before she gave up and passed out. She smelt like wine and evil. Like sweat and sadness. Of all the feelings that hit me at that moment, I felt...bad. Looking back, I pitied her.

Michael and I stood there, staring dumbly at our unconscious mother. Michael's eyes were hard in the darkness, tiny pinpricks in the black. I wonder, did he feel hate toward her? Did he still love her? Did he feel loved? Or was he as confused as I was, forever mixing up love and hate and fear and females. I'll never know. I don't think I even care.

The spell of shock wore off when we heard another sound from the kitchen. My father was stirring. My first instinct was to run and hide. I feared him in a different way. That I'd get a spanking for wetting my pjs. That I'd be told I was nothing but a fuck up (not so much in those words, I was six after all, but I got the gist. I'm no dummy). But he didn't notice in the darkness. He appeared in the doorway, standing over my mother, with an expression of hopelessness and utter disdain on his face. *This is what I get*, it said.

Instead he said, "You boys are getting a nanny. We can't live like this."

Same difference, I suppose.

My name is Dex Foray and I'm a hypocrite. Proud of it, too. I call my mother a monster but I'm the one who took her last name. Maybe because unlike my dad, she never left me. There's something to be said for sticking around...even if it kills you.

I'm a hypocrite because I can't stand weakness in others, even though I'm born of weakness myself. I dish it out and then laugh when they try and dish it back. Like I'm above it. And sometimes I think I am.

I'm a hypocrite because I hunt ghosts and I've pretended all this time that the ghosts haven't been hunting me.

And I'm a hypocrite because I judge people. I judge the fuck out of everyone I meet, from their music tastes, to their jobs to their lifestyle choices. I judge them but fuck them if they dare judge me. They think they understand this monster in me, the monster in all of us. But they don't.

They don't know where I've come from.

They don't know my side of the story.

But now you do.

AFTER SCHOOL SPECIAL

"Hey Dex. Way to fuck my girlfriend, you dick!"

That was the only warning I had before Chase Huntington – steroid monkey and douchefucker extraordinaire – punched me right in the face. I don't know if you've ever had a fat, pharmaceutically pumped fist meet your eyebrow ring and eye socket at the same time but I gotta tell you, it's not fun.

There was a black explosion of pain and I stumbled backward and hit the wall, dropping my joint to the ground. My friend Toby gasped and I couldn't tell if the fuck was upset about the joint or that his bandmate was injured. I was seeing stars out one eye and squinting angrily at Chase with the other.

"What the hell was that for?" I cried out as Toby quickly scooped up the joint from near my feet.

"Are you fucking deaf?" Chase bellowed, taking a step forward, his fist raised.

Oh right. The whole girlfriend fucking thing.

It was true. Not a misunderstanding by a long shot. But I was going to play it that way, especially as I saw the hungry eyes of our nearby classmates focus on us from across the yard, sniffing the potential blood in the air. Kids, they always liked a fight, especially one between a jock and a skid like me. This was David and Goliath level here, people. One scrawny, pierced 15-year-old fuck up against an 18-year-old who failed high school twice because he couldn't spell his name properly.

I mean, what, they were really going to believe that Amanda Layne, Chase's gorgeous, straight-A student, gymnastics champion girlfriend would sleep with someone like me?

Well she did. Don't ask how I did it. I think I give up some kind of "I don't give a fuck" charm or maybe it's the long hair and eyebrow ring. Or maybe it's because I'm very, very persistent and I more or less cornered her in the darkroom after photography class and shoved my tongue down her throat and gave her a taste of something she couldn't say no to. A Dex sample, totally free. She didn't have to buy the thing, but she did.

I'm a good product.

For whatever reason it worked and a few days ago I was going down on Amanda underneath the bleachers (yeah, yeah how cliché but chicks dig clichés). I think I ate as much dirt as I did pussy but she seemed to like it. No, scratch that, *love* it. I could tell from the way she screamed out my name until I had to put my hand over her mouth in case someone heard us. The bleachers soon led to her car (she's a year older) and I took some perverse pleasure in the fact that I was screwing something Chase prized very dearly. It made me feel like I was *The Shit*. She wanted me. He wanted her. I walked away clean.

Or at least I had until Chase found me during lunch hour. I knew this was coming, I just had hoped I wasn't stoned at the time so I could have had a little more warning. I could have devised a better plan than the one that came into play.

"How dare you accuse me of something like that?!" I hollered back in mock disgust and rubbed at my eye which I knew was going to black and swollen very soon. "I wouldn't touch that skank with a ten-foot pole."

Big mistake.

The gathering crowd gasped.

"Dude," Toby said under his breath before toking away.

This time I did see the fist coming. I planned on it. No guy worth their salt wants to hear their girlfriend being called a skank, even if she was a skank (and, come to think of it, she really was – though I was no better).

Chase lunged for me, but I was smaller and went lower. I tackled him at the waist and it was only surprise that allowed me to knock him off his feet. We hit the ground and fumbled for a bit until I managed to straddle him much like I wanted Amanda to straddle me (she was too shy or some girly bullshit) and I delivered a few quick jabs to his jaw and a crushing one to the nose. He cried out in pain at the crunch and blood and then literally threw me off of him.

I rolled for a few feet expecting to have Chase's overpuffed Nike sneakers crushing my face at any second but there was nothing. I opened my eyes and blinked at the sky. Something was blocking it. Something fat and round like the sun.

Principal Gould.

From what he saw, the scruffy, troublesome Dex Foray had randomly attacked Chase Huntington, one of the star football players and heroes of the school. No wonder Chase kept failing. Why leave a place where even the Principal worshipped the ground you walked on?

I (barely) had the chance to defend myself physically but there was no way I could do so by talking. I opened my mouth to say something, anything, but Gould shot me that look that said I would only harm myself more by talking.

I took my chances.

"He attacked me!" I protested, trying to get up to my feet. I shot Chase a look and wasn't surprised to find him shrugging and looking totally innocent. I then looked to Toby.

"Tell him what happened," I said frantically.

"Uhhhh," Toby said through glazed eyes and at that moment we realized that getting in a fight wasn't our biggest problem. Toby was caught red-handed with a joint in his hands. I admired the balls (or blunted stupidity) on the kid because instead of sticking up for me he puffed on the joint at supersonic speed before Gould snatched it out of his mouth.

"You boys are coming with me."

I had been at my new high school for two years now but time hadn't eased anything. I had been happy at my old school in Manhattan, happy with my life before my pa decided to up and go. Leave me and my brother Michael behind with nothing but our crazy mother. OK, maybe not happy as a "pig in the shit" type happy but I was certainly *happier*. Here, in Brooklyn, I never found my place. I coasted through life fucking around, barely going to classes, doing a lot of drugs fifteen-year-olds should never do, doing a lot of girls fifteen-year-olds should never do. Ha.

At my new school I came in as the brooding, mysterious fuck-up and I remained that way in the eyes of everyone, Principal Gould especially. This wasn't my first fight either. The first day of school some drooling asshole found out I had come from the Upper West Side and said I was a tight-assed prepster. How the hell he got tight-assed prepster from my uniform of cargo pants, Misfits tee shirt and boots was beyond me, but it pissed me off enough to lay the smack down on him. Unfortunately, the drooling asshole was also bigger than me and that fight ended with my face in the dirt. Still, my reputation as being a scrapper was sealed.

Gould ushered us into his office, the dungeon of doom as we liked to call it, and gave us a threatening lecture that made his cheeks puff out and turn all red. He said he was going to call our parents...actually he shot one look at me and decided that Toby was the bigger issue here.

It was a smart move. My mom would have been drunk on her ass and he would have gotten an earful from her. As much of a mess as my mother was, you didn't fuck with her children. Only *she* could fuck with her children.

So Toby's mother heard all about how her son broke the law by smoking pot at school. Of course Principal Gut had to bring me into it any way he could and made it sound like I was the bad influence on Toby. Phhfff. Toby was bad before I even showed up.

I'm not sure how much Toby's mom, who was a whippet-shaped dream muncher, really cared about the fact that I got in a fight and it must have gotten through to Gould, because when he was done with her, hanging up the phone in a sweaty huff, he looked at us both with frustration.

"You're both suspended for the rest of the week," he growled. "Go home."

Woo hoo! All right! No school!

That's what most kids would say. I mean, with suspension you had the lecture and grief and disappointment from your parents, but after that you didn't have to go to school, and your classmates would talk about you for months like you're a real bad ass.

Notice I said most kids. That wasn't the case for me.

I actually liked school. No, wait, I take it back. I actually liked *being* at school. Classes and teachers could kiss my perky ass, but school wasn't home. And any place that wasn't home was a place I wanted to be. My mother worked nights and she was home during the day. It was bad enough having to see her for a couple of hours after class where, if I was lucky, she'd throw a cheap frozen meal in the microwave for me and Michael. If I wasn't lucky, Michael would be out with his friends, my mom would be in rage mode, and I'd have a belt mark on my neck for looking at her wrong.

I exchanged a grim look with Toby, who no doubt would be grounded during his suspension and thus no band practice nor access to weed. This was going to suck.

In the months to come, I'd look back at that moment and want to pull my hair out. I wanted to yell at myself, tell myself to not go home. Go anywhere else. I wanted to hold onto that feeling that things couldn't get any worse when they very well could. I wanted that ignorance back.

But there was no turning back.

I went home. I was hungry and bored and even though I hung out at my favorite record store for a few hours, killing time, my house was calling me.

I knew it was a mistake the minute I walked in. Our place was small as all hell, with sad, peeling blue walls that looked silly against the relatively fancy furniture that we salvaged after dad left. The apartment normally had this moldy smell about it, like death clung to the walls, but that evening it was another smell. It was the stench of melted plastic and it stung my nostrils something bad.

I quietly placed my backpack on the floor and shut the front door behind me. Living in an apartment was hard when you had a mom who liked to scream and yell and cry and puke a lot. The neighbours, even the drug dealers, must have hated us. I had this weird feeling that this was going to be another epic disturbance and I hoped the other tenants weren't home.

The next thing I found weird, aside from the gross stench, was the silence. Usually the TV was blaring, or you could hear the sound of my mom pouring herself a drink, or she was yammering en Français to far-off distant relatives who didn't want anything to do with her nonsense.

But there was nothing.

It was fucking creepy.

I crept down the hallway, wishing I'd worn my Vans to school instead of the combat boots. Wherever my mom was, she knew I was coming.

I looked in the kitchen. Empty.

I peeked in her room. Empty.

I peeked in Michael's room. Empty

I stopped outside my door. It was closed. I always closed it but I knew she was in there. The god awful smell of burning plastic filtered out from under the doorframe.

Along with a tuft of smoke.

Holy fucking shit.

I put my hand on the knob and before I could hesitate any longer, I whipped the door open.

My mother was on her hands and knees in the middle of my room. I had a terrible sense of déjà vu, like I'd seen this before. My mother wasn't very original with her drunken terrorizing.

But that's not what caused my heart to fill with ice. That's not what made my skin crawl with disgust and righteous, bubbling over anger.

All of my records were sprawled out on the floor in front of her. My precious vinyl collection that I had worked for so long to acquire, paid for with the paltry change I scrounged up over the years. The music my mother said was the work of the devil.

She hadn't said that lightly. It turns out she very much believed it for my mother was lighting my records on fire. Let me repeat that. She was lighting my fucking record collection on *fire*. Half of them were reduced to a nauseating pile of melted black vinyl, producing a stench that made my eyes water. Maybe I was crying too, I don't know. Call me a pussy for shedding a tear, but those records meant absolutely everything to me and she was destroying them.

"I'll cast you out!" she screamed with a wicked smile, holding a lighter in one hand and Pink Floyd's The Wall in another. She was destroying it and loving it.

I don't know how long I stood there in stupor as the smoke began to flood the room. She had left the window open but it wasn't helping. The carpet around the melted records began to flicker a little from budding flames. My room was about to turn into an inferno if I didn't do something.

It was a tough call. I wanted to save my records, what was left of them. I wanted to prevent my room from going up in flames. And I wanted to go over there and hit her so bad. And fuck you if you think that's wrong. I was so angry at her and this horrible thing she'd become. Angry that I came from her and angry that she made my dad leave and angry that she always loved Michael, but not me.

Never me.

I didn't hit her, even though it would have been karma for beating me up all these years. I gathered my wits at the last minute and ran out of the room and to the kitchen. The rage was blinding me, taking over but I had to think. THINK! I needed to get water to the fire and fast.

I pulled out a bucket from under the sink and flipped on the rusted tap. The water wasn't coming out fast enough. Fucking plumbing in the building had always sucked.

I heard her coming behind me.

Please don't come any closer, I thought to myself, closing my eyes and gripping the bucket even harder. I was afraid what would happen if she did.

I turned and looked. She was walking unsteadily toward me, her clothes stained with ash and grease. She pointed at me, fixing her dark eyes on mine. Oh how I wished I didn't look so much like her.

"Mom, go away!" I cried out, my voice cracking shamefully. I looked back to the bucket. Half-full. Just a few more seconds.

"You're not my son," she said in this low, utterly deranged voice. "You're not my son."

Fuck, this again? If I had a nickel for every time she told me I wasn't her son, I'd be able to re-buy my record collection.

I caught a whoosh of sound from around the corner and beyond my mother's sad form, there was a hint of light on the walls. The fire was growing. The bucket would have to do for now.

I lifted it out of the sink, the water spilling to the sides.

"I wasn't me when I had you."

That one was new.

I turned around and looked at her, the water sloshing in my hands and dripping to my feet.

"Mom, please I have to put out the fire."

I took a few steps forward hoping to walk past her. But she came toward me, putting her body in between myself and the fire. I tried not to look at her eyes, tried not to see the madness and shame in them, but I was doing exactly that.

"I wasn't me when I had you. I wasn't me! You're not my son!" she bellowed, her rotten, booze-filled breath blowing hotly in my face.

"Get out of my way mom, please," I begged, my voice wavering. We didn't have time for her lunatic rantings. She wasn't herself? What did that even mean?

"I wasn't me when I had you!" she screamed.

"Mom, move!" I screamed back. I took the bucket of water and shoved it against her.

Hard.

A little too hard.

And that was all it took. I was so angry, so out of my mind, that I shoved my mother a little too hard.

Water spilled on to the floor.

She lost her balance.

The ground was slick.

She fell backward.

She reached for me in slow motion.

I didn't drop the bucket.

I stepped back. Away from my mom's reaching hand.

She fell to the floor, almost hitting it at once.

But she had stumbled a little too close to the edge of the counter.

Her head hit the corner of it first. The sound of something being split, like a cracked watermelon, filled my ears.

Blood clung to the counter's sharp edge.

My mother landed on the floor with a thunk.

There was more blood mixing with the water, creating a pale red soup.

Then there were more flames.

Then there was nothing.

DEAR ABBY

Life can be pretty screwy. Hectic. Random. That was my life anyway, and most of the time. But, occasionally, things just fall into place. There's a feeling of fate. Kismet. Order. I prefer the up-and-down jumble and unpredictability. I liked that shit happens for no reason sometimes. There's something easy about that.

When things align themselves in my favor, it makes me suspicious. Maybe because I don't like the idea of my life being part of some overall cosmic plan. I don't want the universe to pay attention to me. I just wanted to put my head down and go.

Sing Sin Sinatra (why the hell did I name it this?) had been doing really well until Toby up and left the band. Toby, my last remaining friend, a leftover from high school, decided smoking crack in the Bronx was better than playing bass in my band. OK, our band. But really, it was my band.

Not that I wouldn't have had to fire him at the rate he was going but still. It would have been my choice and my decision. Instead, just before the fall season, when we had a shit ton of shows (good shows too) to do, he decided to say see ya.

Good riddance and fuck off, said everyone else in the band. They were sick of him being late, being incoherent. He could barely play the bass anymore and that was saying a lot, especially with most of our songs. I mean, fuck, we did the classics. They were as simple as shit. But it burned me a little bit. Like I said, he was my last high school friend, a connection to my past. Did I like my past? No. I didn't even speak to my own brother anymore. But it was something.

It also sucked balls because he was going to be my editing partner. He wasn't in school, but he had the talent and the equipment. Well, before he sold it for crack. We worked well together. Well, before he started wigging out.

Fuck. I should have seen it coming.

So there I was, gathering my books, getting ready to leave my afternoon editing class. Everyone in my class was a dick so there was no way I'd feel comfortable making side projects with these people. Anyway, I needed someone who would want to fuck around with film with me. I know I'm not easy to work with, so there was that too.

I started toward the door, the last person to leave the room.

Before I got there, a gigantic redhead appeared in the doorway, panting and out of breath. A layer of sweat lay across his freckled forehead.

"I missed it didn't I?" the ginger said, his arm propping his body up against the frame. His voice was unusually smooth and he had a weird accent that was Southern but also not quite.

"Missed the class?" I asked. I walked toward him but he was still leaning against the door and his whole massive body blocked it. There was something weird about him, about the way he was, but I couldn't quite put my finger on it. Oh well, no matter. It wasn't my problem.

"Yeah. Shoot. I signed up for editing. Missed last week's too."

I gave him a false nod of sympathy. I had places to go, a girl to fuck. I wasn't about to stand around and shoot the breeze with this guy. Looking at him gave me a headache and made me want to rub my eyes vigorously. Maybe with salt.

"Better luck next week," I told him with a placating smile, then gestured for him to move.

He did. Reluctantly. I quickly glanced at him as I passed. If I'd known better, he looked confused. Maybe even hurt.

"You're Declan Foray," he called out after me.

I stopped walking. I slowly turned around.

"Yeah. Who are you?"

"Jacob." He smiled. He had pretty white teeth for a Southern boy. Then he frowned, catching himself. "No. Jacobs."

"Jacobs? With an S? Do you know your own name?" I frowned at him.

He wiped his hand on his jeans and thrust it out at me. "Maximus Jacobs."

"Oh, you have many names."

He eyed me and his hand expectantly. I sighed and dragged my ass over to him.

"Nice to meet you Maximus Jacobs. I'm *Dex* Foray." He shook my hand in a very strong, cold hold. He kept it there a little too long. I narrowed my eyes at him. He smiled in response and dropped it.

I took back my hand and wiggled it a bit. Fucker could have broken it. Who let this animal out of the zoo?

He smiled again like he'd heard what I thought and found it funny. I ignored it.

"So, Maximus Jacobs."

"Just Max, please."

"OK, Max please. How did you know who I was?"

"Word on the street was you were looking for a new bassist," he said.

"Word on the street? Who says that?" I scoffed, taking in his purple plaid shirt. "Where are you from?"

"The South," he said. He scratched at his orange sideburns. He had a very wannabe Elvis type do. It looked retarded.

"Oh, the South," I remarked dryly. "Always wanted to go there."

A smile tugged at the corner of his mouth. "Louisiana. Outside of New Orleans. On the coast."

OK. Now his accent went from odd and slightly Southern to full-on Cajun. Like he was trying to sound neutral but eventually failed.

I needed a cigarette badly. I sighed and pinched the bridge of my nose. I don't know where the headache had come from but it was apparent that standing around talking to the burly Cajun wasn't helping. Still, I had to know.

"So you say word on the street?" I mused. "Who told you?"

He shrugged. "I just overheard."

So, so vague. "All right. Do you play bass?"

He smiled broadly. He almost looked angelic. "I play everything but I love bass."

Did anyone really love the bass? I mean, I could play everything too. I loved the sound of the bass but playing the bass? Unless you were peeling off some Les Claypool riffs, it was boring as fuck.

"I can play just like Les Claypool."

I flinched. "What?" Had I said that shit out loud?

"Les Claypool. You know, he's in Primus."

"Yes, I know who he is," I snapped. I eyed him warily. "You don't know what kind of music we play. It's not exactly Primus."

He nodded. "I know. I've seen you live."

That startled me. Did I have a stalker here?

"When?" I demanded.

He shrugged. "When I first got here."

"Our last show was a month ago…"

"Then I got here a month ago. Look, I really liked your band."

I could see how sincere he was. But still.

Reading the doubt on my face, he quickly said, "I'll even audition. I reckon I'll win you over yet."

He'll *reckon*? My god, why didn't he just stick to the banjo and pots and pans? Fucking hillbilly. Still, we needed a bassist and finding one in New York City that wasn't either an asshole professional or drooling crackhead wasn't easy. My bandmates might even like the jolly red giant.

"Thank you," he said.

"I didn't say anything," I muttered, annoyed and feeling deflated.

"I know. I could just tell. Do you smoke?" he asked.

I perked up. "Fuck yes."

He fished a packet of cigarettes out of his shirt pocket. They were in a bright yellow box, with Spanish writing. "Ever had Cuban cigarettes?"

"No. How did you get those?"

"I have ways. Come on," he nodded toward the exit and I was suddenly aware that there was a school around me with students and teachers going back and forth. It was the weirdest fucking thing, like I'd been in a dream or something.

I had a few smokes with the Cajun. The smokes then turned into beers. Beers soon turned into jamming. I didn't need to audition him. We had our bass player. Could he play like Claypool? Not quite. But he was polite (annoyingly so), kept good time and was open to anything.

Then we got to talking about film. He had some skills in the editing department and wanted to collaborate on student films with someone. It was like God plucked Max out of the sky and handed him to me. An answer to the prayers I never made.

So, you can see why it made me suspicious. The big dude in the sky usually never gave me anything but shit. But here was Max. Ginger Elvis. A bassist and editor all in one. The perfect replacement for Toby.

Well, almost. Toby knew my history. He knew I was on some medication. He knew what made me tick. Max didn't know any of that and I fascinated him for some reason. He was always asking me questions. Questions I didn't want to answer, like about my parents. About my brother. What my childhood was like. Did I have any nannies growing up. Who were my friends.

Did anything strange happen to me when I was young.

"Like what?" I asked. We were sitting in a dark bar in the Bowery on a Thursday night. The weekend before we played one of our best shows yet. Seemed there were parts of New York that got the joke, the campy fun of lounge music turned rock and roll. Max and I were taking over the city.

"Oh I don't know," he said. He was eyeing a girl in the corner of the bar. She was blonde, short but pretty enough and staring at us like she knew us. I leaned my head back, looked past his shoulder at her and winked. She giggled. I knew it. She was staring at me. She was staring at me like she wanted to bend over and let me stick it anywhere.

I turned my attention back to Max. She'd be there later, and then hopefully in my bed. What Max had asked me was weird and distracting.

"Are you trying to get all serious with me?" I asked, leaning into him. "No one touched me in private places, if that's what you're getting at."

He took a sip of his drink and smiled. It was lopsided which meant he was getting drunk. It took a lot for the big guy. Almost as much as it took me.

"No, no. Just wondering if perhaps you ever experienced something supernatural," he said lightly, like it was an every day topic.

I didn't like it. It hit way too fucking close to home. Never in a million years would I reveal the ghosts I used to see, particularly the one who tormented me the most. She had only appeared to me the night before, sticking her accusatory finger in front of my face and screaming at me until I had to fuck my way out of it. Yeah, that's right. I'm not proud of it but I'd been having a different girl in my bed for the last who knows how long. It's easy for me, to just pick them up. Chicks dig men who can sing. Fucking them is a lot of fun too but what was most important is that it distracted. It made the ghosts go away. Not always, but often. And if it didn't, well, no harm done. The girl got what she wanted, even if I didn't. At least I got laid.

I turned my attention back to the girl in the booth, suddenly afraid she'd lose interest and leave. Conjuring up the image of the ghost in my head made my blood and breath flow cold. I didn't want to be alone tonight.

I noticed Max was staring at me intently, like he was trying to pluck my thoughts from my brain. Sometimes I thought he was the paranormal one. If not paranormal, at least a big fucking weirdo.

"What?" I asked him.

"You never replied."

"It's a dumb question." I motioned the bartender for another Jack and Coke.

"It's perfectly reasonable. Some people believe in UFOs. Others believe in ghosts. What do you believe in?"

He was still watching me, his eyes hard and patient.

I plucked my new drink off the table and took a bigger gulp than I intended. "I believe in Dex Foray. What do you believe in?"

"Dex Foray," he agreed with a smile and raised his glass. We clinked, drank the rest and that was the end of that.

Oh, and I did take the blonde home. The ghosts never came *and* I stuck my cock up her ass. Win win.

~~~

All right, I know what you're thinking. I'm a crude man-whore. And I couldn't argue with you. If it looks like a pig and fucks like a pig, it's a pig.

But crude man-whores don't last forever. Eventually they meet someone who puts all the other women to shame. Sometimes it's someone you least expect.

Abby wasn't quite a groupie, but she certainly was a fan. I'd seen her around at shows before. She never approached me and barely looked my way half the time, but when the lights hit the room just right, I'd catch her watching me. And yes, I know, I'm the singer and everyone more or less watches me. But this was different. It wasn't lust or frenzy or acceptance I saw in her eyes. It was something akin to awe. Like she admired me. I liked that. Shit, I liked that a lot.

After one show of ours, in a tiny little club packed with more douchebags than I could count who clearly thought our band was a little more hardcore and less weird, I saw her ordering a drink by the bar. I was intrigued by this shy girl and for once I wasn't thinking with my dick.

I approached her and told the bartender that I would pay for whatever she was having.

She barely turned to face me. She just shot me a look – one I couldn't read– then turned away.

"Hey," I said. I wanted to follow it with: *I bought you a drink, say thank you*. But I didn't want to seem like an ass. So I left it at "hey" and bit my lip.

She ignored me. Walked off.

What the fuckity fuck?

I'd never had anyone do that to me. Who the hell did she think she was? She wasn't even all that pretty. She was attractive, I guess, but there was nothing remarkable about her. She had dark eyes and strawberry blonde hair that was neatly curled in waves. She was wearing a dress that was far too girly for a club and flat shoes. From what I could tell from her body, she was of average weight, not fat nor skinny, and of average height. She was pretty...average.

So why was she walking away from me? And why did I care?

Regardless, I found myself at her side again and grabbed her arm.

She looked scared. Up close, with her facing me, I could see she was a little prettier than I had originally thought. Nice lips. Nose had a bump on it. Brows were a bit too low and thick. But sparkling eyes. They made me feel kind of crazy.

"Hey," I said and smiled most handsomely. "I'm Dex."

She continued looking scared until I dropped my hand off of her arm. Then she relaxed. She took a sip of her drink.

I raised my brow and leaned into her. She smelt like soap and lavender. "Do you have a name?"

She swallowed hard and nodded. "It's Abby."

Her accent was pure Fargo. Later I'd find out it was Minnesota, but same difference.

I held out my hand. "Nice to meet you, Abby."

She gave it a light shake. It was weak but her touch lingered. I don't know what it was but I felt her touch all the way down to my toes. Now my dick twitched a bit in my pants. So much for not thinking with it.

"I hope you enjoyed the show," I said, trying to ignore the rising erection. I swear it popped up at the most inappropriate times.

"I did," she said. "I've seen all your shows."

"You're a fan?" I asked even though I knew.

"Of the band," she clarified.

"Not of me?" I teased.

She shook her head. "You're a bit of a chump."

Whoa. And my pants deflated.

I laughed awkwardly. "Ouch. Now I feel like an idiot for buying you a drink."

"I could have warned you." She smiled coyly. Was she flirting with me or wasn't she?

I eyed the drink. It was fancy looking. "I bet it was pricey too."

"Aviation club cocktail. With top shelf gin."

"Well that serves me right for assuming..."

She raised a brow. It looked less bushy now. It suited her face. She was actually very pretty. "When you assume..."

"You make an ass out of you and me," I supplied.

"No, I was going to say when you assume, you make assumptions."

I grinned at her. "Aren't you a clever girl?"

She looked down at the floor and in the dim light I caught a hint of color growing on her face. Success! I made her blush. "I've been called worse things."

I held out my arm for her. "Well since you're such a fan of the band, would you like to meet them?"

She nodded excitedly. "Yes please. Especially Max."

I kept the smile on my face while I frowned internally. Wasn't easy. Fucking Max. This wasn't the first time girls were going after him. It pained me to admit it but he was one good looking dude. But it was the first time a girl I wanted showed interest in him.

A girl I wanted. There you had it. And it wasn't just in a fuck your brains out till morning, avoid the ghosts and get the goods, type of want, either. Oh it was there, but I had a strange inkling to actually spend some time with this girl. Talk to her. Figure out what she's about. *Then* fuck her brains out.

But I sucked it up. I brought Abby over to meet Max, even though he was dating a girl named Kate at the time. I also introduced her to Dennis (our drummer), Travis (our guitarist) and Pete (our keyboardist). She was actually quite shy and reserved around all of them but they were nice enough and Pete even bought her another one of her weird gin cocktails.

She flirted with Max all night, sitting on his lap and giggling into his ear as she got progressively drunker. Something told me that she was drinking to cover up what she was feeling. Shyness? Nervousness?

Either way, even though she wasn't in my care or even my friend, I felt strangely protective of her.

At one point we were in the back room of the club with our gear and Abby and Max had started making out. He was drunk too, so I had to go over and tap him on the shoulder and very clearly say, "Where's Kate? You know, your girlfriend?"

That barely got his attention. So I tapped Abby on the shoulder. "You should probably go home Abby. Come on I'll call you a cab."

She pushed me away but eventually Max came to his senses and put an end to it. I didn't want him to take her anywhere because that wouldn't have ended well, so I put my arm around her and escorted her to road.

She stumbled a bit, drunk as anything. A cab came up but I realized I didn't have the heart to send her on her way. I didn't know where she lived and she probably wouldn't know either. She was that wasted.

With a sigh I got in the cab with her and we left for my apartment. That was the beauty about being the singer. Never had to help the band load in and out. I just showed up and left as I pleased.

Believe it or not, we didn't have sex. I wasn't an animal. She ended up with her head in the toilet most of the night just puking her guts up. And yes, I held her hair back. She was right. I was a total chump.

But whatthefuckever. I guess it bonded us or something because after that we were inseparable. We had sex the following morning and didn't stop for days, weeks, months. I only stopped to eat, shit, go to school, drink, play a show, write a song, make a movie. Every other spare moment we were in each other's beds, screwing like our livelihoods depended on it, as if we were trying save humanity with each moan, with each thrust.

It was a good few months. The best.

Then things started to change. I started to change. Abby had gotten under my skin. She was all I thought about, all I wanted to do. I was addicted to her, physically and mentally. I was obsessed. I was paranoid. I was jealous. I was head over heels in love. So far down the rabbit hole that there no way out. I was wedged in there, helpless and needy. Oh so fucking needy.

It...disgusted me.

No one had done that to me before. I had never given a girl that type of power. I didn't trust females. I didn't want them close to me. I wanted them close enough that I could see their eyes flutter when they came but I didn't want them inside me. I was inside them - it wasn't the other way around. I didn't want them anywhere near my soul or my heart but fucking Abby, she clawed her way in and set up camp.

The Dex Foray I knew was gone. If I thought I was out-of-control before, I was wrong. I was always in control. Wild but on purpose. Crazy but free. With Abby I was locked down and trapped because I couldn't go a single day without feeling her wetness around me, without looking into her deep eyes, begging her for some sort of acceptance.

I'd fallen. And it sucked.

And really, it was my fault. I gave into love and it chewed me up and spit me out.

I became a man I never wanted to be and I drove her away.

I accused her of cheating on me when she wasn't. And when she inevitably did, I blamed it on myself. So did she. Or, I guess she did. I never knew because she died.

Another death on my hands.

I forget all the details. It doesn't matter that she drove drunk and had many DUIs before back in Minnesota. It didn't matter that I was just the angry boyfriend and she had been having an affair. It didn't matter. She's dead. My fault through and through.

I'd never experienced such pain in my entire life. And that was saying a lot. Losing Abby...I lost a part of my own life. My own future. There was chunk of my heart and soul buried with her in that cold, cold ground and I was never, ever going to get that back.

And Max. Where was he in all this? He was my closest friend, the guy who was always around, like a flame-haired shadow, asking me questions about weird things, taking me out for a drink when Abby and I had a fight (which, by the way, was often). He went from, I don't know, a (shitty) guardian angel, or even a brother figure, to someone who despised me. Maybe that's not the word. He was disappointed in me. It's like he gave up and decided I wasn't the type of person he wanted to be around anymore. I thought Max being in my life was fate. An answer to something.

I couldn't have been more wrong.

To make matters worse, because he was pushing me away, I found comfort in his girlfriend, Kate. At first she was just a shoulder to cry on. She was Abby's best friend now too and she was also hurting. Eventually though, things got physical. Max thinks I only slept with her once, and that's because he caught us in a very compromising position. The truth is, I was sleeping with Kate every chance I could.

Because, you see, the ghosts were back. I didn't have Abby to distract me from them.

This time, the ghost *was* Abby.

SPOOKSHOW BABY

The room smelled like shit. Shit, seaweed and decades of decay. It was too bad Smell-O-Vision never went anywhere, because the smell of the old lighthouse would have been just as terrifying as the sight of it.

Speaking of, there wasn't much to see here. Downstairs was empty. This floor gave up nothing except doors that wouldn't open and I was beginning to doubt Old Captain Fishsticks was actually haunting the place. Just because pansy-assed ghost hunting shows were clamoring to film the lighthouse, didn't mean anything was actually here. Had I been duped by the hype? No. Not me. That was impossible.

I stopped in the middle of the room and sighed, the camera feeling extra heavy on my shoul-der. A migraine tickled my temples and I pinched the bridge of my nose, hard. I hated feeling like a fuck-up failure. I couldn't go back to Jimmy empty-handed. I suppose I could, seeing as the Nazi didn't really know what I was up to, but it didn't matter. He'd sniff it off of me like some fucking dog. He'd know I was down here, trying to find something better for myself.

Then there was Jenn. She was worse. She said she was sad when I left the show, but I could see through those tears of her. I knew what they meant. She was secretly pleased I took off with the tail between my legs, like she won yet another battle or something. Three years with someone and you get to know their tactics pretty well. You can see that smug smile beneath the "But I'll miss you." The one that says I'll be nothing without her, that I'll fail on my own.

I didn't want Jenn to be right. But looking around this disgusting, dark relic with the kelp and the crashing waves outside, waves that seemed to laugh at me, well, fuck, she probably was right. Again.

I chewed on my lip absently and looked above. I had more of this place to see. I wasn't going to give up yet. After all, I was here. And even though the monsters were hidden behind veils of prescription, I was still the same boy as I was back in New York. They still wanted me, even if I couldn't see them.

My pride would be the death of me one day.

THUD.

A loud clatter sounded out from the floor below. It sounded hard, like something had toppled over from a great height.

I froze, feeling just a little spooked. I walked across the room and paused near the staircase, waiting for more.

From downstairs came a scurrying noise, like a very large rat was poking around. I carefully turned off the camera light and waited. My ears listened hard, trying to figure out just what the hell it was. From what I remembered, ghosts didn't usually make much noise. They didn't move around like they were trying to be quiet and failing at it. Rats didn't move like that either, especially not on the West Coast.

I picked up another sound now. Footsteps. Then a metallic jangling.

It was definitely a person.

I was definitely fucked.

I took in a deep breath and ignored all the possible scenarios that waited for me below. What was the point in figuring out who it was, or what was going to happen? If I got out of there without them seeing me, then worrying was fruitless.

I made my way down the stairs, pausing every other step to keep track, until I reached the bottom floor. I could hear tiny gasps of ragged breath coupled with a whimpering sound. I could see only darkness, except for weak light that spilled in through one of the rooms. There was a window where there hadn't been a window before.

You need move your ass now, I thought to myself. But before I could do anything, I felt this...this...I don't know what the hell it was, like a magnetic pull, like the air before a thunder-storm. An energy rolled toward me like a freight train. It made me stop, stunned and still.

There was another whimper, almost like a sigh, then feet slapping the damp ground.

Before I had chance to process that the footsteps were coming toward me, something collided straight into my chest. There was a scream, a girlish shriek (not my own), and I was shoved backward by something small and solid. The ground smashed into my shoulder, then my head, but it didn't matter. The CRASH of my camera was the most painful thing of all.

I groaned and rolled over, feeling for the machine.

Oh please, please, please, please, please, I thought in a panic. *I can't afford this, I can't afford this!*

I heard the other person, the beast that hit me, stirring and moaning, then they hit the ground again with a thump that sounded painful. Part of me didn't give two shits about the asshole that might have ruined the most important thing in my life. The other part of me felt kind of bad, especially when it became apparent that the asshole was some fucking chick. She was making little terrified squeaks.

Then she made no noise at all.

Motherfucker. Now I had a broken camera and some trespassing broad who was either dead or unconscious.

I hoped she wasn't a cop.

My hand made contact with the camera, and from the initial feel I was copping, it didn't seem like much damage was done to the outside. My fingers instinctively found the light and switched it on. I let out a breath of relief as the darkness was violently illuminated.

As was the girl, lying on the ground beside me. Her eyes were closed and she wasn't moving.

Shit, shit, shit.

I got on my knees and placed my hand on her neck, feeling for a pulse. She stirred a little and moaned, which meant she was at least partially alive. Not dead. I hadn't killed her. So I had that going for me.

I couldn't see her properly in the competing darkness and blinding glare, but she seemed damn young. She was small, with a round face that glowed ghostly pale. A camera hung from her neck and onto the floor. Without thinking, I reached up and brushed a strand of black hair off of her forehead. She was warm, almost feverish. Still not dead.

At my touched she moved a little and tried to open her eyes, raising her arm up to block out the light.

"Don't move," I said, my voice coming out broken and hoarse. The last thing I needed was for her to wreck herself even further. Just because she was alive, didn't mean she was well.

She dropped her hand reluctantly and I took the light away from her face, placing the camera down on the ground beside her head. It created crazy shadows along the planes of her face. Her pert nose turned into a beak. If I let my imagination run away with me, there were a million things she could have morphed into. I was lucky I hadn't skipped my pills earlier, like I had been thinking about doing.

I touched her face again, just to make sure she was still a person. She was. She was still soft, and warm, and alive.

Was I being creepy?

Her eyes fluttered open and I could barely make out a shade of blue in them before panic tore them wider and she tried to jerk away.

I pressed her shoulder down to the ground to keep her still.

"Seriously," I told her. "You might be really hurt. Please don't move."

She obeyed and lay back down.

"I'm OK," she said through dry lips. Her voice was light and scared. But she didn't sound like she was in any trauma. Her eyes searched my face without really seeing me.

I still had one hand on her shoulder and the other on her face.

I was definitely being creepy.

I took my hands away and inched back a bit to give her space to breathe - and me space to run. She looked no older than 20, so she obviously wasn't a cop but she was here, in a place I had no right to be. I eyed the hall in the darkness, wondering if getting out of the building was going to be as hard as getting in. I hoped she wasn't about to call for help. Or press charges.

She eased herself up and looked warily around the darkness, her eyes focusing on the camera. I could see the wheels turning behind those shadowed eyes, wondering what the fuck was going on.

"I'm so sorry," I said. Even though she technically ran into me, I had to placate things before they escalated.

"I was upstairs and I heard this crazy clatter from down here," I explained, my voice speeding up as my heart raced. There was too much adrenaline in my system and the medication was screwing around with it. "And I thought maybe it was the cops or something. I didn't know what the fuck to do. I thought I could get out of the way I came in, but I saw you there, and then I saw the window probably at the same time you saw the window and I'm...I'm so sorry if...well, you're obviously OK."

There was a pause. She didn't seem to buy any of that.

"Who are you?"

The million dollar question. What would my answer be today?

"That depends on who you are," I said honestly.

In the shadows I saw her cock her brow.

"I asked you first."

Why did I have to run into the most questioning people? I exhaled and reached back into my pocket. My new business cards were printed just last week – she'd be the first person to have one.

Whoever she was.

She took it from her hands, hesitant, like I was handing her poison. So suspicious. Tsk, tsk.

I picked up the camera and aimed it at the card. It gleamed under the light. So did the chipped polish on her gothy-looking fingernails.

She read it out loud and flipped it over, then looked up at me, somehow even more confused. The light lit up her face better.

"Are you from West Coast Living or something?"

I let out a small laugh. "Fuck no."

I started to rock back on forth on my feet, needing an outlet for the energy that was rumbling inside my bones. She was a curious little thing, but something about her made me nervous. Wary. Like she could be even more dubious than I was. Like she had a million secrets to tell and I would never hear any of them.

Whoever she was.

"Well, Dex Foray, I have a feeling that whatever you guys are doing here tonight, you're doing so without the permission of my uncle, who owns the lighthouse."

Shit. Fuck. Shit.

Her uncle owned the lighthouse. I felt the routes in my brain rewire as they prepared for the extra adrenaline, the gallop of my heart.

But...wait...

"There's no one else here," I said. "It's just me."

She laughed, clearly not believing me.

"Look, I don't care," she said and there was just enough ease in her voice to make it true. "I'm not going to report you. I shouldn't even be here myself. Just get your crew together or whatever and get out of here before you do get in trouble."

I stopped rocking. What the hell was she going on about? My crew?

"It's just me," I told her again. "Did you see someone else here?"

She frowned but kept her gaze on mine. "Yes. I heard you upstairs, and I was going to go out the window, but I saw the shadow of someone pass by. Outside."

A shudder ran down my spine and roll of nausea waved through me. I skid a bit closer to her, my pants dragging on the damp ground.

"Are you sure you saw something?"

If she had seen something, and it obviously was not me, then I was hooped up the ass. Maybe she was too, but I just couldn't get a proper reading on her. That weird energy slinked off of her in bursts and messed with my head a little bit.

"Yes, I saw someone," she said with a tinge of doubt. "Someone walked past the window, swear to God."

I wasn't sure if her God was one I could hold truth to.

"Where did you come from? Did anyone come with you?"

Like your uncle...or the cops...or your 250-pound MMA boyfriend.

She shook her head. I placed the light closer to her face, feeling like I needed to do a bit of interrogating to get to the bottom of this. She winced at the glare.

"Sorry," I mumbled. "I...well, nevermind."

"Nevermind?" she spat out. Her eyes narrowed and not from the light. "You just broke into my uncle's lighthouse. Don't you tell me to nevermind."

Whoa. All I was going to do was apologize again for doing exactly that. Well, fuck. Forget it. I was done. I was out of here.

With a grunt, I got to my feet and stretched up into the moonlight that was now creeping from the nearby window. It would be an easy escape. I picked up my foot to go, but I stopped.

I couldn't leave like this.

She looked so helpless at my feet. And I did have manners somewhere.

I reached for her hand. She eventually took it, feeling all too tiny in mine, and I brought her to her feet. She staggered a bit, almost keeling over, her camera swinging, and all I could think about was maybe she fell a lot harder than I thought. Maybe she wasn't really "all there" and we'd need an ambulance after all.

I put my hands on the sides of her arms and stepped closer to her, trying to keep her from faltering. She was short as hell and that was saying a lot since I wasn't very tall to begin with.

"You OK?" I asked, already knowing she was the type who'd say she was fine even if her limbs were chopped off. I saw a flash of something – hope? – in her eyes before she twisted us around and I was illuminated and her face was hidden in the dark. I searched out her features but couldn't get them. It was unnerving to not see the round pale face and watchful eyes.

"Just a bit dizzy," she said. The fact that she admitted that much didn't sound very good. I began to think where the nearest hospital was, whether I could get her there in the Highlander, if I would need to call her uncle first. Who would then slap me with some trespassing charges and a possible assault charge, because men were dicks and no one would believe a girl could run into me, especially not one pixie-sized.

"Good," I said, trying to look into her eyes, trying to keep things light. I smiled, thinking it might help my cause. "Promise not to sue?"

"I won't. Can't speak for my uncle, though."

Damn it! Just where was he anyway? Why was she exploring a lighthouse in the dark without him?

"Why are you here?" I asked, more and more curious about this little goth girl.

She dropped her gaze to the ground, even though I couldn't see her anyway.

"We're having a bonfire at the beach," she said. Her voice went higher, younger, and I got the distinct impression that she was feeling guilty about something. "I got sick of hanging around teenagers and wanted to come here. My uncle never let me come here when I was younger. I didn't tell anyone, I just left. I was hoping to film stuff."

Hoping to film some stuff? As if she couldn't get any more intriguing. What kind of stuff, exactly. What had she heard about the lighthouse?

She let out a small gasp and started fiddling with something. Her camera. I picked up mine and shone the light on her and while she was squinting uncomfortably at the glare, I took her SLR in my hand and peered it over. Aside from scratches that were probably there before, there was no damage.

"It's fine," I told her, trying to sound reassuring. "I thought you wrecked the shit out of mine when you ran into me."

I patted my camera which made the light bob against her face. She didn't look very impressed. Who could blame her?

"You're right," I said, before she could. "Who cares? I probably deserve to have this camera smashed."

Even though it would put me back at square one. I couldn't think about that.

Thump.

I froze. The sound had come from upstairs. Where I had just been. Where nothing else had been. Unless...

I looked at her, putting the light closer to her face. It was Bad Cop time again.

"You sure you came alone?" I whispered.

She replied, "Are you?"

I nodded. She didn't. It then occurred to me that I had no clue what her damn name was. She never offered it up. I didn't know anything about her.

This could have all been a trap. They might have known I was coming here. I don't know how, but maybe they saw the Highlander from a distance. Maybe trespassers were a weekly occurrence. Maybe they lured ghost hunters here and then robbed them. Or raped them. I'd probably let Little Miss Doe Eyes do the honors, but I had no idea how strong her uncle was.

She dropped her eyes from mine and looked at the window. The only easy way of escape.

But if she was thinking of running, that meant she was afraid. It meant she didn't know who, or what, was upstairs.

And if they didn't come with her...they were already here.

I leaned into her and smelled something like a fresh breeze radiating from her neck. It took me a moment to find my tongue, find the words to say, "Are you one hundred percent sure that no one else came with you here?"

I wanted to pull away for her response but that energy, that smell, kept my nose and mouth locked near her neck for just a few more seconds.

EVEN DEEPER

"Oh come on, just shoot the freaking zombie already!" Matt or Tony yelled at me. I couldn't tell which one. They both looked the same and sounded the same – deafening.

I'd been playing video games with Perry's cousins for the last hour while she checked her emails and we waited for night to fall. My zombie-hunting "skills" seemed just as useless as my ghost hunting skills and the noises and the graphics were fucking up my equilibrium. I mean, shit. After what went down in the car, running into that psycho, Dame Edna lady again, I was surprised it took me this long to realize everything was doing my head in. I had enough.

"That's it," I said, throwing my controller down on the couch and getting up. "I've died for the last time."

The twins made a noise in unison. It sounded like false disappointment. It was eerie.

Then they continued playing like I had never even been there. Also eerie.

And nerdy.

I made my way over the kitchen and started to pull out my notebook from my overnight bag. It still smelled like apple pie here, the one that Perry managed to bake earlier. What possessed her to try baking was beyond my cloudy brain. Just one more thing to scribble down on my mental notepad headlined PERRY and sort things I needed to get to the bottom of.

It was good too. Not the best thing I've tasted in my life, but it was good considering she ran-domly cooked it in her uncle's place. I couldn't even remember the last time I had homemade apple pie. Had I ever? The only time I could think of was the God awful Christmases with Jenn and her white-ass rich folks, and if I knew them, they probably ordered those pies from some epicurean pie catalogue for old farts.

But the thing is, it wasn't so much what it tasted like but what it smelled like. The damn pie smelled like home to me. But apple pie didn't exist in my fucked-up youth, and if it had, it wasn't at the hands of my mother. Perhaps a nanny had baked every now and then. I don't know, I didn't care to remember that shit. That whole period was blocked out for very good reasons.

But the smell still stirred up memories that never could have existed. It felt...like, warm. Good. Honest. How the hell did those things belong in my life?

I looked at Perry as she came into the kitchen and sat down at the table across from me. Her face was anxious, like she was having another battle inside that head of hers. There was something about her that stirred up the same feelings. Maybe this had nothing to do with apple pie at all. Maybe it's that she made it, and when she handed over that first slice and met my eyes, I could see she made it for me. And no one had ever made me anything.

Naturally, I wasn't about to tell her that. It was retarded, actually, to even think this funny little girl thought of me more than some crazy mustached fucker in her uncle's kitchen. She just met me. She didn't know me. And if she thought she did, she was mistaking me for someone else. Someone who didn't hide medication in a hollowed-out book.

I kept my mouth shut and began to write an overview of the day. I still managed to watch her at the same time, watch her debating whether to tell me something or not. A glint of something gleamed in her blue eyes. It was almost...hot. Was she thinking something naughty? I found myself shifting uncomfortably in the chair.

"So," she said, her voice high and self-conscious. "A local ghost hunter's club in Salem was hoping I could come aboard their team and perhaps show them around the lighthouse.

The...fuck? I stopped writing, trying to process what she was saying. Competition? Already? I knew I should have fucking got her to sign a contract. I knew I was being a fucktard by just trusting that she'd stick with me and not go to someone else with this fucking access, someone who actually knew what they were doing. All that shit we said to each other in the car, all the things I said – that didn't mean shit, did it? Fuck I was a fool.

I cleared my throat and tried to sound casual. "And?"

She shrugged. "I haven't gotten back to them."

How considerate, I wanted to say but I shut my mouth. This was not the time to fly off the handle. I knew I wasn't thinking straight lately, especially today, I knew I was predisposed to say shit I didn't mean, hell, shit I didn't even think. I couldn't fuck everything up now, not when we were so close.

"Well, you can do whatever you want to do," I lied through my teeth. "You're a free agent. We haven't signed anything."

Cuz I'm a dick-grabbing monkey, that's why.

My cell phone rang, preventing me from saying anything else ridiculous. It was Jenn but I was grateful for any distraction.

"Hey babe," I said.

"Dex?" Jenn's voice sounded tinny through the poor reception. "Sorry to bug you on your little adventure but Cynthia and Reece wanted to have a girl's night out and…"

She droned on but I had quit listening and was watching Perry again. Her nose twitched (how cute was that?) and a faint flush of red crept up her neck and onto the side of her face. She straightened up in her seat as soon as she noticed me looking but it didn't stop the girl from looking like she'd rather be in a million other places than sitting here in front of me. I hoped she wasn't seriously thinking about that pussy ghost hunting club. Who the fuck decides to form one of those?

"....and I know you won't be home till late, but I won't be there until probably much later. Is that OK?"

"Yeah, that's fine."

"You sure?" Jenn asked and from her tone I knew she didn't give a fuck if I said it wasn't. She'd still go out, as she always did. I didn't even know why she was calling to ask. Maybe she wanted to check up on me.

"Seriously, I don't mind. Go do whatever it is you girls do."

After I told her I'd be home in the morning now, I hung up the phone and decided to jump right back into it.

"OK, where were we?" I said out loud. What did we need to know for tonight?

"She doesn't mind you staying another night?" Perry asked.

I raised my brow. Odd question. Why did she care?

"No," I said, not wanting to talk about how pathetic our relationship truly was. I let my gaze fall to the window where the wind was shaking the trees loose. I breathed in and let that smell of home bring my heart rate down a notch.

"Do you have anymore pie?"

"There's a slice or two I put back in the fridge..." she said, as if she wasn't sure.

"Would you mind getting me a piece of pie?" I asked. I wanted to see if she'd do it. And if she'd hand it to me again with that look in her eyes. I needed that look right now. I sensed some changes inside, the wiring coming loose and needing a good cauterizing. My thoughts were getting lost.

She tried to look annoyed but she failed at it big time. Cuz she still got out of her chair and walked over to the fridge. She opened the door and had to bend over in front of me to get a bottle of milk. My God she had one hell of an ass. Not too big that your dick would get lost but just big enough to get a good, meaty hold and squeeze and smack and come until the cows came home.

I must have been pretty obvious in my leering. Wasn't I trying to impress her, not creep her out?

"Were you staring at my ass?" she said. She sounded surprised but she was glaring at me, so I had no idea what the fuck she was thinking. Did she like the idea? Was she going to tell her mafia uncle to pour cement in my shoes and chuck me out in the Pacific?

"Yes," I told her. Why lie? I'd put on the cement shoes if I had to. I've done worse for a woman.

She made some exasperated sound and shook her head. But she still came back with a piece of pie. She was beet red now and avoiding my eyes. Maybe she liked my attention after all.

"Obviously, I'll need a napkin too," I told her. Pushing buttons, pushing buttons.

"Obviously," she muttered and she tossed one to me. I took it with all the grace of a dandy and folded it in my shirt pocket. I was a gentleman over everything. An ass-appreciating gentleman. We are the finest kind of man. I should open my own ass-appreciating gentleman's club one day.

I shoved the pie in my face (pie-appreciating gentleman that I am) and noticed she wasn't having any. To think of it, she hadn't had any earlier either. That's probably why I thought she baked it for me...she certainly didn't bake the desert for herself.

Oh no, don't tell me she's one of those self-conscious girls who have absolutely no reason to be self-conscious. I eyed her full breasts and couldn't fathom why she'd want to diet.

"You're not having anything?" I asked, pointing my fork at her in an accusatory fashion, hoping she'd prove me wrong.

"I don't like pie," was her stupid answer.

I laughed and a piece of pie shot out. "You don't like pie? What kind of person doesn't like pie?"

I poked her with the fork to make sure she was still real. "You can't be trusted."

She took a swipe at the fork, looking annoyed. "You're the one with the fork."

Without thinking, I reached over for her hand and opened it, soft and warm. I placed the fork in it and gently closed her fingers over it.

"Now you have the fork," I said softly and sat back in my chair. She stared down at the fork, thinking. I stared down at the paper. Thinking. Sometimes you came across women who had every-thing going for them…looks, personality, smarts, and they had NO fucking idea what they were worth. How amazing and beautiful, they were, how they oozed sex and secrets. Then you had those women who knew they had what you wanted and used it. Repeatedly. Just to get what they wanted. It was an unbalanced universe.

Now I could see that Perry was the former. She did look self-conscious and unsure of herself at every turn. She was always pulling down her shirt or tugging up her jeans, or keeping her chin as far away from her neck as possible. She'd cover up her breasts with heavy jackets and boxy shirts, like they were something to be hidden. The girl was fucking nuts and for all the wrong reasons. It made me feel strangely helpless.

"I just want you to enjoy all the pies in life, Perry," I said, gazing at her, trying to get her shy eyes to meet mine. "That's all."

I wondered if she'd let me try.

BIG DUMB SEX

It was nearly five in the morning when I finally pulled the car into the garage. I had been so close to taking out a few trees and road signs on the drive up from Portland that I started blaring shitty pop music with the windows down, just so the disgust and cold would keep me awake.

It worked. I didn't crash the car though as I staggered over to the elevator with my duffel bag in tow, I kinda wished I had. I had Rebecca Black in my head, a fate worse than death.

My plan was to enter the apartment as quietly as possible. If luck was on my side I'd be able to sneak inside without waking up Jenn and I could put off facing her until a reasonable hour, until I had ten cups of black coffee and a few sneaked cigarettes.

Lady Luck, that saucy bitch, was *not* on my side. As soon as my keys started to jangle in the hole, the door flung open and there she was. And, as I thought, she was ready to kill me.

Yeah, the thing is even though I spoke to her earlier in the day when I was at Perry's uncle's and told her I'd be coming home in the morning, even though she said she didn't care and that she was going out with her bimbo posse anyway, I knew she'd be mad. I just knew it. And I was right. I was always fucking right.

"Hey babe," I said quietly, trying to flash her a smile she once thought was charming.

She narrowed her eyes and didn't let me in.

"It's the middle of the night," she hissed.

"I can see that," I said and blinked at her hair. It was in a wild fro on top of her head, her face was without a lick of makeup. She did look gorgeous but she also looked evil. It was the heat seething from her eyes. "Are you going to let me in or shall I sleep out in the hall? There's a cozy spot in the stairwell, I discovered that the last time you –"

"Last time I what?" she asked carefully. She raised her chin and eyed me down.

Last time you got totally jealous because I was hanging around some girl. Even though it was Rebecca. Even though she's a lesbian.

"Las time we had disagreements," I said. I put my hand up on the door and pushed it in a few inches. "Please. Babe. I've had a rough day."

"Where the hell have you been?" she asked though she stepped away and let me in.

I walked in and tossed my bag on the couch.

"I told you earlier. You called *me*, remember?"

She folded her arms across her chest and tried to stifle a yawn. "I thought you'd wait until morning. Maybe have some respect for my beauty sleep. It's *Wine Babes*, not *Wine Hags*, you know."

Boy, did I ever.

"Perry had to get home, she works in the morning," I explained, my voice hesitating only slightly. I watched her reaction and wondered what ground I was treading on tonight.

Her eyes flashed like lightening, almost too quick to see. Then the mask of indifference slid on her features and she looked at me with a perfectly blank expression.

"Who is Perry?"

She wasn't fooling anyone but I let her play her game.

"You know, the girl with the lighthouse." As if Perry wasn't the sole reason Jenn had called me earlier.

"Girl?"

I shrugged. "Yeah, girl. She's like twenty or something."

White heat erupted from her gaze. I'd forgotten that the younger another woman was, the worse things got.

For me.

I sighed and turned away from my glowering girlfriend, ready for bed, ready to turn off my brain. I had bigger things to worry about than Jenn. I mean, fuck, the lighthouse actually fucking exploded. It exploded! I had nearly died tonight. We both nearly did and it would have been on my conscious if anything had happened to Perry. I spent the whole drive home trying not to think about it, trying not to think about what I thought I saw. What I couldn't have seen.

"Dex?" Jenn asked, her voice breaking into my thoughts before they foundered. I felt her hand on my shoulder, her grip firm and warm. "Are you OK?"

I turned my head slightly and spied her out of the corner of my eye.

"I'm just tired. It's nothing. I'm hitting the sack."

I started to step forward when her grip tightened on my shoulder and held me back.

"Dex," she said again, using my name in a deliberate way. There was warmth to it, enough to make me realize she was...what was this? Concern about me? My heart lurched around in my chest. Tricky little bastard.

I turned to face her and her hands immediately went to my waist. With hooded eyes she took her delicate, long fingers and started stroking back and forth along the waistband, teasing my skin.

I knew those moves all too well. Did she care or did she just want to get laid?

Fuck, why did I even bother thinking? I didn't care either.

The fear I felt turned to flames. The night turned to need. I needed to be distracted, from Perry, from ghosts, from death. As usual, this would do.

Oh, this would do all right.

With one hand she popped the button on my pants. She dropped to her knees. I got hard instantly, knowing what was coming next.

Me.

Out of all the women I'd been with, Jenn knew her blessed way around a cock. Sometimes I wondered if she'd been a man herself in a past lifetime. Not that I liked to think that when she was unzipping my fly with her teeth, but there was no question she was a woman who knew exactly what you needed and wanted and was never ashamed to give it to you.

Sexually, anyway.

The minute my cock came free of my pants, heavy and twitching with anticipation, I grabbed the back of her head with both my hands, making a tight fist in her hair and yanked her toward me. She gave a little moan from the pain and took all of me in her mouth, and then some. She expertly gripped me in a squeezing motion with one hand, and let her fingers play with my balls with the other.

In seconds, I didn't have a thought in my head, except that I wanted it harder, faster, more, more, more. Part of me wanted to come now and hard, the other part wanted to prolong the pleasure as long as possible. As selfish as it was, I didn't really care if she got off or not. This was about me, my need to forget, my need to only feel this dirty high. Jenn didn't really care either, she could always take care of herself. There were no tallies with us. We both always got what we wanted in the end.

She started to twirl her tongue along, rubbing it hard along the ridge. Fuck, I was going to lose it quickly if she kept that up.

Then she pulled away and wiped her mouth before grinning at me. If my mind wasn't so clouded by lust, I could have sworn she looked positively fake.

"How about you take me from behind?" she purred. Without waiting for me to respond, she slipped off her short shorts, her thin top, and she was bare ass naked. She flung herself down on the couch and arched her back invitingly.

Fuck me. I could never *ever* say no to that.

I guided myself in, grabbed her around the small of her itty, bitty waist and pushed in hard. She moaned some more, loudly...too loudly.

"Yes, fuck me harder Dex," she yelled.

I almost laughed. *Fuck me harder Dex?* Was she kidding? Now Jenn was always delightfully nasty and vocal at times, but it sounded like she was trying a little too hard. It sounded scripted.

I slowed the thrusting down and tried to get my mind back on track. Who cares if she was putting on a show, I was getting laid, wasn't I? My dick was full-up inside her, what was the problem? No problem.

"You're so good," she cried out again in a breathy voice.

I bit my lip. What the hell was she doing? I liked porn but I liked it realistic and raw, not cheap and tawdry and that's exactly what she was acting like. For the first time ever she was acting like someone else, someone...insecure.

Then it hit me. This was about Perry, wasn't it? Oh of course it was. I was a fucking idiot for not seeing it.

Naturally, I was turned on, inside her to the hilt and my load was threatening to blow at any minute, so her cheesy porn star act and insecurities weren't enough to make me stop or distract me. But the thought of Perry herself, well, that was distracting.

And pleasantly so.

I moved my hands down to Jenn's tight ass, increased my speed, and closed my eyes. No one could complain about Jenn's body, but I wondered what it would be like to have Perry on all fours in front of me. If it was her I was fucking, with that big, gorgeous ass of hers, I'd have a lot more under my hands, soft flesh I could squeeze and knead and lick and bite. I wondered if she'd like it from behind, if she'd moan with every inch of me. I wondered if she'd let me grab her thick, dark mane and hold it like a pair of reins, if I could make her come with my girth alone or if I'd need to reach down and stroke her until she literally dripped on the carpet.

Fuck.

I came hard.

The hardest in a long time. I dug my fingers into Jenn's ass, causing her to give a legitimate whimper of pain, and bit my tongue to stop me from screaming out Perry's name. My legs shook as the deluge pumped into Jenn in endless, brain-seizing waves. I couldn't stop seeing Perry's face, someone so innocent that needed to be defiled. Someone who might possibly need me to show her some things for a change.

When I was finished, I pulled out of Jenn and walked to the bathroom, feeling dizzy, my heart firing at a million beats a minute. I heard her cry out in indignation at something or other, but it didn't matter. I went in and closed the door behind me and leaned against the sink.

What the fuck is wrong with me? I thought.

I just got off thinking about Perry, my 22-year-old potential partner, and it was the best orgasm I'd had in months. Years.

I wiped the sweat off my brow and looked at myself in the mirror.

You, sir, are asking for trouble.

I closed my eyes to my flushed reflection and bright, dilated pupils. Immediately an image of Perry sprung up on my head again, this time she was on her back, lying beneath me, her breasts rising, anticipating me.

I quickly locked the bathroom door and stroked myself at the thought.

I came again and right away.

Fuck trouble. I wasn't asking for it.

I was inviting it.

BUTTERFLY CAUGHT

"So have you made love to her yet?"

I shot Maximus a look. "Made love to her? What the fuck is wrong with you dude, it's not the 50's."

He shrugged and kept a stupid smile on his lips while turning his attention back to the desert. His flaming red hair matched the dust that blew past the jeep.

"Anyway," I said, trying not to grip the wheel too hard, "and not that it's any of your damn business, but no. I have not *made love* to her. Nor have I fucked her. We're just partners."

"Good," he said. I didn't like his tone. It sounded like he was patting me on the back or something.

Fuck that. It seemed ever since Max randomly stepped back into my life in Red Fox, every second with him was rubbing me the wrong way. Apparently, I still had an axe to grind and if I didn't know any better, he had one to grind with me. He was just hiding it behind his stupid drawl and fake air of decency.

I bit my lip until I tasted blood. With no meds in my body, I felt royally screwed up and I was constantly battling the urge to act up and out. What I really wanted to do was pull the car over to the side of the road, tell him if he wanted to keep his dick attached, he needed to stay far away from Perry. Then I'd kick him out and make him walk to the ranch. Perhaps he'd get eaten by a coyote while he was out there.

Wishful thinking. Deranged, but wishful thinking.

He gave me a sly look out of the corner of his eye.

"What?" I asked testily.

He shrugged again. My grip tightened. I wanted out of the car. Why did we have to go all the way into town to do the atmospheric shots? It was too damn hot and I couldn't spend another moment in this inferno with him. All his red hair just fanned the heat.

When he didn't say anything, I flipped on the stereo, letting the Deftones distract me. Unfortunately angry music doesn't help an already angry guy.

"She's cute, you know," he commented, his voice raised over the music.

"Yeah, so?"

His shoulder's lifted up.

"Don't you dare fucking shrug again!"

He smiled and looked down at his all too clean fingernails.

"I'm just saying, she's cute. I'm surprised you haven't made a move on her," he said. Then he added under his breath, "Since you make a move on pretty much every woman you come across."

Ah, here was the axe. Grind, grind, grind.

I cleared my throat. My god I needed water. Or a beer. Or a bottle of bourbon with a bucket of ice. It felt like I swallowed the contents of a vacuum bag.

"I have respect for Perry, believe it or not," I told him.

He chuckled to himself. "Right. I'm gonna guess you already tried to put the moves on her and the little lady turned you down? What did you do, the good ol' Dex Foray special, tried to put your Johnson up her ass?"

"What the hell is wrong with you?" I countered. "I did no such thing, and you know that's not the Dex Foray special. The Dex Foray special involves two lubed fingers, a lot of tongue and a cigarette for afterwards."

Speaking of cigarette. I fished one out of my pocket and lit it with one hand.

"Do you mind if I smoke?" I asked not caring what his answer was.

"Yes."

"Didn't you used to smoke?" I brought the cigarette to my lips and inhaled. I blew the smoke out at him and grinned.

He coughed and waved at me, annoyed. Good. "I used to do a lot of things Dex."

"So where you been keeping yourself all these years?"

"I already told you. Nice way to change the subject. You're still the king of that."

"Better than thinking I am *the* king. When you going to get rid of the Elvis do, Max? Guess that's a thing you still do. You know, look like a douchebag."

"Funny," he remarked. "Same insults."

"I'm the same boy, Max. So are you."

"I'm not. And it's Maximus," he shot out. He looked back to the dry scenery flying past, the hills of stark rock and dark chasms. In the distance lay the ranch. We had arrived, thank god.

Just as we were pulling up to the Lancaster's house, Max had to get one last thing in.

"So is she single?"

I slammed the jeep into park. "Who?"

"Oh, you know. Perry. The little lady with the...nice endowments."

I wanted to wipe the shit-eating grin off of his freckled face. I couldn't even answer. If I said no, I'd be lying. If I said yes, he'd start going for her. And given the weird way I felt about Perry and the even weirder history I had with Max, that was one hell of a bad fucking idea.

So I didn't say anything. I just shot him a dirty look and hoped to god he didn't round up the courage to start hitting on her. He had a strange sense of confidence though. I guess being built like a small giant had its advantages. Chicks always fell for it. I had to rely on my good looks and goddamn charm.

We walked back to the house, me leading the way. The sad sack that was Will was standing at the foot of the front steps, his dark eyes searching the rugged horizon of his ranch.

"Hey Will," I said. I stopped beside him in the dry dust and tried to follow his gaze. "Whatcha looking at?"

"Bird," he replied absently.

"Fair enough."

I left him in the desert and went with Max inside. It was wonderfully cool in the house, though I'm sure having a frigid bitch like Sarah as a wife probably had something to do with it. I went straight for the couch and flopped down on it. Sure, I was a guest here and it was probably rude to just put my sweaty body on their furniture, but whatever. It's hot out. Deal with it.

After a few seconds, I realized the frigid bitch herself was sitting on the chair across from me. She was staring right at me. I mean, she had those damn shades on so I couldn't see her eyes, but I could feel them. Blind as a bat and I could swear she was watching me. That and sucking the thoughts out of my brain. I shivered despite the heat.

"So, where's Perry?" I asked, wanting to make some conversation. I knew she was probably upstairs in our room anyway. I had an image of her reeling from the heat, lying down on our bed in next to nothing. Crap. I really hoped Sarah was blind because she did not need to see the rise in my pants.

"She's gone. Missing. Bird has gone looking for her," she told me calmly.

My head snapped up. "What?"

"You heard me. You really ought to keep your wife under control. She's becoming a nuisance."

I heard her, barely. I got to my feet, shoving down the panic that was building up in my chest, and ran for the door. Max, who was nearby in the kitchen (always fucking nearby) followed behind me.

I flung myself down the steps to say something to Will when out in the distance I saw Bird and Perry walking together. Well, Bird was walking. Perry was limping. She looked like she'd fallen off a cliff.

She was alive, which was a plus. But she was hurt and I had a feeling it was all because she didn't fucking listen to me.

Fuck. I was mad. Mad? I was livid.

Whatever anger I felt earlier because of Max, it was coming out now and there was nothing I could do to stop it. I let my emotions run wild and ran up to her, throwing my hands in the air.

"What the fuck happened to you?"

She looked scared at my reaction but I didn't care.

Bird gave me a sympathetic bullshit smile. "She took a little tumble, she's fine."

"She's not fine," I spat out, struggling to keep my voice down.

She was scraped from head to toe with a giant bloody gash at her cheek. Her tank top was ripped and bloodied and she was barely standing up straight. I'd never felt such an intense rush of anger and sorrow before. I wanted to yell at her, then take her under my wing and make sure nothing like this ever happened to her again.

Bird knew when to leave. "I'll go get the first aid kit."

I gave him a look and then turned back to Perry. Looking at her was breaking my heart into a million pieces. I wanted to hurt the bastard who did this to her and it was hard knowing there was no one to blame except Perry.

"I'm sorry," she said. "It's no big deal."

I anxiously rubbed at my chin, feeling too much and having nowhere to put it.

"What happened?"

She explained. It didn't help. First there was going off and walking by herself when I told her to stay put. I wasn't saying those things to be a dick, I said it because I knew she attracted danger and, goddamn it, I cared about her. Then she had to literally fall off a cliff, get attacked by a crow and almost get bitten by a snake before Bird annihilated it with a gun. The results of that were all over her shirt in sticky patches.

"Well I hate to say I told you so, but, I so fucking told you so," I said. "You want to listen to me next time?"

She didn't look ashamed in the slightest. I guess I was putting her on the defensive, as usual.

"It depends, Dex," she said with a glare, giving my name special hated emphasis. "You're not normally the voice of reason here."

True.

"Neither of us is. You better wash up."

We went back into the house. I watched Maximus's eyes seeing if he was dumb enough to lay the Southern charm on but he looked mildly horrified and only offered up "My Lord" as we passed by.

Perry went up the stairs to the room and the minute she shut the door behind her, I turned to her Bird who was coming out of the kitchen with a first aid kit in his hands.

"What the hell, Bird?" I yelled.

"Easy, Dex," Max said.

"Oh shut the fuck up," I told him without a glance. I snatched the kit out of Bird's worn hands. "Why did you let her go off like that?"

Bird put that oh-so-wise and patient look on his face, his lines growing deeper. He didn't say anything for a few seconds and calmly folded his arms. Those eyes of his had a very calming effect on me.

Finally he said, "I did not know she had left. As soon as I found out she had, I followed her tracks into the mountain. I arrived...just in time."

He let those last words sink in a little. AKA you should thank me you white asshole.

I shot him a weak but appreciative smile. "Well, thanks then. I just..."

Bird nudged me and gestured to the ceiling. "Go tend to your wife. She needs you."

I nodded, hoping my face wasn't portraying the sudden heat I felt at the mention of "wife" and went up the stairs.

She was in the bathroom but I didn't hear the shower running.

I gave a quick rap on the door.

"It's Dex," I said giving her enough time to cover herself. I tried the handle. Locked. Guess she thought I was the type of guy who would ambush her in the shower.

Guess she was kind of right about that.

The door eventually opened a crack and Perry gave me a suspicious look. That's all I noticed before I spied her breasts which were spilling over the top of her towel. And by towel, I mean dishcloth. The girl was dangerously close to having a nipple slip.

"Hello there," I said in an extremely sleazy voice. Didn't mean to, just slipped out. I hoped her breast might follow suit.

"How long have you been standing there?" I heard her ask. She sounded far away. All I could see was skin and cleavage and beads of water rolling down full mounds and...

She reached over and pushed at my forehead until my eyes were forced to meet hers. That was OK. I liked staring into her eyes as much as I liked staring at her boobs.

"Did you just see Sarah leave?" she asked, tension in her voice.

"Why?" I looked at her closely. She looked more scared than annoyed at my leering, and when my head cleared of the blatant sexuality on display, I remembered why I had come up there. Her pale skin was marred with rough, red scratches up and down her arms, on her hands, her face.

She closed her eyes and sighed, getting ready to close the door. "Nevermind."

I quickly put my arm up to stop it. "Nuh uh." I pushed my way into the bathroom and shut the door behind me. "You need some attending."

"Oh yeah, you'd like that wouldn't you?" she sniped and took a step back from me.

Sheesh. What the hell was her problem? I wasn't the one who told her to go off into the desert with her arms wide open yelling "Come to me my animal friends!" I told her to do the opposite.

I raised my brow at her in warning. Then I sighed, opened the kit up in the sink and said, "Actually I'd like it if you were being the sexy nurse, not me."

I tried not to imagine that hot little fantasy of mine and concentrated on the task at hand; pouring alcohol on gauze and cleaning up her wounds. Time to man up and quit thinking with my dick.

She flinched as I pressed the solution into her arm but she held it together for the most part. I have to admit, it was a bit unnerving being so close to her when she had on just a towel. Hell, if I was being honest here, it's unnerving being close to her in general. The way she smelled, the feel of her skin beneath my hands, it was intoxicating. And confusing.

And there I was with my dick thinking again. Although...it wasn't just that. And that was the confusing part, wasn't it?

Fuck, forgetting my pills was a bad, bad choice.

I rerouted my brain and concentrated on getting her better. When I was done wrapping her hands with a shitload of gauze, I met her eyes. We had a moment. I tried to read her. There was too much going on inside both of us for me to get a clear picture.

"I'm sort of waiting for you to tell me how this happened," I said softly. "I mean, not the *Cliff Notes* version of things."

Now she looked embarrassed. She took in a deep breath and explained everything down to the dream she had before she even came to Red Fox. Now that pissed me off. I know that we barely knew each other and we were just partners when it came down to things but, I don't know, I felt strangely betrayed that she hadn't confided in me about it. It was like she didn't trust me with things for fear of what I would think. That would have been flattering if it wasn't a little off-putting. I wanted her to trust me but it was apparent it would be slow going.

When she finished telling me how the crow attacked her and how lucky she was for Bird to have showed up (luck didn't even begin to cover it), I was pretty much done. All I had to do was clean the cut on her cheek.

"You know the drill," I told her. I touched her face with my hands and leaned in closer. My eyes tried to stay focused on the wound but it was hard. I wanted to look into her eyes at this close of a distance. I wanted to let her know she was going to be OK. There was something so vulnerable and restrained about Perry, something that made me want to do stupid, ridiculous things to keep her safe. At the same time, I wanted to draw her out and make her strong, like a diamond from coal.

Without even realizing it, I found myself gazing deep into those blue eyes, totally fucking lost in them. My heart did a little flip. Christ, this was not a good idea. My heart of all hearts did not need to be flipping.

I broke away, broke the tension, broke the connection, and gave her one final dab of iodine on her cheek. I gave her a forced smile, already feeling distant. Distance was good.

"You're going to have a rusty blotch on your face from the iodine, but I think if you wash it in an hour you should be good to go."

"Thanks Dex," she said, her voice barely above a whisper. She looked away, staring absently at the sink. She felt the distance too. This was for the best.

For now.

SHE'S GOT A WAY

"Sexually frustrated?" Perry asked, her voice struggling to be heard in the noisy bar.

I turned my head away from my beer bottle and looked at her in surprise. The girl must have been psychic, though I could see from the way her round eyes were slanting at the corners that she might just be drunk.

I had to smile. "Yes."

There was really no use in denying it. Even with all the bullshit going around and the feeling that my brain was splitting in two, it was having to sleep next to her every night – and just sleep – that was fucking me up the most. I looked down at the beer bottle label that was sticking to my fingers in moist chunks. Christ, I couldn't be more obvious.

She didn't appear put-off. She rarely did. It was one of her annoying super powers.

"Because your girlfriend isn't here?"

"Sure." That was part of it. But even if Jenn were here, God help us all, it still wouldn't have gotten rid of the constant boner adjustments.

I took a long gulp of my beer, hoping that she would get the hint and not pry any further. Perry didn't seem to have control over her lips half the time and not in a good way and it was only a matter of time before I said something really stupid. I didn't trust myself without the meds.

I glanced up at Maximus and Bird talking across the table from us. I hated Max again. I didn't know if it was being off the meds or whatthefuckever but his rockabilly bullshit act was wearing thin. I didn't like how he acted like he knew everything and I didn't like the way he was trying to win Perry over. He would deny it, but I knew exactly what the fucker was trying to do to me. And Perry was too innocent, her self-esteem too ravaged to pick up on it.

To cement my point, Dire Straits came on and after Perry proclaimed her sudden (and surprising) love for the band, the douchefucker stood up and asked her to dance like he was a Cajun Rhett Butler.

She agreed, taking his hand with a look that was pretty close to glee, and he led her to the packed dance floor. I looked back at the beer just in case she wanted me to notice what was going on, notice them together. My fingers started picking at the label again. I wouldn't give them that satisfaction.

"You care about her a great deal," Bird said in his 'I'm an old man' voice.

I shot him a look and resumed concentration on the beer, taking respite in the monotonous movements. I didn't say anything. There wasn't anything to say. It was the truth, that's all it was.

"It's OK, Dex," he continued. "I would too. But you have to respect each other. You have to move slowly. You are both too much the same."

"What does that mean?" I snapped at him. I felt bad, once again I wasn't in control of my emotions, but Bird's face was impassive and gave nothing away.

"You know what it means," he said and he left it at that. I did know what he meant. That's what made the whole situation harder.

We sat in silence for a bit, then he excused himself to go to the bar, promising to bring me a beer. I wanted to stick my fucking head in a pitcher but I needed to take it easy. Drinking never really helped me in the way I thought it did. And those thoughts always came when I was three sheets to the wind.

I managed to avoid looking in Max and Perry's direction but that all went fuckaloo when U2 came on and Perry wasn't back at her seat with fingers in her ears.

Instead she was still on the dance floor. Slow dancing. With ginger fucking Elvis. They were dancing close, way too close. Her breasts were crammed up into his chest, he was holding her like he was about to turn her over his knee and spank her six ways from Sunday.

And she was letting him. She looked like she was enjoying the body pressure as much as he was. I could only imagine the way his chubby must have been grinding against her. Not that I wanted to imagine that. I shuddered, feeling the curious mix of disgust and envy carry through me. Feelings, fuck, I wasn't used to this.

I was still making a disgusted face when Bird came back but to his credit he just handed me my beer and didn't say anything. It was taking all my willpower to peel my eyes away from the couple and concentrate on something else.

This came in the form of Cheri and Amanda, two MILFs who had been eyeing me since I sat down. I'm sure they probably went after any guy under 35 who didn't clean his ears out with his car keys, but I decided to be flattered. I grinned at them and as expected they teetered over to me on tacky plastic heels, smiles broad, breaths rank.

I didn't really hear a word they were saying, I was just trying to look handsome and not breathe in through my nose. One of them, Cheri, maybe, took a liking to Bird, which he didn't seem to mind. Bird didn't strike me as someone who had a wife waiting for him at home, though he could have certainly done better than some old lush with wrinkled cleavage and brown-speckled teeth. I felt like throwing up in my mouth but I played up my virility and asked Amanda, maybe, if she'd help choose songs from the jukebox with me.

We walked to the box through the sticky crowd and I kept Perry and Max in my peripheral vision. On the outside it looked like I was having fun, on the inside I was paranoid as fuck. I kept fearing that he'd grab her and take her away somewhere dark and private. The thought of him touching her, kissing her, bothered me to no end but Amanda was watching me and looking confused at my expression. I smiled at her again, all good vibes and good sex, and let her select some shitty songs first before I requested mine.

We had just gotten back to the table (where Bird was trying to give Cheri a very polite GTFO) when Max and Perry finally removed themselves from the floor. I wanted to make some cutting remark to him and cut him down a peg but there was a weird aura of tension just steaming off. Something had gone down between them and even though it soothed the spite in me, I was a bit concerned for Perry.

Apparently, so was Amanda. The minute she saw Perry's sweet, worried face she grabbed my arm, sinking her Pepto Bismol–colored talons into my skin.

"You're dancing with me, sugar," she commanded. She was surprisingly strong for her size and her sun-raped arms had no problem dragging me to my feet.

"Like I have a choice," I said, trying not to laugh. This was one hungry cougar.

I gave Perry a quick wink as we went past and decided to give Amanda what she'd been waiting for: Someone young. Someone fun. I grabbed a cowboy hat off of some random Joe Blow and gave "Crocodile Rock" my best moves.

It had been a while since I was able to use some of my theatre school skills, other than fucking

Michelle in the orchestra pit and taking hits between monologues. I knew it didn't matter if I screwed up or looked like a retard because that wasn't the point, but I was surprised how easily it came back to me. Again, all I could think about was how deep I felt the music, how deep I was feeling...everything. Though I was swinging Amanda around, my mind dwelled on what my medication was hiding half the time. Besides the very obvious.

"You're good," Amanda said to me, holding me close to her, trying to take back the control. People were clapping and watching us with amusement and she was basking in the glow.

"It comes naturally. But so does being bad," I said with a smirk.

"I can see that. Your wife must be pretty pissed."

Wife? Oh right. Fuckity fuck. I didn't need to eye the ring on my finger to remember the whole charade. Not that the town of Red Fox gave two shits whether I was really married to Perry or pretend married, but it didn't hurt to keep up appearances.

"She's pretty understanding," I said.

Amanda nodded. I noticed her earrings were clip-ons and dangerously close to slipping off. This was one sweaty, stanky ass bar.

"You're the understanding one. Most men here would be all macho about it if their wife was dancing with another man. But I could see he wasn't a threat at all."

Oh really? I wanted to pry her for her cougarly wisdom but I bit my lip instead. We danced some more and then we were interrupted by another woman. She said her name was Mary Sue (naturally) and she was years younger (possibly even underage) with desperate eyes that screamed at me, like dancing with Dex Foray was the most excitement she'd ever get. That made me really fucking sad. How pathetic this town must be to find a fuckup like me as their savior.

I danced with Mary Sue, going through the motions, thinking about the fake wedding band on my ring finger. When the song ended again and I could see more women approaching me (look, I get that I can look pretty hot, but no one should attract this many rednecks), I decided I had enough. I knew what song was next and I knew who I was dancing with. My wife.

I walked toward her, ignoring the women and focused on her face until her big blue eyes met mine. She looked so small and dainty sitting there among Max and Bird, drinking and trying to have fun even though a world of danger whirled around her. I could see the strain on her face. I knew she was always hyper-aware of what lurked in the dark. I knew because Bird was right. We were too much the same.

I stopped in front of her and tipped my hat in the most awkward imitation of a cowboy.

"It's our song," I said to her over the piano notes of Billy Joel's "She's Always a Woman." I held out my hand, hoping she'd take it.

Her eyes lit up and she took my hand. I quickly grasped it, cool and white between my fingers. I led her to the floor and put my arm around her, bringing her in hard and fast to my side. She was mine. For the sake of appearances, she was my wife, but she was mine anyway. She didn't know it yet, but I did. It was wrong and it made no sense, but she belonged with me. No one else, not any-one else.

It was a shame that I was the one who belonged to someone else. I wondered if I'd ever have the strength to correct that or if I'd punish myself forever.

We started dancing slowly, side to side, and I put one hand behind her back, where it was hot and small, temptingly close to her ass. The other held her hand. I kept her as close to me as possible, but I didn't want to impose like Maximus did. Besides, the last thing Perry needed was to feel my hard-on on her hip, even though it was fucking tempting to let her know what she was doing to me. I entertained the idea that she might even like it. It was a high school dance all over again.

I had to know. I stared into her eyes, lost in the storm, and started singing along with Joel. Softly, and at a distance to start, then I leaned into her ear where it smelled like sunshine and baby powder. I closed my eyes and sang, feeling my breath bound off of her ear in hot clouds. It was taking all of my willpower to not take this further, to not wrap my lips around it and lick the lobe to see what it would taste like. See if I could make those eyes roll back and make her forget everything that had happened to her. I didn't want to be Red Fox's savior, but I wanted to be hers.

As if hearing my thoughts and welcoming them, she laid her head on my shoulder. I tried willing my heart to beat slower, knowing how fast it was racing now. This felt so perfect, a perfection I didn't deserve but I would take it if I could get it.

And then *wham bam thank you ma'am* the spell was gone. Perry raised her head back and looked wide-eyed and vaguely frightened. I couldn't figure her out if I tried. But I wouldn't let her go. The song ended, but I kept my arms wrapped tight around her, not letting her move an inch. If she was having some internal battle again, she could do so in my arms.

"Whatcha doing, wifey?" I joked, secretly enjoying the sound of that.

She gave me a look of forced casualness. "Song's over."

Right. Like that's what happened behind those deep eyes of hers.

"Is it?" I asked, knowing exactly what was coming next. Yep, I was a smooth one tonight. Found two Billy Joel songs on the jukebox and bogarted them both. I was sure the hillbilly folks of Red Fox would be put out without their country incest bullshit, but I was in town and I had a fake wife to impress.

I don't know if she was impressed, though. She looked shocked. I didn't know if that was good or bad.

"Don't look so worried," I told her, trying to put her at ease. "Best fifty cents I ever spent."

"What, did you select Billy Joel's *Greatest Hits* or something?"

Er, maybe she wasn't finding it as charming as I thought. Maybe I was being creepy. Wouldn't be the first time.

"Well, I tried," I admitted. "But these were the only two songs. I'm afraid it's Poison after this, so you should probably enjoy this dance while you can."

"You really like Billy Joel, don't you?"

Oh, she was just so clueless. Bless her heart. I brought her in closer to me so she'd start picking up on the right idea, which was the wrong idea. Or a bad, naughty idea.

"He's all right," I said, having a hard time keeping my amused grin under wraps. "But I figured you might dance with me if I put this on. Only fair that I get to dance with my wife."

She blushed at my choice of words. "A good wife would dance with you to anything. Especially with you. You're a modern day Gene Kelly."

Now it was my time to blush. Except that I'm a man and I don't do that.

I laughed instead. "Years of theatre school and that's the only thing that sticks."

It was true too. I was a pretty fucking good dancer before I got sucked into the film side of things. Though I gotta say, the tail I got in theatre school was one of the reasons I stuck around for so long.

Her eyes widened. She smiled, her breath hot and sweet. "You're going to continue to surprise me, aren't you?"

"I hope so," I said. "The element of surprise is all I have."

And to make my point, I did something I had wanted to do all night.

I reached down and took a firm grab of her sweet ass. It molded like soft putty in my hand.

I looked over to Maximus, hoping the twatwaffle was watching.

He was. He looked surprised. Bothered. Red brows knitted together.

I grinned at him and gave him the thumbs up.

Suck on that, Max.

"What the hell, Dex?" she whispered harshly.

Oh right, I still had her ass in my hand. I let go and put my hand at the small of her back. Still in reach.

"What?" I asked innocently. "I'm allowed to grab my wife's ass. She's got a nice one."

A strange look came over her eyes, like clouds from an incoming storm.

"What would Jennifer think?"

Oh, fuck man. Why did she have to go and ruin a perfectly good – and innocent, I might add – ass-grabbing moment like that? Jennifer. What the hell did she have to do with anything? This was about me and her. This was about now. Why couldn't she have left it like that?

Reality bites.

"There is no Jennifer in this scenario," I told her.

"You're skirting dangerous territory, Dex," she warned.

It's too bad that was the best territory to be in. What a little buzzkill I had in my hands.

"What do you mean?" I wanted to hear her say it.

She thought about it. She knew I was baiting her.

"Your girlfriend is awfully trusting of you, that's all."

It wasn't all. But it was right.

"We have a relationship based on trust. Just like you and I do."

The trust that I wasn't going to do anything to jeopardize either relationship unless I had a damn good reason. And, well, I hadn't seen the reason yet. It needed to be foolproof.

Oh, I had no fucking idea what I was thinking about. All booze plus no meds makes Dex a crazy boy.

I felt eyes watching me every move so I looked away from her sweet face and scanned the bar. There were two idiots in their twenties sitting nearby, staring intently at Perry. It gave me a very bad feeling. First of all, one of them looked like he got chewed up by a lawnmower and hastily put back together. The other was just dripping with Perry lust. It was a little nauseating. Fuck, I hoped I didn't look like that.

"Looks like you're attracting some yokels at ten o'clock," I told her, trying to sound breezy but wanting her to know it wasn't something flattering.

She observed them for a moment. They never broke their stare, even though now I was full on giving them the Dex Foray glare.

She looked back to me and I softened my face.

"Lovely pair," she joked. "Are you suggesting I go for them?"

I twirled her around. "Only if you want to add another cut to that cheek."

We danced for a little bit more until the song ended and then I regretfully took my hands off of Perry and left her to go to the bathroom. It had felt so good to be holding her but it was back to reality and the tawdry, beer-soaked morons of Red Fox.

When I was done, I came back to the table where Maximus and Bird were talking. Max's head snapped up the moment he heard me approaching and the look in his eyes was brilliant. As in, he was still annoyed about the ass-grabbing move. Well good. Her ass wasn't technically mine to grab (not in the real world) but it sure as hell wasn't his either.

Perry wasn't at the table but I didn't want to ask where she was in case Maximus had some stupid answer. So I just slid in the seat beside him and started talking to Bird about the history of the town. Not that I hadn't learned quite a bit all ready, but I liked Bird, and Bird seemed more relaxed when he was talking about boring shit.

I don't know how much time had passed before it was apparent that Perry wasn't coming back anytime soon. Max had gotten up to go somewhere, so I asked Bird.

"Where's Perry?"

He looked over at the crowd, his stern eyes scanning every person.

"I don't know....she-"

I didn't hear what he said. The slight spark of panic in his eyes was enough for me to jump to my feet. I marched to the edge of the dance floor and tried to pick her out there. Then I went around the bar area, searching every table and booth. I went to the bar, still as packed with stanky people as ever, and then I went to the washrooms, hanging around the woman's one for a few minutes before I had this terrible, ball-grabbing sensation that she was in major trouble.

I hoped my instincts were wrong but when it came to Perry they never were. It was like I had some sort, I don't know, it sounds lame to say *connection*, but that's kind of what it was.

I ran away from the washrooms and pushed my way through the crowd to the front door. Outside people were smoking, puking, making out. Perry wasn't one of them.

"Fuck," I swore under my breath and went back inside, the wall of sweat and heat hitting me like a bum paddle.

When I looked around again, I noticed the two yokels I spotted ogling her earlier were gone. Again, my balls seized. This was not good.

Not good, not good, not good, not good.

I spied an exit sign at the back and another door and scrambled my way through the crowd. At one point my borrowed cowboy hat fell off but I wasn't about to retrieve it.

I burst through the back doors and into the still of the night, the sounds of the bar fading as the door closed behind me.

But, fuck.

Wait.

I heard noises coming from around the side of a truck.

I saw. Oh god. I saw feet sticking out. Perry's worn and dusty shoes.

My heart lurched, anger pulsing through my veins at the speed of light. It was a violent feeling. I shut down to everything except swift justice.

I couldn't even think. I walked slowly toward the back of the truck. I spotted a shovel in the back of the truck with some farm equipment and quickly yanked it out. The scraping noise of metal on metal was a dead giveaway so I had two seconds to act.

I leaped around the corner and brought the shovel down like I was batting a home run. It connected with the face of the ugly bastard and he went flying backward.

It was only then that I saw Perry underneath him, blood on her hands, life in her eyes.

"Perry!" I screamed. I went for her, falling to my knees beside her. I put my hands to her cheek, seeing how hurt she was. She was still clothed, but from the way her pants were unzipped, the way her stomach was bloodied...

I could barely choke out the words, "Are you hurt?"

She shook her head. At least there was that. I slipped my arms underneath her and brought her gently to her feet.

"I got you," I whispered. Then I remembered the other dude at the bar. "Was it just this guy?"

She didn't say anything but she didn't need to. I heard the crunch of gravel and saw her eyes go circle-wide. I turned on my heel, without thinking, without planning, and swung the shovel at my target.

And there I found the other guy, his face underneath my shovel as it connected with a sick crack and he went flying backward onto the ground.

I don't really remember what happened next. Something in me, something I tried to keep buried and starving, it came out. It overrode my entire body and all I could think about was wanting to, needing to, kill this man. This beast. This animal. I wanted to rip his heart out and eat it in front of him for what they did to my Perry.

I didn't rip out his heart but this got pretty ugly with the shovel there. It was only Perry's cry, her protest for me to stop, that made me realize there was no use. He was down. She's the one who needed me.

I dropped the shovel and ran to her. She was barely staying up right and her eyes were closing in lid-fluttering daze. I was losing her.

"Perry! Hang in there!" I yelled, holding her up. She went completely slack in my arms. I hoisted her above my shoulder, finding the strength deep inside (she was small but, fuck, boobs weigh a lot) and brought her to the door.

Just then, Bird came rushing out with Max and Rudy, a flashlight in his hand.

One look at Perry and the guys on the ground and they knew what to do.

I was ushered through the crowd toward Rudy's office.

We did get a lot of looks from the drunk patrons, but none of concern. Just curiosity. It made me wonder if hauling bleeding women around was a part of their nightly scene. It wouldn't have surprised me.

Luckily, being a medicine man didn't mean Rudy relied on just flowers and hocus pocus to heal people. He had syringes, vials, antibiotics and a whole mess of clinical stuff under his desk.

He cleared it off and I laid her down on top of it. He lifted up her shirt. The wound near her bellybutton...it made my skin crawl. It made that beast want to come out of me again.

I spent the next hour trying to keep the rage under control. A police officer showed up and I had Maximus show them to where the two guys were. I couldn't go myself. I would have finished the job. They deserved death but I knew better than to give it to them.

When Perry was finally patched up, we took her still unconscious body to the jeep and gently placed her inside. I had hoped the rolling movement and noise of the car would have woken up, but whatever she was drugged with (Rudy said she exhibited all the signs) was far too powerful. She was there but not there. I wanted all of her to be there. I wanted her to be awake and know she was OK. I had her.

We brought her into the house where Will immediately started fussing and flipping out. Everyone was on edge, angry, wanting answers and justice. So was I, but I had to take care of her first.

I brought her up to the bedroom, alone. I was about to put her on the bed when she started making noises. Gurgling noises. Puking noises.

There wasn't enough time. I made it as far as the bathroom with her before she puked up on herself. Trying to ignore the smell, I took her over to the toilet – she was walking a little now, but not talking – and held back her hair as she brought up the rest of the night.

When she was finally done, weak and dirty, I ran a bath for her, lukewarm. I took off her clothes and there was Perry below me, naked. She looked as vulnerable as a baby bird.

I gently put her in the bath and quickly bathed her myself, sponging her with a soapy shower puff, trying not to get her bandages wet. Her pajamas were next. She was now coherent enough to help me by putting her arms through the sleeves. Bird was now in the room with us, a shotgun in his hand. It didn't make me feel all that better. It felt like the damage was done.

I scooped her up in my hands and lowered her into the bed. Her eyes opened wider, taking me in for the first time in hours. There was a flash of horror as she regained memory of the night. Then there was something else. Something reserved especially for me.

Maybe it was a thank you.

Maybe it was something more.

It didn't matter. She was looking at me in a way I'd always dreamed. It's too bad I had to save her in order to get it.

I'd never stop saving her.

STRIPSEARCH

"Where are we going?" Perry asked from beside me, taking in the sights of the city. They weren't too pretty at the moment. Granville Street was Vancouver's entertainment district, which meant street punks with suspiciously acquired dogs, pushy homeless people, jonesing drug addicts and stumbling, drunken idiots in Tap-Out shirts. Not to mention the Canucks had just won the hockey game against the Rangers, so everything was multiplied by a billion beers and douchebags.

I didn't want to tell her where we were going. If she knew, she'd back out. I was on a mission to expose her to my world and let her hair down a little bit. I felt like a king earlier when I convinced her to wear the Canucks jersey I bought. It looked so fucking hot on Perry, barely fitting over her breasts, and it was taking all of my willpower to stop me from ripping her jeans off and bending her over in the hotel room. In the bathroom. Anywhere would have done. I was getting hard again just thinking about it.

So, naturally, I decided to take her to a strip club. Fuck, the way I figured it, she needed to loosen up a little. Let her hair down, like I said. And if I walked around with an erection in there, no one would be the wiser. At least she wouldn't think it was attributed to her, which 90% of the time it was.

And honestly, I needed the distraction like nothing else. After the news from Jenn...my mind was in dire need of shutting down. It couldn't happen fast enough. There was no way in hell I could deal with that shit this weekend of all weekends. Call me a coward, call me weak, I don't give a fuck. I had the rest of my life to deal with it.

Just not now.

For now, I was going to pretend.

I gave her a coy smile. "You'll see."

I was tempted to grab her hand and hold it as we walked down the streets; there were men leering at her from all directions and it was quite obvious I wasn't her boyfriend. I hated that. It happened all the time.

Instead I walked by her side, the chilly November breeze whistling in between us. I tried not to notice the way it turned her breasts into headlights. We couldn't get to the dark, anonymous club fast enough.

"What the hell is this?" she asked, eyeing the door to The Cecil. The strip club down-at-it's heels, nowhere near as classy as Brandi's Showgirls, but Brandi's cost a lot of dough and I wasn't about to spend that much on Perry, who looked like she was going to start running over the Granville Street Bridge any second and all the way home to Portland.

"It's our fun for the night," I told her, motioning her to go inside.

"I thought the hockey game was our fun for the night," she said and crossed her arms.

Oy, convincing her to partake in naked ladies might be harder than I thought.

I decided to turn on the charm. It was always tactic number one.

I leaned in closer to her. "Kiddo, the fun never ends when you're with me."

She narrowed her eyes into two rather seductive looking slits. "If you think I'm going into a strip club..."

"Oh, don't be such a pussy," I sniped. Tactic number two. Call her a pussy.

Her eyes widened for a second, then she brought an equally amusing sneer to her face. "I am not a...*pussy*. I just don't have any desire to see some tonight."

"But I do," I whined. "Please, Perry?"

Tactic number three. Beg.

"Seriously?"

I smacked her lightly on the arm. "You're no fun."

"I'm more fun than you can handle," she said and wagged her finger at me. Then she turned on her heel, flung open the door and marched into the club. She was extra hot when she was angry.

And there I was getting turned on again.

I sighed and followed her.

After the doorman collected our cover money (which I paid for - because I'm a gentleman), I led Perry straight toward the stage. I recognized the girl up there, wriggling her ass away. I didn't remember her name but I'd had a lap dance from her before. Not the best, not the worst.

I snuck a peek at Perry. She was putting on a brave face but I knew she was feeling as awkward as all fuck. You can always tell with her. Her shoulders hunch over a bit, like she's shielding herself from the world and though her mouth is set in a "don't mess with me" line, her eyes are sad, like she's about to be found out at any moment. She's vulnerable and she hates it.

I thought bringing her to the stage where the leerers and jeerers were would have been a good idea. Fun. I immediately knew it wasn't. I didn't like her like that. I liked her with her chin high and her chest out.

I put my hand on her shoulder, just for a moment, just for comfort, and pointed at an empty booth in a dark corner. I could only imagine how dirty it was (it's not like they sanitized the seats every hour) but I knew it was out of the way and hidden.

Once there, being careful not to wince at the sticky seat, I ordered us two Jack and Cokes and tried to put Perry at ease.

"Just pretend you're in Disneyland," I told her.

She managed to snort and look scared at the same time. "Yeah, a Disneyland where Ariel walks around topless."

"Hey, either way it smells like fish." I smiled.

She gave me a disgusted look. "You can be really gross sometimes."

I took that as a compliment. It meant I was getting under her skin.

We watched the dancer do her thing for a few moments, Perry trying to look and not look. Our drinks came and I told her, "Look at it this way. You pay cover going into any other bar nowadays. Might as well get a show to go with it."

I held up my drink to her. She did the same.

"Even though these drinks are probably ten dollars each?" she pointed out. I noticed her eyes moved away from mine. She probably didn't believe in that whole ten years of bad sex thing. Not that bad sex could ever happen if I was in her bed.

Jesus, Dex, I thought. *Get back on track.*

"Oh, it's worth it." Our glasses clinked. I watched her intently for any signs of loosening up. So far it wasn't going very well. She was looking all over the place, taking in everything in nervous little spurts. Her eyes eventually settled where everyone else's eyes were settled: the stage.

And why not? It was Marla up there. I didn't try and memorize the names of the strippers here but Marla was a gorgeous creature and gorgeous creatures deserved some of my respect. Unlike some of the snaggletoothed dancers who could barely waddle out a song, Marla had this old Hollywood vibe to her. She was still a bit of a whore, but at least one you could take out for dinner.

"Marla always has the best moves here, doesn't she," I found myself saying out loud, hypnotized by her movements. I'm sorry, but when there's a stripping naked woman nearby, you can't help but watch. Especially when it's Marla.

"You know her name?" Perry sounded incredulous. And a bit pissed off. If I had known any better I would have thought she was jealous. But the idea of that was ludicrous. It was probably her fuckload of insecurities coming into play again.

"You always remember the best ones," I explained. "That's not saying much."

I watched her squirm in her seat and wrestle with something in her head.

"Is this making you uncomfortable?" I asked her.

She gave me a brief but nasty look. "You'd like that, wouldn't you?"

She was kind of right. That was part of the plan.

I put a hurt look on my face. "You think less of me now."

The funny thing was, I almost wanted her to think less of me. I sometimes caught this starry-eyed gaze on her face, like she was looking at me with...I don't know, adoration. It was unwarranted. And dangerous. Yet, I still wanted to push her buttons, prod her over the edge. I wanted to challenge her, make her live beyond her bounds. And a major part of me wanted that adoration from her. But that was the part I let out only when I was jerking off. It was safer that way. Just a sore wrist to show for it.

I don't know if anything I was thinking had shown up on my face because Perry suddenly flushed even deeper. Then she laughed. "If anything, I think more of you."

I grinned.

"Good," I told her and tipped her cup so the drink was going faster into her mouth. Fuck. Talk about another turn on. She could hold a lot in her throat. "You're learning."

I held her eyes for a moment before we both looked away. We watched Marla grind until there was nothing left to her but pale skin and moody lights. We drank.

The waitress came by and I ordered two more doubles for us. She eyed Perry. I couldn't blame her. Perry had taken off her jersey because of the dirty sweat and heat in the room and her little black tank top did nothing but show off her breasts. I wasn't even sure how they were staying so high and perky. Young age, I guess. I had been trying not to stare at them for the last five minutes but now that the waitress was, I could too. And I couldn't have gotten harder if I tried. Thank god for the table.

The waitress gave me an appreciate look. "This your girlfriend? She's cute."

Perry was more than cute and no, she wasn't my girlfriend but I nodded anyway. I looked at Perry slyly. "She is cute, isn't she?"

Cute, pretty, so completely fuckable.

The ever present red of her cheeks deepened. Then the waitress leaned in closer and dear god, I could have shot a load right through the top of the table.

"Honey," she purred in Perry's ear. "With your eyes and those breasts, you should be up there too."

Then she left to get our drinks. Poor Perry, she looked like she wanted to climb under the table and die.

"Guess it doesn't matter what sex you are," she managed to get out, her eyes wide and innocent.

"Don't be so modest," I chided her. I looked at the stage where another stripper was grinding. Perry was better any of these girls, better in so many ways, yet here she was feeling like she wasn't worthy. I didn't understand her problem at all. How could she have gone through life so far without noticing the looks she got from men?

The looks she got from *me*.

I watched her, taking in her unguarded features

"You've got a beautiful face," I found myself explaining to her. The Jack was quickly making its way through my system but I didn't care. I turned my focus to the stage and watched the stripper absently. "Gorgeous eyes. I mean I've rarely seen eyes like yours. Fuck, it's like looking out at the ocean and trying to read it as the weather's changing." OK, I wasn't making sense anymore. I continued anyway. "Perfect lips. The most adorable freckles and the tiniest little nose. You're like a sexy...bunny."

That settled it. I wasn't allowed to talk anymore. I couldn't believe I just called her a bunny rabbit. A sexy one at that. *Real smooth, Dex.*

I shot her a quick look. I would have thought she'd have some snappy one-liner to refute the bunny remark, but her mouth was slightly agape and she had nothing.

"Speechless? That's a start." I couldn't help but feel victorious.

The waitress chose that moment to hand us our drinks. After I paid her ($25!), Perry still hadn't said anything.

"Has no one ever complimented you before?" I asked, trying to get her to talk. I pushed her new drink into her hands, hoping she'd suck her current one back faster. I was feeling buzzed as shit and I needed her to get on board with me. The more sober and serious we got, the more I'd have to deal with that other bomb from earlier.

She shook her head. I still couldn't believe it. Were guys in Portland just fucking idiots or what the hell was going on here? Sure she wasn't model skinny like some people I knew, but she was all woman and what guy didn't want that? More to play with, in my opinion.

I sighed. She wasn't going to get it any time soon. I could sit here and tell her how gorgeous I thought she was but until she believed it, whatever I said was falling on deaf ears. And yes, I went on to tell her she was beautiful and had a devastating ass and whatever else I threw in to sweeten the pot, but really, why the hell should she care what I thought anyway?

I wasn't her boyfriend. I was just her partner.

Her partner with a raging, seam-splitting hard on.

And I couldn't take it anymore.

I shot her quick look, trying to convey nonchalance. "I'll be right back."

Then I left her alone in the club.

There's no pride or shame in where I went. Yes, I went to the bathroom. Yes, I went there to jack off. No, most men don't actually jack off in the bathroom of a strip club. Believe it or not, it's not really a very sexual place. It's a place for frat boys and lonely old men, not a wankfest. It's rare for a stripper to get you so worked up that you have to escape for a few moments.

But Perry wasn't a stripper. Perry was Perry. And this was bound to happen, from the beginning. It was just better this way for me, to get it out of the way before I did something really stupid and started coming onto her or something. Or coming. In general. You know, in my pants.

It didn't take long at all and I came out of the bathroom feeling dirtier than ever. Fuck, just what was happening to me? This was the man I'd become?

In typical fashion I decided to revel in it. I motioned for Marla to come over. She was leaning against the bar, scouting the bar for eager participants. Upon seeing me, her face lit up.

"Hey Sugar," she said in her silky voice. She put her hand on my forearm and squeezed it. "Haven't seen you in a long time."

"Been busy," I told her, grinning cheekily. "I was wondering if you could give my partner over there a lap dance."

"The girl I saw you come in with?" she asked incredulously. "I thought she was your girlfriend."

"No, she's not." I didn't want to elaborate. "But she needs to let loose, I thought you could help her."

"Isn't that your job?"

"Not yet."

She smirked at me through sticky pink lips. "So this is all for her benefit, is it?"

I reached down and smacked her barely clothed ass. "Go on, I'll make it worth your while." I slipped out a few twenties from my pocket and stuffed them in her bra.

She flashed me her expensive veneers. "No problem."

She sashayed toward Perry. By some wonderful luck, the song "Stripsearch" by Faith No More came on. I decided to hang around by the bar, lurking in the background, watching, listening. What had Perry called me earlier? A pervy weirdo? Yeah, that sounded about right. There was no doubt in anyone's mind that I was the biggest pervy weirdo around.

And considering where I was, that was saying a lot.

I watched Marla approach Perry, her fake breasts in Perry's face. They exchanged a few words and I could see how fish-out-of-water Perry was. But surprisingly, she hadn't turned Marla away. I expected to see Marla attempt to grind on her, then see Perry flip out like she often does. That would have been enough to fulfill my dirty mind. But instead, Perry sucked it up and let Marla do her thing.

My eyes were laser beams on them both as Marla slid up and down Perry's thigh. I watched as Marla's top came off and slithered down to the floor. I couldn't have been more turned on if I tried. Yet there was this strange feeling of pride amongst the perverseness. I was actually proud of Perry.

It was mesmerizing. Hands down, the best $40 I could have ever spent. It was a memory I'd draw on in the future when my life was down the shitter and I couldn't remember ever feeling free.

When Marla finally finished, she slipped on a robe that seemed to come from nowhere and worked her past me. She shot me a sly look out of the corner of her eye and I leered at her form appreciatively. Credit was needed where credit was due. Then I took in a deep breath and got ready to face my partner who may or may not have been waiting to kill me.

I approached the table cautiously, putting my feelers out. Perry's face was flushed pink again but I didn't know if it was because she was angry or embarrassed. Or both.

I took the seat across from her. She now looked a bit enlightened, like she was having an epiphany of sorts. Dear god, I hoped she hadn't liked the lap dance *too* much.

"What?" I asked.

"Nothing," she said. *Lying*. What a liar. She got a lap dance from the hottest woman in the club (aside from her, of course), a dance that her partner orchestrated for his own perverse pleasure, and she had *nothing* to say? I'd be lying if I said I wasn't incredibly disappointed. Yeah, the dance was totally for me but I'd hoped she'd, I don't know, at least thank me for the experience.

She pulled out her phone and let out a puff of air as she looked at it. I first thought she had gotten another angry tweet or anonymous blog comment but she was just looking at the time. It was getting late. She obviously wanted to put it all behind her.

"You want to go?" I asked, knowing it was probably the smart thing to do.

She nodded with an unsure smile on her lips. "I had fun though. Obviously you had more fun than me, though you weren't in the bathroom all that long."

Could she have known what I was doing in there? I was probably a hell of a lot more obvious than I had thought. Did she think it was because of her though, and did she like it? That's what I wanted, needed, to know. I studied her face, trying to read the slight melancholy look in her eyes, the tense way her jaw was set, how soft and pouty her lips were when the smile wore off.

"I hope you remember what I've said," I told her quickly before polishing off the rest of my drink. I got out of the seat and held my hand out for her. I was still a gentleman, remember?

She let out a small laugh, one that lit up her whole face. God, she was gorgeous.

"Every time I think of strip clubs, I shall think of you," she said in such a feminine voice that the minute she put her hand in mind, I grasped it hard. I pulled her right up into me, feeling her breasts hot against my chest, her heart beating fast and steady.

My chin grazed the top of her head and I caught a whiff of her coconut shampoo. I closed my eyes for the briefest instance and in that instance we weren't in a dirty strip club in Vancouver. We were somewhere else where it was just her and I and nothing else mattered.

It took all my effort to take a step back and hold her at arm's length when all I wanted to do was lean over, grab her firmly around the waist, and taste the inside of her mouth.

I was just so tired of wanting something I absolutely knew I could never have.

DIGGING THE GRAVE

"Truth or dare?"

The minute Perry uttered those words, I knew I was totally screwed. Listen, people, I don't care who you're playing with and how close to them you are but truth or dare is never a good idea.

Ever.

You're demanding truth when life is better, smoother, with lies. And just in case you didn't feel like being honest, you had a dare. Dares are the stupidest shit ever because no one ever does them. They don't! You ask "truth or dare" and they say "dare!" and then you say, "I dare you to eat this entire jar of wasabi" and guess what? They don't do it! They never do it. Why, oh why, didn't I bring a jar of wasabi on this camping trip? If I had, I would have made Perry eat it instead of pouring her heart out to me.

OK, so that sounds kinda uncaring. Mean, maybe. And really it was the game "I Have Never" that started it all. Truth or dare shouldn't get all the blame.

But Perry is already my soft spot – my weak spot. It didn't make me feel good to hear about how her douchebro boyfriend Mason had cheated on her. It made me feel wretched and terrible to learn that she had an abortion. And when I had to deny her dare...because it was the right thing to do? It broke my fucking heart.

"Truth or dare?" she had asked me.

Perhaps I brought it on myself. I didn't want to say truth because I knew what truth she was after and I didn't want to go there. Oblivious and ignorant, that was my way. Let's worry about the ghosts and lepers, but screw dealing with our real problems.

So I said, "Dare."

And she said...

"I dare you to kiss me."

As I said. Heartbreaking.

Perry was leaning on her elbows, eyes glazed but still beautiful, swaying back and forth from the throes of alcohol. She looked so earnest. So real. So...everything I wanted.

And I was going to have to say *no*.

It broke my fucking heart.

I tried to wipe the fear off my face. I smiled at her, though I don't know if it was convincing enough.

"I can't do that," I said desperately trying to hide the gravity in my voice. She couldn't know how it affected me. I had to treat it like a game.

She looked at me with pleading round eyes. Talk about a dagger to my heart.

"But you have to. You said during the hockey game...if you were dared. This is your dare."

Crapity crap crap. Of course I said that as a joke, and even if I wasn't joking I didn't think she'd hang on to it. I never thought she take that as word. I never really thought she'd *want* to take that as word. But that was all before Jenn's phone call.

That one phone call.

Everything was so different now. I knew the dare. And I knew the truth. And the truth was that if I did as she dared, I would lose myself to her completely. There were so many times already on the trip, when the ghosts spooked me out and I was afraid and my adrenaline was running higher than anything, that I wanted to turn to her. I wanted to shut her up with my lips, to take her in my arms.

But I couldn't.

There was Jenn. And even though sometimes I thought Jenn didn't matter, she did now. She mattered and so did my unborn child. I swallowed hard. This was the most I thought about it in days.

"It's kind of inappropriate," I explained weakly. I know how lame that sounded. I wanted to tell her that I wanted nothing more than to kiss her. But what fucking good could ever come of that?

She tried not to look rejected. She really did. But it was clear as all hell on her face. In the way she bit her lip. The way she stopped swaying. The sadness in her eyes.

"Whatever, you have to take truth then."

She smiled at me coyly. It was false. Oh so false. She was shutting down. Turning her soul away from me. She laid herself out there and I turned it down.

It fucking burned.

Well, if she was going to shut down, I was going to open up.

"Ok, give me the truth then," I encouraged.

She smiled. And I knew what was coming.

"What was the phone call about?"

See. I knew it. I knew that was the plan for this game all along. But it didn't matter. I owed this to her. I could at least explain why I couldn't kiss her...and why she and I could never ever be.

I took in a deep breath.

"Jennifer is pregnant."

WHEN GOOD DOGS DO BAD THINGS

I was already awake when the terrible wailing sound came crashing through the trees. I couldn't sleep at all with Perry crammed up next to me in our sardine can sleeping bag, especially when my thoughts were torn between her and Jenn. It was all starting to sink in. I had never been so fucking screwed in my whole life. I couldn't even blame anyone for this except myself. Jenn was on the pill and we'd been having frequent sex for three years straight. The pill wasn't magic. Logic says that one of the little guys was bound to slip past the barrier. I suppose most guys, if they weren't freaking the fuck out, would be a bit proud at this accomplishment. You know, "my sperm is so powerful it punched that pill in the uterus" or something like that. But I felt scared shitless.

If I'm being honest here, there was a time when having a child wouldn't have been so scary. When I was with Abby, and in stupid, retarded love, I often thought about us having a family together. A baby, marriage, the whole shebang. I wanted to give a little version of myself the life I never had. I wanted to live vicariously through them and pretend my whole fucked-up life never happened. That's a pretty selfish way of looking at having children, but come on, it's me we're dealing with here. If you looked up "selfish" in the dictionary, my picture would be there.

I guess I should have been happy then when Jenn told me that she was going to have the baby whether or not I was involved. That stung. And that was a weird feeling. Our relationship had always been an easy ride. We never expected much of each other. No one's heart or feelings were on the line. We had an understanding of companionship and sex. Did I love Jenn? No, I didn't. I never did. And it was for the best. It was for the best, for my best, that I never loved anyone.

But now that she was prepared to take this baby and do it on her own, without me, I felt rejected or something. Like I wasn't needed. I was just the sperm donor and she would take off with a little part of me that I secretly wanted...just under different circumstances. So, naturally I would tell Jenn I'd stick by her. And I'd even marry her if she wanted. But either way, I was going to be unhappy. Talk about making your bed and lying in it.

Thankfully the horrible wailing crashed into my thoughts like a jackhammer and stopped my late night downward spiral. Now I had something more pressing to fear.

Lepers.

The scream continued, coming closer and then moving away in spurts, curdling my blood with each wail. It sounded like a cat being raped by a sad monkey; pained, terrified and sad.

I was terrified and Perry was sleeping away, looking peaceful. Well, not if I could help it. I wasn't going to go through this all alone. If I had to suffer she had to too. And yes, if you look up "chickenshit" in the dictionary, my picture's there, too.

I put my hand on her shoulder and shook her awake.

She looked up at me with clouded eyes.

"What? What's going on?" she mumbled.

A gut-wrenching, piss-your-pants cry shot through the tent.

"What the hell is that?" she exclaimed, the fright filling her face where ignorant sleep had been just seconds before.

"I don't know, it just started. I think it's the nut."

She looked at me as if I was the nut. I explained to her about the nutty leper that once lived in the colony.

"Jesus," she swore.

Won't save you now, I thought. Actually, now that she was awake, I felt less scared. This was exactly the type of thing I should be filming!

"We have to get this on film!" I very ungracefully wiggled out of the sleeping bag and made a dash for the Super 8.

"What, no! You can't go out there," she cried out from behind me.

I grabbed my shoes. I couldn't miss this.

"Yes, I can, I have to."

"No!" she screamed. Her pitch matched the lepers. It made me put down my shoes and look at her. I hadn't heard her that scared the whole time on the island. She looked frightened as hell too. She was literally shaking in the sleeping bag, two seconds away from one of her panic attacks.

"You can't go out there!" she continued. "There are things out there that want to hurt you."

Say what?

"What things, what are you talking about?"

She gave me a pleading look. "Please, Dex, just trust me."

That wasn't a good enough answer for me.

I shook my head. "No way, I'm not missing this. You stay here."

I unzipped the tent, a fresh blast of night air whipping through, when she reached over and grabbed me by the arm, her nails digging into my skin.

"Don't leave me!" she pleaded, her voice strained with fear and agony.

I relented, letting her hands pull me away from the flap. She looked like she was on the verge of tears. I didn't think I could leave her in this state.

"I need you," she whispered.

That was a new one. It stirred up something strange and foreign in my chest. No one ever needed Dex Foray.

"You need me?" I asked, my throat feeling thick.

She pulled me closer, her grip growing tighter. Something was happening. Something that made me forget all about that nut in the forest. I barely heard the cries anymore. I was too caught up in Perry's eyes, the way they shone in the darkness. Whatever this something was, it was crackling with heat, drawing us to each other like a tightened rope, burning around each other.

"I need you," she said with such determination that it was like declaring war.

I watched her lips as she said it.

If she wanted war, she was going to get war.

I smiled.

Then I threw caution to the wind and did the thing I'd been dreaming about doing.

I lunged for her, grabbing her face in my hands, bringing her mouth to mine. It felt better than I thought it would, feeling her, tasting her, my tongue going after hers like I was trying to tame it. If I kept this up I would fucking eat her alive.

I pushed her back onto the sleeping bag and tried to devour her as much as I could. None of this could wait, there was urgency involved, the explosion of too many feelings and missed opportunities. This was what I always wanted, what I fucking jacked off to every damn night. And now she was beneath me, her soft hands touching me around the waist, trying to bring me into her, as if she couldn't get enough too. She pulled my shirt off, scratched her nails on my chest like a cat in heat. I retaliated by sucking on her neck, tasting the sweat and whatever else she was made of. I pushed the envelope, not caring if we were going too far, and began to take off her pants. Fuck these fucking clothes, I wanted skin on skin.

I put my hand under her shirt, feeling the goosebumps of her skin at my contact. Her nipples were sword-sharp and begging to be squeezed along with the rest of her breast. She felt like a dream, a cloud. But it wasn't enough.

She wanted more too. She reached down and pulled her top over her head and I saw Perry's succulent chest in all its glory. I wished it wasn't so dark, so I could see more than just the hint of creamy skin on a hot, rounded silhouette. Her eyes were heavy with lust, begging for me to continue. Oh god, I was trying so fucking hard not to come and I didn't even have my pants off.

I went for her neck and chest again, licking every inch of her, consuming every good thing she was. She moaned and I almost couldn't handle it.

Then her hands were at my pants. I was more than happy to get them off but when her firm grip found my cock, felt how stone hard I was, I knew I was in big trouble. I groaned with pleasure. Loudly. I wanted more but an extra second of groping and it would all be over very fast. And I still had plans. Very wet plans.

I moved back and out of her reach.

I was in control now.

I parted her soft, full legs with my hands and brought my head south. I had a few moves to give her before the main course.

I took my finger and flicked the yielding skin underneath her knee. Then I twisted my head around and did the same act with my tongue, flicking it gently in teasing motions. Her leg tensed up and she made a whimpering sound. She was relishing it like I hoped she would. Her legs even parted more, an obvious invitation.

I accepted.

I took my hand and spread her lips open, running a finger up and down her clit. She was swollen as fuck and as wet as a Slip N' Slide, and it was only going to get more slippery.

I put my lips to her thick wet ones and pushed in my tongue. She was perfect. She tasted perfect, her own type of musky perfume that made my cock even harder until it was flat up against my stomach. It cried out for her touch, begged to come but I couldn't indulge it. This was about her.

She needed me and I was going to give her what she needed.

Her hips were rising, trying to meet my face. My tongue was pushing her over the edge. I didn't want her to go over yet. I wanted to see her, all of her, when she did.

I pulled back and brought my chest onto hers, our sweat mingling. I put two fingers inside of her where they disappeared into the wetness, like she was hungry. With my other hand I grabbed hold of her soft hair and made a fist in it. I pulled it back slightly and her eyes flew open at the delicious pain. I tugged and stroked, hands and fingers, hair and slickness. I did it over and over again until I was almost coming myself. It was painful for me, to hold it back, but I had to.

When she finally came, it was the most beautiful, amazing, fucktastic, heart-grabbing moment of my life. She cried out, an act of instinct. I could hear the pleasure rolling out of her mouth in waves before it slowed to a whimper. It almost sounded hurt but I knew better.

I brought my fingers out of her and rested them on her stomach. I was tempted to lick them off but that probably would have skeeved her out and I didn't want to do anything to ruin the moment.

When she came back down from her high, she rolled her head over and stared at me. I stared right back. We had just crossed a major barricade. I was as turned on as fucking hell and we needed to leave things as they were. I gave her what she needed and that's all I needed.

She reached for my face with her hand and tenderly stroked the side of my cheek. Her look said everything and it was too much. Reality began to sink in, competing with my dick for bragging rights.

What the fuck just happened? What the hell had I done to *us*?

Perry might have picked up on the change, I don't know, but she started reaching for my cock and I wasn't having any of that. Believe me I wanted nothing more than to ram it in her, to really feel how wet she was, to know her from the inside and embrace me like no one else could. I was hard as iron and it was going to go to waste without being inside her.

"I'm sorry," I said feebly. "I can't."

"You can't what?" she asked. She didn't know. She didn't know how things would go if I continued. How further down the hole she and I would fall. We didn't even have a fucking condom, did she really want to end up pregnant? Perhaps with another abortion? Did I want to end up with another version of Jenn?

No. That wasn't fair. If Perry got pregnant that would be something entirely different. But that wasn't our reality. I wasn't with her. I was just her partner. I was with Jenn and that's who I deserved to spend the rest of my life with.

I just got Perry off, gave into the tension that seemed to wrap around us every time we were together. It was a mistake, even if it was the most unregrettable mistake I ever made.

"I don't want to hurt you," I told her. "And I will."

And I knew from the look in her big eyes, I already did.

If you look up "Biggest Douchebag on the Planet" in the dictionary, you'll see my picture.

SHE LOVES ME NOT

Sometimes you can foresee certain moments in your life. For me, it's usually a moment based on a lie. Cause and effect. You lie, you hide something from the world and you know one day someone will uncover the truth. And you know when that happens, it won't be pretty.

It will be ugly.

It will be the screaming face of your partner and she howls at you. The tears in her eyes that she's trying so hard to hold back. It's that look in her face that you just stabbed her in the gut and kicked over the side of a cliff. It's all the trust she ever had in you coming leaking out like an invisible stream of lost promises.

This was Perry the moment she found out that it had been Jenn all this time leaving the anonymous comments. I didn't imagine it going down any other way. I knew I'd be driving that sword into her. I knew she'd break inside. Suffer.

Or maybe it's that I'd be the one breaking. I'd suffer, from knowing what a dipshit I was. Perry and me, it was always one step forward, two steps back. I'd felt like we were finally making ground and then I had to tell her the truth.

The truth always sets my ass back.

She had turned away from me, whimpering her words through anger. "Why the hell didn't you tell me?"

What a place for it all to come out too. Locked in the dark basement of a haunted mental asylum. Actually, it was quite fitting. We had been driving each other insane for too long.

I reached out for her in the darkness, my hand resting on her shoulder.

She whipped around like a caged animal. A glimpse of feral hate in her eyes.

"Don't you fucking touch me!" she screamed, her voice echoing in the damp room.

No. I couldn't listen to that. I couldn't bear to have this between us. I needed to touch her, to know there was some part of her still mine.

Instinctively I grabbed her wrists and held on tight.

"I'm sorry," I said, searching her eyes for something. Anything.

"Let go of me!" she roared. I had found something. She was about to punch me in the face. I knew that look all too well.

Fuck, I was a jackass.

"Fine, punch me!" I yelled back at her, frustration rising. "But you have to listen to me first."

She wouldn't have any of it. "You're a fucking liar!"

And I was. I gripped her wrists tighter and pulled her up to me, needing her to listen, to see me, to hear me out. She relented, her dark hair whipped around her face in a frenzy. But she let me hold her up to me. She let me speak.

"Put yourself in my shoes Perry, please," I begged. "She's my girlfriend, you're my partner. What was I supposed to do? Who was I supposed to protect?"

She closed her eyes, shutting me out. It felt like she was giving up. I didn't want the fire to die in her, I just wanted her to give me a chance to explain.

I sighed and let go of her hands. I didn't even know if explaining would help.

She slowly walked away without giving me a glance. Perry was defeated, and after all the strength I'd seen in her lately, it pained me to know it was me who did it to her.

"Baby," I called out to her, my voice trailing in the cold air.

"Don't you fucking call me that!" she exploded. "You don't get to. Especially after what you just said."

She was hurt. More hurt and angry than I had thought.

Why? What else was there?

I took a few cautious steps toward her. "Why is this bothering you?"

She let out an evil laugh. I couldn't see her face but I knew there was no humor in it. "Heaven forbid this should bother me."

"Did you want me to tell you?" I asked carefully.

"What the hell do you think?"

"Did you think I owed it to you?" And there I was again, digging, poking, looking for something to satisfy me. God, I knew what I wanted to hear.

Did she?

"I guess," she admitted. "I would have told *you*."

"Why?" I coaxed. I took another step toward her.

She slowly turned her head to look at me, maybe to warn me not to come any closer.

"Because..." her voice trailed off. I saw the outline of her throat as she swallowed hard. "You're..."

What? I'm what?

"Perry," I said, my voice shaking a bit.

She was now looking at the ground. In the shadows I could see her brow contracting. She was having an inner argument with herself. I didn't know if the side I wanted to win - would win.

"What?" Fear rippled from her in waves.

She knew what I was going to ask. And I had to ask it anyway.

After all these months together, sleeping in the same bed, the night in the tent, the way my thoughts revolved around her very essence twenty-four hours a day. After almost dying, always saving each other, always pushing and pulling and hurting each other. I had to know how she really felt.

If she answered yes, I'd give in. And I'd tell her everything I was hiding. Everything I fought against every day. I would tell her the truth.

No more lies.

"Are you in love with me?"

And there. It was out there. I was admitting nothing myself but it had to be obvious that I was asking for a reason. That I wanted her to say yes. I needed her to say she loved me.

Then I would be a bit safer when I fell.

Her eyes went wide at the question. I guess it caught her off guard. Or she was a good actress. She'd certainly improved on camera.

"Excuse me?" she squeaked.

I took a few more steps toward her, filling her with my shadow.

"Do you love me?"

Please say yes.

Oh fuck, say yes Perry.

There was nothing but silence. That was bullshit. I had to know.

"Perry," I said again, more urgent. "Do you love me?"

She breathed in deep, a short sharp sound. She steadied herself and looked me in the eye. I looked back. There was no softness there. It was only hard edged and glinting, like a sword. That stabbing blade.

"No," she said simply. "I don't."

I was wrong. I had it all turned around.

I didn't put the sword into her. I only gave her the sword.

She's the one who just put it in me.

MAXWELL'S SILVER HAMMER

Sometimes things end out of the blue; one minute it's going, next minute...it's gone. Sometimes they crumble slowly, like your favorite pair of boxer briefs. You wear them every day cuz they cup your balls just so and don't ride up the legs and sooner or later they become a second skin. You even avoid washing them too often, as rank as that is, because you fear the washing machine will agitate things, shake them up, pull apart those fibers. But eventually, it's going to end. Your underwear will disintegrate. One tug in a fit of mindless passion or just pulling them down to use the can, and SNAP. There's nothing left to hold it together. You're naked. And your ass is cold.

I knew things were over, really over, when I was about to pull my own underwear off. And couldn't.

Jenn had gotten out of the shower and was done slathering her naked body with that Victoria's Secret arsenic-scented lotion. She was flashing me the come hither eyes, the ones that usually created a 0 to 60 boner in five seconds. But though the lil dude got a bit hard – it does that when I see naked women, I can't help it – it never got past the chubby stage.

And that's when I knew this was it. This was the end. If we didn't have sex, what did we have? Nothing. Absolutely butt-fuck nothing. Just a pair of miserable people hanging onto each other for the sake of...I don't know? Not companionship. Not love. Maybe Fear. Boredom.

Loathing.

"What's wrong?" she purred. She didn't understand why my hands weren't pulling down my drawers, why I wasn't stroking myself in anticipation.

What was wrong? Are you really that clueless? I thought. It was all hitting me now like a ton of bricks. How about Perry, Rebecca and Emily being just outside the door? How about finding out you've been fucking screwing around behind my back for who the hell knows how long? And with Bradley? Sir Swagger Douchington the Fuck?

I didn't say these things though. I didn't want her to know that I knew. I just knew it was done for. And whatever chance I had for happiness, happiness that I didn't really deserve, it wasn't in our bedroom. It wasn't with a Wine Babe in all her gorgeous, black-souled glory. It was out in the kitchen. Where a brave, dark-haired beauty was giggling with her new friends.

"I'm not in the mood," I said brusquely as she started reaching for my waistband. I had forgotten that she liked it when I said no. Not that I ever really said no.

She wiggled her perfect bum in the air. Anyone else would have said I was gay for not being turned on by Jenn there on all fours, golden naked honey on white sheets. But making out with a guy seemed like a mighty fine alternative to getting sucked into a vortex of lies and fake nails.

"Dex," she said, her voice getting pitchy.

"I need to get ready. So do you, it's a big night and we're running out of time," I told her and stepped far out of her reach. To cement my point I quickly slipped on my black dress pants. They were itchy as hell and rarely worn but I wanted to look good tonight.

I had someone else I needed to impress. I hoped they would do my ass justice.

I ignored Jenn, turning my back to her and searching for matching socks. I was sort of mindlessly looking, purposely busying myself until she dropped it and lost interest. It didn't take too long. Jenn knew she had to get ready too and I'd bet my dog's farts that she was trying to impress Perry as well.

I heard her sigh and get off the bed. She slipped some ugly 80's 80s Kim Cattrall type dress over her head, pottered about finding her heels, then finally left the room.

As soon as the door clicked shut, I breathed out a sigh of relief. Believe it or not, I felt a bit bad. Jenn's self-esteem was surprisingly fragile and I didn't like going out to a party with both of us off-kilter. But then again, she brought this on herself. So had I.

Maybe you belong together after all, I thought. Who was I to judge her when I was just as much of an ass?

A giggle resounded from outside the door and shook the pity party out of my pants. Perry. She was all I needed to think about tonight. Not Jenn. Not even myself. Just Perry. I needed to do right by her and no one else. Maybe then that nasty voice in my head would shut the fuck up.

I slipped on a white dress shirt and black jacket and stared myself down in the mirror. Maybe it was because I wasn't especially tall, but I always felt like a monkey in a suit. But it looked OK. I knew I looked handsome, maybe even dashing in that wannabe Bond way. I also looked strangely alert for someone who nearly died the night before.

I stopped looking at myself before I turned into one of those guys who give pep talks to their reflection ("Yeah, work that mustache, you stud, chicks fucking dig the rapist look") picked up my tie and made my way out into the apartment where Beastie Boys was blaring.

Jenn was leaning against the counter with a glass of wine in hand. She raised her brows invitingly, which meant she wasn't all that mad about earlier. Perhaps she was already drunk.

"Tie or no tie?" I asked as I walked toward her.

Then, like I was pulled into some cosmic pulse, I paused and looked over at the stereo.

It was a vision of teal satin. And breasts. Oh my god, the breasts.

My eyes locked onto Perry and my breath was stolen. It wasn't just the breasts though – or the nip and curve of her waist and hips, a rolling highway that made me break erection speed records. She looked truly beautiful, comfortable. She was fresh, alive, glowing and...just so fucking real.

I don't know how long I was staring at her from across the room, my eyes taking a dip in her own blue pools, but it was enough that my dick was straining hard against my fly and Jenn said something about taking a picture to make it last longer.

I didn't need to. That moment would always be burned in my head. That moment when I knew that I was way in over my head. I was fucked.

MR. SELF DESTRUCT

When we entered the apartment, the tension followed us in. There wasn't even any Fat Rabbit to break the newly formed ice between us,; he was locked in the bathroom. It was a peculiar kind of ice too. It held us tightly wound, unable to let our guard down. It was a wall that came up as soon as we broke apart in that snowy alley. Fuck, I wanted that again, that feeling of her legs wrapped around me. I needed us to thaw.

Perry walked across the kitchen and leaned against the island counter, her back to me. She kicked off her shoes, the berry heels dangling seductively off her foot. Her head was down, her upper back arched up, leaving the expanse of her shoulders and creamy smooth skin ripe and open for the taking. I kicked off my own shoes and took off my jacket in anticipation.

We needed to thaw. Ice melts with heat and I was packing enough heat in my pants that it pained me. Something needed to be done, for both of us.

I walked toward her carefully, feeling like I might scare her off and ruin the opportunity if I made any sudden movements. Keeping with that theme, I cautiously pushed some of her hair off of her shoulders, all to make room for my lips.

She didn't flinch from my touch. She had expected it.

She wanted it and I wanted her.

I wanted nothing but her, now and forever.

I placed my lips where the wasp had stung her. It was sign of what she was willing to risk for me and I owed her so much more than just my kiss.

I kissed along her back, down her shoulder, feeling her shake beneath me. I tried to get her to face me, but she wasn't thawed yet. I pressed my chest against her, pressed everything against her, and kissed at the corner of her mouth. I needed her to turn to me, give herself, all of her.

She did. She barely made it around before I was all over her, my hands searching her face, her hair, trying to take her all in at once.

There was no turning back tonight.

I put my hands at her small waist and lifted her onto the counter. She wrapped her legs around me again and I responded by hiking up her satiny dress until it was above her hips.

Oh, holy fuck.

I almost drooled on her as I stared at her open on display. My hunger was already insatiable before this.

As was hers. Her eyes looked ravenous, uncontrollable. She reached forward and ripped open my shirt. The buttons flew off. It would have been funny if my head wasn't so clouded with driven lust. I unzipped her dress and pulled it down until her full breasts spilled out like heavy, round dreams from heaven. I tried drowning in them, tasting, licking like I couldn't get enough.

She leaned back and I realized she wanted more. I pushed her gently with my hand until her back was against the counter. Then I grabbed both her thighs and took a dive. I started by swirling my tongue up the soft inner part before I had enough teasing and got to the heart of it. Just like that time on D'Arcy Island, I was rewarded with hot, perfumed wetness. I ate her until she grabbed my head and pulled it up.

Had I done something wrong? I don't know what I'd do if this wouldn't go farther. Jack off for eternity, probably.

"Do you want me to stop?" I asked. Had I been too soft? Too rough. Fuck what the hell was it!?

"No," she said in a voice that made my hairs stand straight. "I want you inside me."

My eyes widened.

Done.

"Yes ma'am," I told her.

In seconds we were both naked as fuck, a first for us at the same time. She let her eyes rest on my cock and I was more than happy to say she looked scared. I couldn't blame her. I felt like I had been having blue balls for thirty-two years and I had a large rod of steel to show for it.

She wrapped her legs around me and brought me into her. I brought my fingers down and rubbed at her until I knew she was slick enough to handle me then I gripped my cock and put it inside. She was tight. So tight. I could barely handle it and my brain started going over the weirdest things to keep everything under control. I wasn't going to go this far and blow my load in two seconds. I wasn't in high school.

I let out a few short bursts of breath, trying to take it as slow as possible. She had other ideas. She put her nails into my ass and encouraged me to speed up. I tried to keep pace without losing everything. I let my hands and face roam all over her upper body, holding on to every moment, watching her every chance I could. Who knew when I'd get this chance again?

And then it came to the point where I couldn't take any of it anymore. Having sex with Perry was...well, I was surprised I lasted so long, especially when she'd smack me on the ass lightly and then grind me into her. But I wasn't about to come first. Somewhere I remembered my manners.

I started rubbing her again, feeling how warm she was. I went for broke. I thrust into her deeper and deeper, faster and faster until we both lost it. A mess of groans.

I came into her like a high-pressured hose. There was a moment where I saw her eyes and she saw me and suddenly we were somewhere else, another world of shimmering air. It seemed to last for all eternity.

And in that eternity I got a glimpse of myself.

That wasn't just fucking. That wasn't just long overdue.

This was love.

I was head over heels in love with her. No, that didn't describe it. I was tear my fucking heart out and throw it at her, beg her to take it into hers. I was falling from the greatest heights with no safety net below. I was giving everything of my own life for hers, giving up every inch of my soul so she could wear it proudly. I was a former king on my knees in front of the queen. A jester begging for a chance. I was powerless, helpless and at her mercy.

And that was the one place I swore I'd never be again.

To love was to hurt.

I wasn't strong enough to survive it again if everything went wrong.

Against all my instincts, I pulled out of her and walked toward the bathroom without even a backward glance. It was all too much. Way too fucking much.

I lost everything before it even began.

I was reduced to a coward, hiding from future pain. How could I love someone who didn't love me? Even I didn't love me.

Eventually I came out of the bathroom and saw the door to the den closed. She was in there and lord knows what she was feeling or thinking. I felt so terrible having to hurt her the way I was going to. But I had no other choice. It was better this way, now. It would be superficial to her.

I slipped on my pajama pants and went to the couch. I was dazed, empty. Whatever ice had thawed was freezing over again, starting somewhere in my heart.

There, I thought. *This is safer. Better.*

I put my head in my hands and wondered what I'd say next.

Then she came out of the den. I heard her walk up to me. I didn't need to look at her to read the worry she was giving off.

"Are you OK?" she asked, her voice wavering.

Fuck me. And she was being polite about it. She cared. She really did.

But she doesn't love you, I told myself, almost yelling in my head. *She told you she doesn't love you and you saw the truth in her eyes. To love her means to hurt yourself.*

I could take pain but not that road again.

She put her hand on me. I jumped.

"Dex," she said, "Talk to me."

Right. Like talking would do any good. I tried talking to her before this whole mess started. I know what she said.

When I didn't answer her, she grabbed my arm and tried to pull it away from my head.

"Dex, please!" she yelled.

I looked at her. I had no idea what she saw.

Neither did she.

She leaned forward. "What is it? What happened?"

"Nothing happened," the words just fell out of me. "And I hope you remember it that way."

She sucked in her breath. "What do you mean by that?"

Oh, she knew.

I yanked myself out of her grip. "What do you think I mean?"

She wasn't biting. She looked defiant. Stubborn. Naïve.

"Dex, just tell me what you're talking about, you owe me this much."

I had to laugh. She didn't get it.

"I don't owe you anything, Perry."

It probably came out a little meaner than I expected. But this wasn't about me owing her. She had the chance to owe me and she turned her back.

"Dex, what the hell is wrong with you? Why are you acting like this?"

"Why are you acting like this," I shot back, annoyed. "All in my face and bugging me every fucking second."

OK. Now I was just being nasty. I couldn't help it. Whatever good there was in me was being replaced by anger. Anger was so much better than fear. To be the one inflicting pain was better than being in pain yourself.

"Bugging you?" she repeated. "We just had sex and you're freaking out like-"

"I'm not freaking out about it!" I snapped.

She was unfazed at my obviousness. "Then what the hell is this? Because we were all fine an hour ago before this happened."

I put my head back in my hands. She was right. We had been fine. We had been us. We had been perfect. Now the tables were turned and I didn't know which way was up.

"I knew this was a mistake. This changed everything."

I thought I heard a gasp from her. I didn't care anymore.

"This wasn't a mistake," she cried out. "How could you say that?"

I decided to drive the point home, enjoying my nastiness.

"Typical. You're reading too much into this."

Let's see if she had any real feelings over that.

She looked like I had punched her in the face. She leaned against the couch, gasping for breath and kind of crumpled over on herself. She looked like she was dying and I was the cause.

I didn't drive that point home, I speared her with it. My words were ripping her apart from the inside. But why? It was just sex to her, wasn't it? She didn't love me. Did she? Why was she hurting like this? It was just me. Just Dex.

"Perry," I asked cautiously. She stayed in her huddled position, like the life was being sucked out of her.

Her head snapped up and someone had replaced her eyes with that of a viper's.

"What was this to you, Dex?" she sneered with bottomless hate. "A rebound? An itch you had to get out of your system? Another notch to add to your bedpost? Another person to screw around with, mentally and physically?"

Oh fuck. I couldn't speak.

She continued, her eyes fixing on mine bitterly, "OK then, guess it was all of the above. Glad I know how you finally feel."

Me feel?

Before I could process that she took off for the den. She was throwing all her clothes in her bag.

Packing.

I leaped to my feet and came for her. "Where are you going?"

I grabbed her arm but she got free and shoved me back, hard. I was shocked at her strength, at her anger that was bleeding out of her. I never expected this.

"You made your point Dex," she said as if she were spitting out old gum. "You've now been very clear."

"Perry, wait," I protested weakly, "you can't leave now, it's snowing, you're in your pajamas." I had no idea how I was going to explain but I had to do something. The last thing I thought she'd do was actually leave me. I thought we'd fight then talk about it. Like we always did.

"I'm leaving and I'm not coming back! Rebecca was right about you, you're nothing but a scared little boy!"

Rebecca had said that? No matter, I had to stop her. She was acting crazy. It wasn't supposed to go this way. She didn't care enough. She wasn't supposed to!

I grabbed her in a panic, anything to keep her. I brought her up to me, my grip tight, trying to understand, to hold on.

"Why do you care so much?!" I yelled at her. My voice cracked over the next bit, "You told me you didn't love me!"

With a huge gust of strength, she wrestled out of my grasp and stumbled to the door. I reached for her but she turned to me in fury. She looked me right in the eye and I saw the truth. I saw it all. And it was all too late.

"You're not the only who knows how to lie, Dex!"

And there it was.

The truth.

She loved me. She had lied. She loved me all this time.

She loved me, *me*.

And I ruined it.

She left into the icy night, her anchor bracelet ripped on the floor. She was gone out of my life, out of the show. I had everything I wanted in my hands, in my actual hands, and I destroyed it before it could even become anything. I crushed everything we already had. I drove the only relationship that meant anything to me into the ground and then buried it with six feet of dirt.

I collapsed to my knees, unable to come to terms with what I had done. At the precious thing I'd lost. It was more than missing a part of me. It was feeling like there was nothing left of me to exist in her absence.

When my knees didn't feel low enough, I fell to my side and curled up on the floor.

When the floor still wasn't low enough, I began to cry.

I remained that way, a mess of tears in the hallway, my hand clutching the remains of the bracelet, until Jenn returned from her night out. Even she took pity on me.

Anyone would have. What else can you feel toward a man who once held the world in his hands only to throw it all away?

You think, "How can he live with himself?"

Good question.

I'll let you know.

DEMON CLEANER

"Dex, over here!"

I scanned the restaurant looking for the source of the smooth English accent that called my name. I swear, Rebecca's voice was on par with Morgan Freeman's in the voices I'd like to narrate my life category.

I saw her in the corner of the room and made my way to her. The restaurant was a hipster-ish pizza joint not too far from my apartment and at six p.m. it was absolutely bustling. She looked delicious as usual, dressed from head to toe in a form-fitting black dress that gripped her hips and set off her vampire-pale skin. Any man would give his left nut to have a night with Rebecca. Unfortunately for everyone she enthusiastically played for the other team.

She got out of her chair and went for a hug, her smile wider than normal. It had been a few weeks since I'd seen her last and it seemed we both were in a darker place then.

She wrapped her arms around me for a few tight seconds, then she stepped out of the embrace and placed her soft fingers around my bicep and gave another, heartier squeeze.

"So you've been sticking to it," she remarked, looking proud. "Good for you. You look fantastic."

I felt fantastic. OK, that was bullshit. But I felt better than I had in weeks.

"You look gorgeous," I told her honestly and sat down at our cozy booth.

She gave me a coy wave, simultaneously brushing off the compliment and reveling in it as only she knew how, and ordered herself a drink when the waiter came by. I ordered a Jack and Coke, naturally.

She waited for the waiter to leave before she looked at me, surprised. "Really?"

I leaned back against the soft leather seat. "What?"

"I thought you were turning over a new leaf."

I snorted. "I have. I'm going to the gym every day, running, I quit smoking, I quit my meds. I can't give up all my vices. I'm not a superhero."

She twisted her cherry red lips around. I could tell she was thinking back to Xmas, when she and Em came over to take me out for a holiday gathering at a pub. Thank fuck they had Jenn's old key to the apartment otherwise shit could have really gotten ugly. They found me faced down on the balcony in my underwear, unconscious, a half-empty bottle of bourbon beside me.

"That's...all done with," I said, feeling defensive. "You know I was in a bad place at that time."

She smiled sadly and gave me a slow nod. "I know. I'm not judging. Frankly, I don't think I could hang out with you if you weren't the vice type of guy."

"Well then you'll be pleased to know that I'm still drinking and I'm still wanking to porn."

"That's my boy," she said appraisingly. The waiter came back with our drinks and we cheersed over it.

"To friends," she said.

"To friends," I agreed.

I took a big slog of my drink, the bubbles fizzing my nose, causing me to tense up. With watering eyes I looked at Rebecca. She was staring at my arms with an odd look on her face.

"What?" I asked.

She shrugged. "I don't know Dex, your arms, your shoulders...you look really good. It's nice to see."

"Good enough to make you switch sides?" I joked knowing she was a lesbian until the day she died.

She took a sly sip of her drink. I had missed the harmless flirting with her.

"Well you better not tell Em then," I continued. "Actually, maybe you should tell her. See if she wants to get in on the Dex action too." I winked at her.

She giggled. "Oh you. Once a pig, always a pig. At least that hasn't changed."

I gave her a forced smile even though what she said stabbed at me a bit. Was that what she really thought of me? Is that what everyone thought of me now?

Her face fell, which meant I wasn't doing a very good job of keeping my emotions under wraps. It was harder now when I was off the medication. I felt everything ten-fold and it was impossible to ignore at times. I felt sorry for women for having to deal with this emotional shit most of their lives.

I cleared my throat and anxiously picked up the menu, absently looking for something to eat. Going off the meds also made me hungry – too hungry – another reason why working out was so important now.

"So how is Jenn?" I asked innocently.

Rebecca looked a bit shocked. She lowered her voice and leaned in slightly. "Do you want me to tell you or do you want the truth?"

I shot her a quick glance, trying to play it cool. "It doesn't matter, I don't really care."

"She's doing well then. I'm not too happy about it but it makes working with her easier."

I sucked in my breath and nodded. "Oh yeah?"

Fuck Jenn. Why did I even ask that? Wait, I didn't care.

"Yeah," she continued, watching me carefully for some sort of meltdown. "I guess Bradley makes her happy. It's a weird sight to see. She's still an annoying cunt though."

I humored her choice of words with a smile and went back to trying to pick a pizza. I *was* grateful that Jenn was out of my life but it still hurt to hear what Rebecca was saying. I didn't miss Jenn, but I didn't think it was fair that she was happy and I was absolutely miserable most hours of the day. The only time I was vaguely OK was when I was running, lifting weights or jerking off.

Rebecca reached over and placed her hand on mine, trying to get my eyes to meet hers. "You did the right thing Dex."

"Right," I mumbled.

"Just because..." she trailed off.

I gave her a sharp look. I didn't want her to finish that sentence.

She didn't. She just tapped my hand. "You know you did the right thing. You and Jenn breaking up was long overdue. You deserve someone better than that."

I didn't. But I appreciated the lie.

I smiled quickly and went back to the menu. I was distracting my head with the different toppings I could order when my phone rang.

I shot her an apologetic look and wondered if it was Jimmy. He had been hounding me lately about coming back to Experiment in Terror. After Perry quit and after I had my little downward spiral full of shame and loathing and Cheetos and bourbon, the show was the last thing on my mind. When Perry left, I left too. Now that I was pulling myself out of the greasy orange-stained hole, Jimmy wanted my services again. Talk about a company that sucks you back in. But without

Perry, I didn't see a whole lot of point to going forward. Without her, I wanted to do something, anything else.

I fished the phone out of my pocket and quickly glance at the screen. It wasn't Jimmy at all. It was some other number.

My heart stopped beating. I looked at Rebecca.

"Where is area code 503?' I asked quickly.

"Huh?"

"Area code 503!" I repeated in a panic.

Her face grew paler. "Portland."

I couldn't move. I couldn't breathe. Luckily Rebecca snatched the phone out of my hand and answered it for me before the caller hung up.

"Hello?" she asked. She frowned, listening. "Yes he is. May I ask who is calling?"

I bit my lip, my chest was growing tight with lack of oxygen. She looked at me, her eyes wide, her mouth dropping a little bit.

"Hi Ada, it's Rebecca," she said. "What's going on, are you OK?"

I immediately put my hand out for the phone. I still wasn't breathing but I was functioning.

She eyed me and nodded. "OK, calm down, I'm just going to give you to Dex here."

She placed the phone in mine and twitched her head in the direction of the doors. It seemed like it was something I'd need to take in private.

I gave her a quick smile and put the phone to my ear as I got out of the booth.

"Ada?" I asked, making my way past the crowded tables.

"Dex?" I heard her young, tiny voice from the other end.

"Hi, what's up? Is Perry OK?" I didn't want to ask it, I felt like I had no right to, but I couldn't see any other reason for Ada to call. It had been too long since we had our falling out, the time to be reprimanded had past. And somewhere in my black heart, the minute I asked it, I knew that Perry *wasn't* OK.

I was lucky to have made it out of the restaurant and onto the chilled street when Ada said, "No, she's not OK. Something's happened to her."

I almost dropped the phone. Something had to give, so I did. I leaned against a brick wall and let my legs give out, and slid down until I was sitting on the ground.

"Dex?" she cried out. "Are you there?"

I closed my eyes and swallowed the fear. "Yes. I'm here. What happened?"

"I don't know."

"Is she hurt?" My voice cracked. I swallowed hard, shooting out little prayers in between the answers.

"Not really."

"Ada..."

"I don't know Dex. I shouldn't even be calling you. I just don't know what to do. I think she's possessed. She's...she's not herself, I've seen things too, things that are after her. They have her strapped to her bed now."

"Who are they?"

"My parents. Maximus."

"Maximus?!" I roared. People on the street looked at me and quickened their pace as they went past. I didn't care. The rage was almost undeniable. "What the fuck is he doing there?"

"He and Perry are, well I don't know. He's a douchecanoe, that's all that matters. Dex, she's gone. She's going. I don't know what to do. We did a house cleanse and then Maximus turned his back on us and is making it look like Perry is crazy. I'm afraid they're going to put her away. You know, in a crazy house. But the thing is killing her, Dex, it's *killing* her."

I was vaguely aware of the restaurant door opening and Rebecca coming out of it. She stood beside me but I couldn't look up at her. I couldn't move. I couldn't even process what was going on. Something had Perry and it was killing her. Something so bad that Ada had to call me – of all people – and ask for *my* help.

"I'll do whatever I can," I told her, trying to get the determination in my voice heard over the phone. "You have to promise to keep her safe until I get there."

"What if I can't? They don't listen to me. They've got her like an animal...and she is an animal, she's an animal now!" Ada broke off as her words got clogged by the tears. Ada was one tough teen cookie. Little fifteen. To hear her cry over Perry put the final dagger into my heart.

"Ada, listen to me. I'm going to take care of this, OK? I'm not going to let anything else happen to her, you understand me? I am going to do whatever it takes to make sure she gets out of this. Give me a day, give me a few hours, I will be there and I will fix her. You understand, little fifteen?"

I heard a sniffle and a pause. Finally she said, "OK. But please hurry."

"I'll text you when I'm on my way," I told her.

"Thank you. Thank you, Dex," she said. "I knew you weren't as big of an asshole as everyone said."

Oh, gee thanks.

"Yeah, well, we'll see. Hold tight, OK?"

"OK, bye."

I never made out my bye before the line went dead. I looked up at Rebecca who was watching me in horror. I was shaking all over.

"I have to go to Perry," I told her, voice wavering. "She's in trouble."

Her eyes widened and then she helped me to my feet before people started thinking I was a crazy street punk.

"Anything I can do?" she asked. I saw the fright in her face. She cared a lot about Perry too. It suddenly hit me how disappointed Rebecca must have been since Perry and I parted. No wonder she went all the way to Portland when I had asked her not to. She was hurting from it too, from the mistakes I made.

I couldn't have felt like more of an ass. More of a horrible human being. Not even. A pig, as Rebecca had said. But I couldn't let myself dwell on it anymore either. I had months of that under my belt. I wanted to better myself. This was the best chance for me to prove myself. It wouldn't undo anything but...I couldn't live with myself if I did nothing. Like it or not – and I certainly didn't like it – Perry was still the most important thing in the world to me. Knowing she was out there was painful enough. But knowing she might not ever be out there again...that was something I couldn't live with.

I shook my head and took Rebecca's hand and kissed it. "Thank you for being there for me, through all of this. I've got a few phone calls and bribes to make, then I'm out of here."

"You'll get her back," she said, even though she couldn't have known what trouble Perry was in. "Then when you do, you're going to bring her here and we'll all have pizza together."

I promised her and ran off down the street, into the dusk.

BAILOUT

Rage makes you stupid.

It's one of the things I learned today, along with "trust your instincts" and "shitting in public is impossible."

I'm no stranger to anger problems. I try not to let it rule me though fuck if I don't have a lot of shit to be angry about. But I think I have been pretty good about it. I can blow up on occasion but most of the time I just shove the rage somewhere deep inside. Or I don't even process it at all. Like water off a duck's ass. Back. Whatever.

Before I even pulled the car down Perry's street, I knew the clusterfuckery that lay ahead of us. Not even that, I could *hear* it. Don't ask me how, in fact. In fact, be prepared to not ask me a lot of things. Trust me, I don't have answers. But I could hear, in my head I guess, Max's voice telling everyone to calm down. I could sense a gathering of people, authority figures, more than just her family. So when we came to her house and saw the cop cars, I wasn't all that surprised.

I was just unprepared.

I should have had a better plan than to just get out of the car and walk toward the house, hand in hand with Perry as a show of solidarity. I just wanted her parents, Max, the cops, to see that I hadn't kidnapped her, she had gone willingly. I selfishly wanted to prove myself to them. And jab them in the eyes a little bit. You know, the whole *oooh but look who your daughter chose in the end, muahaha.*

Yeah, I'm that petty. You should know this by now.

But I was totally unprepared for the reality of everything. Knowing Max and our fucked-up relationship, I still didn't think he would so easily turn on me. Or on her. He was supposed to care about her. For fuck's sake, he stuck his... no, I don't even want to think about it. I'll vomit.

And when Perry's father came roaring for me, Mr. Fists O' Fury, I didn't expect him to be so nuts. Did I deserve the punch? Yes. God, yes. For the way I acted with Perry, after, you know...I totally deserved it. I deserved a thousand of them and under any other circumstance I would have gladly stood in line for a firing squad of fat Italian knuckles. But this wasn't just for that. It was for assuming I had stolen their daughter away, abducted her into the night so I could do all sorts of hellish things to her. In an ideal world I could do hellish things to her and she'd love it but in this world I came to save Perry. No one else seemed to give a shit.

So, stupid me, even though one of my worst case scenarios involved some police action, I figured I'd be able to talk to them like they were rational human beings. You know, funny story but this is all a BIG misunderstanding and then we'd all laugh about it. I did not expect them to come after me like I'd just assassinated the mayor of Portland.

Click. Click. Two cold, metal handcuffs around the wrist.

I'd never been arrested before but I thought maybe they'd just tell me to come with them or they'd at least place those plastic cuffs on. I mean, I wasn't a menace to society. But the click, click, was preceded by my arms being grabbed and yanked roughly behind me and followed by a cop reading me my rights.

Part of me felt like laughing at the absurdity of it all and I was this close to telling them to shut up, I'd watched *Law & Order* enough times, I knew my rights. But it was not being arrested that kept the humor sucked out of me. It was feeling utterly helpless as Maximus appeared and went straight for Perry, holding her back with his stupid GI Joe arms.

In that moment time did its funny slow-down dance and all three of us were communicating soundlessly. Both Perry and Max were looking at me and I was torn between trying to figure out what the fuck Max really wanted and letting Perry know she was going to be OK.

The problem was, I was in handcuffs and being shoved toward the cop car. I wasn't even sure if I was going to be OK, how was I going to be sure about her? I was already breaking the promise I made to myself earlier, that I would do absolutely everything in my power to protect her. As if I had some bloody powers, as if I was some kind of hero. All it took was stepping out of the crunched-up Highlander for me to get punched in the face and put in police custody.

Max, never taking his hawk eyes off me, leaned into Perry and whispered into her ear "Don't fight it,

Perry, do as I say. I won't let them take you anywhere but you have to play nice and play fair. Calm down." I felt my blood boil hot, my face flushing, burning. He was trying to take my role again, AGAIN! The nerve of that ginger bastard telling Perry, *my* Perry, to calm down, while she was struggling against him.

Perry wasn't having any of it though and I could feel her thoughts slamming at me. She was more worried about me than about herself. Her eyes were wet with unshed tears and vibrant with the same sort of anger that was seething through me.

I'll be fine, I thought hard trying to get the message across the yard with just my eyes. Whether she got the message or not, I didn't know, and it didn't matter because it was suddenly no longer about me.

A tall man with a patronizing tilt of the head and a falsely distinguished style, like a little kid wearing grown-up clothes, came out of the house and calmly walked toward Perry and Max. It was Perry's shrink, Doctor Freebody or whoever. I never met the man but I had met enough shrinks to pick them out in a crowd. This was the enemy and he was here for her.

I must have grunted or cried out and I was trying to get to her but the cops kept me under control. For now.

They pushed me toward the car and shoved me in the back seat. I yelped, twisting in my seat, fighting them, only to see Perry being engulfed by the doctor's shadow. My heart felt shadowed too, a giant eclipse that squeezed the life out of me.

I had lost her once before. I couldn't lose her again.

I thrashed in the seat as the car lurched and roared away from the house and down the street. I was screaming, yelling, the cops were threatening me with things I didn't understand. English was a language I no longer understood. The only thing I heard, the only thing I responded to, was rage.

And rage makes you stupid.

I *knew* it was nearly impossible to escape out of a moving police car. I knew that if I attempted to kick out the side window with both my hands behind me, my feet would either do nothing, or if I was shit-out-of-luck, I would get one foot stuck in the glass. And then what? Somehow squeeze out of the window while the car is moving at 20 miles an hour?

I knew all these things. But rage doesn't. The power of the anger flowing through me, the urge to get back to Perry while I could, had raised me into another level of consciousness. In other words, I was bat-shit crazy.

Therefore, what happened next was a blur.

With a roar that was neither internal nor external I leaned back in the seat and then propelled my legs forward. My boots met the glass and shattered it with an explosion of light and glitter that filled the car like a snowstorm.

The brakes screeched but the car didn't stop. I didn't have much time. I don't know how I broke the glass so easily and I don't know how I shimmied myself out of the car legs first. I don't know how I was airborne for a few seconds before my shoulder hit the grass at the side of the road and I tumbled along like a rag doll. I don't know how I immediately got to my feet, shaking broken glass out of my hair, and started running back the way we came, not even giving a backward glance to the cop car.

I don't know how any of this happened. All I did know was that I had to get to Perry and get her out of there. If Max, the doctor, *anyone* touched a single hair on her head, I was going to rip shit up. If you think I went Hulk just there, you have no idea. At that moment even I had no idea; I just knew it wasn't going to be pretty.

Unfortunately, even though I felt no pain and was running along with glass streaming off of me, maybe just blocks away from Perry, I was also running with my hands behind my back. It made things a bit awkward. And the closing darkness made things a bit hazy. And my fucking boots that helped me escape the car got caught on the lip of a tree root and went flying for the ground.

Dirt, meet face. That was going to leave a mark.

I groaned and winced, the movement making the dirtburn on my cheek sting. I had no time to wallow in it. I got up to my feet took a step and heard:

"Freeze!"

Just like in the movies. They actually yelled "freeze." Wish they added "punk" at the end of it.

Also wish I had actually froze on my own accord instead of turning around to face them with a sneer. The officer facing me, who looked suspiciously like that douche from those dance movies, had a look of fear and fire in his face. Oh, and he was holding a taser aimed at me.

I sneered at the taser. In rage mode I didn't think anything could stop me. I began to move.

The next thing I knew there was a crackle of electricity in the air. My body went completely stiff, painfully, unbearably rigid like a board as I felt my muscles being hit by a million sledgehammers. My motor skills ceased to function. I had no control over anything. Now I was frozen and yet completely aware of what was going on at the same time. *Please don't let me shit my pants*, I thought.

I was aware I was getting consistently lower to the ground. Aware that my breath was hitched, my body was convulsing in stretched lines. Aware that the dirt was coming up to meet my face. Again.

As soon as I hit the ground like a sack of potatoes, it stopped and I shot off a round of expletives that would even make non-raging/non-tased Dex blush. The pain was over and I was left feeling like I had been run over by a buffalo stampede...if the buffalo were all live wires.

In my state of total exhaustion, the officers were able to handle me and quickly got me to my feet while they called in another cop car. They seemed scared of their captive and when they brought me toward the car, which had been stopped up the road, I could see why. I saw the damage I did when I hit the ground. I saw the glass shattered at the rear window. I wondered how I managed to pull that off and from the looks I saw the officers shooting each other, I could tell they were wondering the same thing.

I made it back to the police station in a paddy wagon. I suppose now I was a threat, if I wasn't already before. They could throw the book at me for trying to resist arrest, for trying to escape. The rage I felt, the need to get back to Perry, was still there ebbing beneath the surface but the rational part of my noggin at least had some control. My balls had been too big for my britches and now they were barely there. I hoped the tasing didn't do any serious damage.

Once at the station I was put through a round of questioning by some surly-looking individuals. I was photographed – and I smiled through it all (why not, I had a nice smile). I would have thought I'd be shown to a doctor since I had been tased, but they never made any mention of the event and I didn't want to press my luck by bringing it up. I was stripped of all my belongings; my cell phone, my money, my notepad.

Then I was given a *very* thorough pat down. I had wondered if my balls were still around and I can tell you, yes they sure are, Officer Zucotti found them. It was sad that ever since Jenn and I broke up, that *that* was the most action I had gotten. Thank god Zucotti was a gentle beast.

With my dignity and male-groping virginity gone, I was then showed to my cell. The guards took me past the holding cells that were filled with a smorgasbord of Portland's vagrants, criminals and drunks (and there were a lot from each category) and put me in a cell that had only one other guy.

He was sitting on the aluminum shitter and emitting a stench that made my eyes water. It was like a stanky-ass car wreck, I wanted, *needed*, to look away and give the man some privacy but it was fucking hard when the cell only consisted of two concrete slabs with thin mattresses on top and the sink. And the shitter. And the man on the shitter.

I would later find out his name was Gus.

Gus and I had a lovely time bonding. He was huge and wide, like a muscular elephant or Vin Diesel's bigger cousin, and covered with tats from head to toe. They literally went up his neck and onto the giant expanse of his bald head. But he was surprisingly well-spoken. He'd been there all day for violating his parole. I didn't ask what his crime was – I didn't know how to react if he said he'd murdered his landlord or something like that ("Oh, that's cool. Right on."). But he was keen to interrogate me. I guess he felt we had no secrets if I'd seen him shit.

"There's this girl," I started and immediately winced at how cliché that sounded. We were sitting across from each other on the cold mattresses. I had no clue what time it was.

"Isn't there always?" Gus replied. Also cliché.

"Yeah. Well, not usually. Not for me. But she's…she's in a fuckload of trouble."

"Trouble and women go hand in hand." Gus squeezed one of his hands with the others. I heard his bones pop. He smiled, showing blinding white veneers.

"That they do."

I wasn't sure how much I could tell Gus without him thinking I was crazy but I figured if you can't tell the truth to your fucking cellmate, who can you tell the truth to?

"Did you try and kill her?"

The glib way he said it, glib and utterly sincere, made me raise my brows to the roof.

"No," I said carefully. Though, if the exorcism had failed, wouldn't that have been a consequence? I felt sick at the thought. The smell in here didn't help either.

"I didn't try to kill her. I tried to save her. She was sick. I wasn't around...we had a fight, I guess you could call it."

He nodded knowingly. I didn't like that he was relating to me. It made me wonder just the kind of person I was.

I continued, "And after the fight we didn't speak for a while. She just cut me out of her life. Did I deserve it? Yes. Did I think she'd actually never talk to me again? No. Actually I didn't. You know, she and I...we fight all the time. In small ways. I think it's because we like to push each other's buttons. You know how some people really get under your skin...and you like it? I fucking loved it. She pushed me, poked at me. She questioned me, kicked me, annoyed me. She was always there, digging, digging, digging, and I loved every second of it. I fucking hate talking about myself but she cared so much to get to the bottom of me, like I was some sort of mystery. I don't think I've ever had anyone like that in my whole life, someone who wanted to know you, the real you, and wanted you to be a better person, a better man."

"Did you become a better man?"

I looked down at my hands. Just the other morning I was holding Perry's hand as she slept, not really knowing if she'd ever really wake up. If she'd be the same. Now my hands were dirty and scraped pink from the fall from the police car, my wrists were rubbed raw from the cuffs.

Had I become a better man? That was the question, what it all came down to, wasn't it?

I had done a lot in Perry's absence. There was more change than I was comfortable with. I ended things with Jenn, which was still surprisingly hard considering what we knew about each other. I confessed to being with Perry, she confessed to being with Bradley. Say what you want about our relationship, about Jenn, but a lot of habits were made over the course of three years. Saying goodbye to something or someone after that long of a time, even if it brought you pain and misery, is hard. It's like living with a gangrene foot. You know you need to just whack it off and you'll be healthier for it. But damn if you don't feel some sort of emptiness when your decaying foot is gone. You look at the end of your leg expecting to see it there in all black and rotting but there's just nothing but air now. And, if I'm being honest here, I do miss the sex. Anyone would. The earlier pat-down aside, who knew when I'd next get laid? It would be a lot of wishful fucking thinking to imagine it would be Perry.

So there was that. No more long-term girlfriend. No more sex life. Then I listened to the tapes, heard what Pippa told Perry, found out about the switched meds. It made me hate her just a little bit, which lessened the pain of having her gone. Then it made me appreciate what Perry did in her diabolical, scheming little way. She did me a favor. And I let that favor continue. I threw out all my meds. Fuck it all to hell, if I was going to see ghosts, I was going to see ghosts. If they could see me, I decided I'd want to see them. And so far, they'd been kind and few and far between. No sign of the one ghost I hoped I'd never see.

With the medication out of my system, my body responded by piling on some weight. It didn't help that I'd also gone from lying-on-the-bathroom-floor-drinking-Jack-out-of-the-bottle to stuffing every single thing in my face. One month of being depressed and desperate as shit and I was going to make up for it with every food possible. So I started going to the gym and directed some of that weight in the right places. I started training for 10K runs with Dean, started feeling stronger. More capable. More of a man.

I even got a new tattoo, one that would remind me of exactly what was important in my life. And what was worth fighting for, every bitter step of the way.

So was I a better man? The minute I heard from Ada I knew that question would be put to the test. Here was my chance to really come through, to prove myself. I did end up saving Perry. I give myself credit for that. I give her credit for actually allowing me to save her too.

But, didn't I also make things worse? If it hadn't been for me, she wouldn't be alive. But here I was in jail with Gus, unable to help her and she was…fuck. I had no fucking idea where she was. The demon was gone but she had new demons to consider. Ones that wouldn't bow to a shaman. For all I knew, Perry could be walking down the same path that her mother pushed on Pippa. She could be alone at this very instance with no one to look out for her, no one to protect her.

She might not even be the Perry I know anymore, medicated to a point of lifelessness and apathy, the passion and fire sucked right out of her.

The thought rattled me. It really fucking shook my organs, stabbed at my heart, squeezed my lungs until my face grew hot and tense and the volcano inside threatened to cut loose.

I had to get out of there.

"Are you OK man?" Gus asked.

I barely heard him. Panic dulled all my senses.

I got up and all I could think was *GET OUT OF HERE.*

Like a raging robot, I put my hands on both sides of sink...

"No man, she's not worth it," I heard Gus like background music.

...and with a terrifying cry of metal and concrete, I pulled the metal fixture out of the ground. Water gushed straight up in to the cell, soaking me in minutes flat.

I smiled.

Someone yelled, "Guard!"

I think it was Gus.

It didn't matter. I wasn't even sure what I was going to do with myself. In my head I saw myself walking over to the sink and ripping it out of the ground and then throwing it at the bars. The bars would break open and I would walk out, free.

Only I knew that was impossible. Throwing the sink would do nothing to the bars but create a lot of noise and ruin their plumbing. But how the fuck was I holding it in my hands? How did I manage to rip it out of the ground?

My muscles were much bigger and I was stronger, I knew that, but...this?

Before I could even contemplate it further, the cell door slid open and a bunch of yelling guards came in. I felt something hard hit the back of my neck and I was down.

The last thing I remember thinking as I lay on the wet, cold, disgusting ground was that I never answered Gus. I never told him if I was a better man or not.

~~~

When I came to, I had a killer headache and I was alone. No more Gus, now I was in another cell. The bars opened up onto a hallway with a guard sitting across from me, which meant I still wasn't using the can in public but at least I no longer had a roommate. Not that Gus was bad, but look where his questions had gotten me.

I rubbed the back of neck, wondering what brutal police instrument came down on me and eyed the guard suspiciously. He returned the favor. I got it. I was more than a troublemaker, I was a force to be reckoned with and I had my own permanent guard. Seemed the more upset I was getting over Perry, the more I was dooming myself to life in prison.

"What time is it?" I asked the guard. My voice sound raw and groggy.

The guard didn't say anything, just kept on giving me the evil eye.

I got up – slowly – feeling all out of sorts.

"Not the talkative type, huh?" I asked. It felt like I'd been in a washing machine with bricks. My clothes were completely dry though, and in the dank jail, I doubted that would have happened fast. I staggered over to the bars and leaned against them, eyeing down the guard. He was a big guy. He didn't flinch. He didn't look away. He was made for this sort of thing.

"Aren't I supposed to get one phone call?"

The guard didn't look away. "Normal perps get them. You ain't normal."

Wasn't that the understatement.

"Is it because I damaged your sink?"

"Not my sink," he said with a haughty sniff. "And it was damaged to begin with. No way you could have pulled that shit out of the ground, so get that higher than thou look off your face and sit your skinny ass back down."

He might have been right about that but I wasn't about to sit down.

"I think I want my phone call."

"No phone calls."

"I think I want to know what time it is."

"Fuck off."

I think I might bend these bars in two, I thought, my hands tightening their grip on them.

Glad I didn't say it out loud. Nothing happened. Hulk I wasn't.

So I continued to stare at the guard. I thought about kicking up a fuss about police brutality and being hit on the head, I thought about threatening them over my rights and how I didn't have. But thinking didn't do me any good. They would just say it was in self-defense, and who would they ask as a witness? Gus? They'd let him out early if they could get him to twist his version of events around.

I wanted to sigh. I wanted to exhale all the anger and frustration boiling inside of me but that would only show weakness. I wasn't weak. I was going to get out somehow, I just didn't know when.

"Declan Foray?" Someone yelled from down the hall.

My head whipped up as did the guard's. He looked less than pleased.

The Step-Up cop was in front of me with a wary smile on his face. He must have been fantasizing about tasing me again.

"You're free to go, your bail has been posted." He stuck keys in the lock and the door opened.

"What?" I asked, shocked, really.

"You sound as surprised as I was," he commented, grabbing me roughly by the arm and leading me down the hall. I heard the guard growl in my wake.

We came into a room where they gave my meager possessions back and I caught a glimpse of a clock. It was at three. And judging by the dim light that streamed in through the windows as I was escorted into the waiting area, it was three in the afternoon, the next day.

Holy fuck, how long had I been out for?

Not only that but, holy fuck, what the fuck is Ginger Elvis doing here?

Across the room, rising up from his seat, like some redneck giant from Planet Flannel, was Max.

It took every bit of control to keep myself from wrapping my hands around his fat neck and squeezing.

So much control that I could barely move. It was like being tased all over again.

"Don't look so happy to be free," he drawled in his stupid accent. He sauntered over to me and laid his hand on my shoulder. "Would you rather they put you back in there? I still have the receipt."

He waved it in the air with his other hand. I was proud of myself for just swatting away his freckled hand and doing nothing else.

"I could kill you," I said, seething the words through grinding teeth.

"I reckon you shouldn't make such threats in a police station," he said in a lowered voice. He turned and ambled out of the room and into the blowing cold wind outside. "Come on, I'll give you a ride to your car. It's at the impound lot. Did you hit a deer or something?"

I was in no mood to talk to him. I was so fucking angry and relieved at the same time and my feet were itching to take me back to Perry.

We got in his truck and I shuddered at the thought of Perry being in this car with him. I knew she had, I could also smell it. He knew too. He had another idiotic grin on his face.

"You could thank me, ya know," he said as he flipped the engine.

"Where's Perry?"

He narrowed his eyes at me. I narrowed mine right back. As the guard learned, you don't play the glare game with Dex Foray.

Finally he said, "She's fine, don't worry about her."

"Don't worry about her," I growled. "You fucking dickwad. Because of you, she's in danger."

"She's not in danger," he said, bringing the truck out onto the street. "She's at home and she's fine. And it's because of you this whole mess started in the first place so if I were you, I wouldn't throw stones."

Throw stones? I was beyond throwing stones.

I headbutted him instead.

I felt nothing but pleasure as my head connected with his cheek. He dropped the wheel for a few seconds and the truck wiggled down the lane.

"What the fuck?!" he cried out, reaching for his face with one hand and trying to regain control of the wheel with the other. A few other cars honked in the twilight until the truck was under his control.

"Pull over," I said, my teeth grinding.

"Fuck you."

"Pull. Over."

Max took one look at my face, his eyes watering, and gave in. I was absolutely seething. I didn't want to do anything to him at the police station, but now that we were a few blocks away, there was nothing stopping me from going apeshit on him.

He pulled the truck to the side of the road outside a small house. I wondered if the owners would mind if I murdered someone in their front yard. A big red-headed someone. He was so full of shit, he'd make fantastic fertilizer for their garden.

I reached over and turned off the engine. My fists curled at my side.

"Do you want to do this the easy way or the hard way?" I asked.

"What the hell are you talking about, Dex?" He rubbed at his cheek while looking pained.

"I'm giving you a choice in how you want your ass kicked, *Max*," I replied.

He frowned. "Maximus. It's Maximus. Why do insist on calling me Max?"

"Because that's the name I know you by. I don't know this *Maximus* who fucks me over and sleeps with my...my...woman."

I cringed at the way it came out and knew Max was going to throw it back in my face.

I was right. He laughed without it reaching his eyes. "Your woman? *Your* woman? Oh you've got to be kidding me, man."

"You know what I mean."

"No, actually I don't. I reckon you've got you and Perry's relationship completely wrong. Your *woman* wants nothing to do with you."

"That's not true," I protested. My protest sounded weak and I hated that.

"It is so. Brother, you have no clue what you did, do you?"

"Don't call me Brother," I barked at him.

"Don't call me Max," he shot back.

"I know what I did, all right? It doesn't matter."

He raises his brows to the roof the car. The look said, *holy shit you are in denial*. And I was. But I needed to win this argument. I still wanted to kick his ass and he distracting me with words.

"If you reckon that it doesn't matter to Perry," he started.

"Get out of the car," I interrupted. "I can't kick your ass in here."

He eyed me wearily. "And why do you want to kick my ass again? Is it because I just bailed you out of fucking jail with my own money?"

Actually, that was part of it. I hated the idea of being in debt to Maximus. Er, Max. Douche.

"I want to kick your ass because you're a traitor, that's why."

He snorted. "Seriously?"

"You took advantage of her." The thought of Max putting his hands on her, his tongue on her...I had to stop thinking about it. If I kept on, Max would be missing his balls.

"I did not," he said. "She wanted it."

"She wasn't herself," I sneered. The anger was getting harder to suppress.

"Well how was I supposed to know that?"

I sat back a bit, feeling smug. "Exactly. You don't know her at all. So you wouldn't know that."

He looked out the window. "And how does that make me a traitor anyway?"

"Have you not heard of something called the Bro's Code?"

He laughed again, this time it shook the car. I had to wait impatiently for him to calm down enough to speak.

"You are really something, you know that pal?" he finally said.

"Fuck off, I'm not your pal."

"And thank God for that. Dex, you slept with *my* girlfriend. Or did you forget that along with everything else from New York?"

"She came on to me." It was true, too. No excuses, but I was in a terrible place when it happened. There was a reason I tried to forget everything that happened in New York. Too many memories. Too many ghosts.

"And Perry came on to me."

I narrowed my eyes at him, searching his face for the truth. His jaw was tense and the skin beside his eye was twitching. I didn't know if it was because I hit him there or that he was lying.

"I highly doubt that," I said, even though my voice wavered with uncertainty. "But even without that, you not only turned on me but you turned on her. She told me everything that happened. You hung her out to dry when she needed you most."

His face went cold. "I did what I had to do."

"What the fuck does that mean? No one said you had to side with her parents and make her look like a nutcase. No one said you had to pretend that all this supernatural stuff was bullshit. No one made you do this stuff. You fucked it up yourself."

He grew silent. I didn't like the silence. I wanted him to come back at me with words. I wanted to keep wanting to hit him.

"That's not true at all," he said quietly. "You have no idea."

"No idea about what? You were being a selfish prick."

"Oh, and you weren't? You destroyed her."

"And you turned her in. Fine pair of men we make."

I clenched my fist and sat back in my seat, suddenly angry at myself as well. All Perry needed, – deserved – was a man in her life that would love her, support her and make her his world. He had his chance. So had I. Now I was afraid it was too late.

"Anyway, I didn't turn on her. Her parents wouldn't have believed me at any rate."

I shook my head. "That's not the point. You should have sided with her no matter what the cost."

"The cost would have been greater than you realize," he said. His drawl was low and there was a hard edge to his voice. It commanded my attention.

What the fuck did that mean? I want to ask him that but I wasn't sure what kind of answer I'd get.

Something about all of this was tugging at me but my brain couldn't really focus on what or why.

"Why did you come here?" I asked.

He twitched then composed himself. "What do you mean?"

"Why did you come to Portland? Why did you contact Jimmy?"

He shrugged. "I wanted a change of scenery."

I watched him closely. He wasn't meeting my eyes.

"You have good timing, you know that?"

"It depends on what you mean by good," he mused.

"Just funny how I'm out of the picture and you immediately swoop in."

"Hey, I had made plans to come here while you were still...in the picture."

That was true. Jimmy had told Perry and I about Max the night of the Xmas party. The best night of my life turned the worst night of my life. Still...

"And in Red Fox..." I wondered aloud.

Max gave me a funny look. "Red Fox? What about it?"

I didn't know, exactly. I wasn't sure where I was going with it, only that something was off, like a missing puzzle piece. I started to think back about

Max and what I actually knew about him. Despite being in a band together, sleeping with his girlfriend, spending most of our NYU days working on the same films, frequenting the same bars, I still didn't know that much about Mr. Maximus Jacobs.

But then again, he could say the same about me.

"Who are you?" I asked, looking him square in the face. "Really?"

He blinked. "Maximus. Just Maximus. Not your buddy. Not your pal."

"Yet, you're always around at the most...pressing moments. Trying to help me out in the most backward way possible."

"Can we go now?" He straightened out his long legs and put his hand on the key. "If you reckon bailing you out of jail is backward helping, you're the one who's got things turned around."

"I don't trust you," I told him but buckled up my seat belt.

"I don't like you."

"Why did you bail me out then?"

He sighed as he started the truck. "Because I like *her*."

His eyes were completely sincere. I know what that look meant. He had it bad for her. Well that made two of us. Whoop dee fucking doo.

"You can't have her, you know," I said. I meant it.

"That will be her choice." He shrugged like it was no big deal. No big deal that he had already lost.

"She already made her choice. I thought that was quite apparent."

"Yeah, well we'll see when she's normal. Which she is now, thank the Lord."

I bit my lip and looked out at the darkening afternoon. "How far away is the car?"

"Not far. Then you're free to do whatever you like."

I opened my mouth to speak but he cut me off. "Whatever you like providing you don't go to her."

"Don't you fucking tell me what I can't do."

"I'm not," he said testily. "You reckon her parents are going to welcome you with open arms if you go back there? They'll call the cops again."

"They can't arrest me for visiting."

"I wouldn't press your luck."

"You care about me again?"

"I'm not bailing you out twice."

"You won't have to." I wasn't just going to show up. I brought out my phone and started to text Perry. But I didn't know what to say.

"What are you doing?" Max asked, looking over.

"Do fuck off." I decided to text Ada instead. I wasn't sure where Perry was, if she was OK. Just because Maximus said she was didn't mean it was true. I also didn't know if her psycho parents were monitoring her phone or something.

I texted, *The douchecanoe bailed me out. Where's Perry? Can I see her?*

I waited a few moments for an immediate reply and when I didn't get one, I put the phone back in my pocket.

"Don't do anything stupid," Max warned. "Believe it or not, I really do care about her. We were lucky that she's fine, that the doctors didn't find anything wrong with her."

"That wasn't luck," I told him. "That was *me*. If I hadn't of showed up..."

"If Ada hadn't have reached out to you."

Fuck. I hated it when he was right. I didn't want to think about what would have happened if Ada hadn't called me that day.

Max lowered his voice. "You know I wouldn't have let anything happen to her. I wasn't going to let them put her away. I wasn't going to let it go that far."

"Just far enough, right? And for what reason then?"

"I told you."

"No, you really didn't. You're acting like you're serving some higher purpose here."

A weird thought struck me. Was he serving some other purpose? I squinted at him, taking in the ginger. I thought about what we had talked about minutes earlier. His appearances in my life. His "ghost-hearing" abilities. Some things fit together, some things didn't.

He didn't say anything. I was tempted to ask the "who are you" question again but I knew it would get me nowhere. He was my old college buddy Max, that's all he could be. That's all I wanted him to be.

My phone beeped and I jumped in my seat. Everything had me on edge.

I looked at the text from Ada: *WTF?! OK I'm glad ur out. She's OK - sleeping. Maybe come by around 11 when the rents R asleep.*

The thought of Perry lying in her bed, sleeping, brought a smile to her face. As creepy as it sounds, there had been so many times I'd watched her sleep.

Just a ratty Slayer concert tee, bedhead, no makeup. She looked so beautiful, so serene, even when she was drooling.

My heart flipped in my chest, a mix of hope and sadness. I swallowed the feeling and buried it by telling myself I was going to do whatever it took to make things right between us again.

Whatever it took.

AFTERWORD

In case you haven't noticed, almost all of the chapter titles in The Dex-Files are songs. Favorites of mine, actually. Check them out:

- **After School Special** – Mr. Bungle (too weird? Listen to Retrovertigo instead)
- **Spookshow Baby** – Rob Zombie
- **Even Deeper** – Nine Inch Nails
- **Big Dumb Sex** – Soundgarden
- **Butterfly Caught** – Massive Attack
- **She's Got a Way** – Billy Joel
- **Stripsearch** - Faith No More (the song playing during the scene)
- **Digging the Grave** – Faith No More
- **When Good Dogs Do Bad Things** – Dillinger Escape Plan
- **She Loves Me Not** – Faith No More
- **Maxwell's Silver Hammer** – The Beatles
- **Mr. Self-Destruct** – Nine Inch Nails
- **Demon Cleaner/Bailout** - – Kyuss

About the author

Karina Halle is a USA Today bestselling author who hides out on Salt Spring Island, BC, in her 1930's farmhouse with her husband-to-be and her rescue pup. She's the author of the Experiment in Terror Series, The Devil's Metal and Devil's Reprise (Diversion), and The Artists Trilogy (Hachette). She has far too many books in her house and far too many ideas in her head. Yet she keeps buying – and dreaming.

Made in the USA
Lexington, KY
07 June 2014